The Degenerate Opportunity

MARK LAKERAM

ISBN: 978 0 9957929 0 6

In loving memory of my father,
Jack Morris Lakeram

CONTENTS

	Prologue	1
1	He Is Kind	13
2	He Plays The Game	24
3	He Does What It Takes	37
4	He Carefully Selects The Guy	51
5	He Can Fake It	64
6	He Has The Moves	77
7	He Has Many Faces	90
8	He Is Helpful	104
9	He Listens	117
10	He Does Not Discriminate	130
11	He Can Be Vulnerable	144
12	He Seduces Men With Ease	159
13	He Is Proud	173
14	He Ties Up Loose Ends	187
15	He Can Manipulate Anyone	201
16	He Has No Boundaries	215
17	He Enjoys Himself	229
18	He Destroys The Evidence	243
19	He Likes Taking Risks	257
20	He Seizes The Moment	272
	Epilogue	286

PROLOGUE

Slowly he began to regain consciousness. All he could see through partially opened eyes was a halo of light. As some of his other senses started to come back to him, he wanted to touch his hurting skull. He tried to move his arms to his throbbing head but he could not, and then the memory of being restrained came back to him. Panic gripped his tormented body, causing all the newly delicate parts to hurt more. He would have started to struggle against his fetters, but his head felt woozy and he lost consciousness again.

A few hours passed before he managed to wake; this time he took things slower and gently lifted up his head to survey his body. He looked up at his arms—each one was stretched out and tied to a bedpost. Then he glanced down the bed at his naked self, briefly stopping at his stomach where the hair was matted and stuck to his skin. Continuing downwards, he saw his legs were spread and also fastened, forcing his body into an X-shape on the bed-prison.

After his visual inspection, he allowed himself to take in all the physical hurt he was feeling. There was the dull ache in his head, his shoulders were sore mainly from the position he was being held in. He arched his body upwards to lift his ass out of the patch of spit, blood and shit that had leaked from him, but this caused him pain.

He started to feel really sorry for himself again, just as he had done since his dream date had turned into his worst nightmare. He was so young and yet he was worried about dying, but more importantly, what would his family say when the details of his death emerged? He had never contemplated his own mortality before this day started. His mind shifted to the events that had brought him here.

* * * *

Being too scared to approach anyone in the real world, he had continued his secret life where he felt safest—chatting to gay men online. At first he was chatting, always in a private dialogue box, to various men; some guys demanded to see pictures before they would even contemplate maintaining the discourse. Others wanted to talk dirty and share sex stories, which he did not feel comfortable with, as he had none at that stage. Then along came Martin Fealy, who he felt a rapport with. Martin was in his mid-twenties, which he found to be exciting because he did not want to be with a schoolboy like himself. Martin was respectful of his age and experience and never pestered him for anything untoward.

They had started talking online frequently. Finally he, Robert "Bobs" Ashton, felt relaxed with Martin. He shared his face picture and full profile with him, but continued to lie about his name. Martin said he could only show Bobs his face in person because of the nature of the work he did, but Bobs's sexual attraction to Martin was provoked by the other pictures he received. Finally, Bobs had found someone he trusted to come out to. So he did.

Telling Martin gave him the confidence to eventually open up face to face with a person, and at the end of that summer he came out to his best friend, Marco. Now he had an actual friend to be his confidant, one who he could go out to bars and clubs with and one who told him not to trust people online—especially someone who would not show his face. Bobs gave up on his online life.

* * * *

There was a noise from the other room, which brought Bobs's mind back to his current predicament. He was not sure what the sound had been, but it could only mean his assailant had returned. This told him he could either do nothing—and be abused and tortured more—or he could try and get away. He decided to stop feeling sorry for himself and to push past the physical pain.

Bobs yanked his right arm hard, as far as the restraint would let him, but as he pulled his limb the knot seemed to get tighter. Maybe it was one of those special knots—one that the more you struggled against, the more it tightened. He switched to his weaker left arm, arched his body upwards and pulled even more against his right one so that he could move his left hand towards the bedpost. It seemed to work...his right hand became numb as the entanglement at the wrist had become very tight now, but his left hand could freely touch the bedpost and attempt to undo the binding. He was fumbling because he was not left-handed and did not have the dexterity in that hand, but mainly because he was scared. After what seemed like a lifetime, he managed to free his hand. He flexed and scrunched his fingers to get more feeling back to them. Freeing his right arm was easier because having one limb liberated had settled him, and since the cross was broken he had more maneuverability.

He sat upright, causing significant pain in his head, but he knew he had to keep on going. He was about to try and untie his legs when he heard the guy directly outside, saw the handle to the bedroom door start to move.

Bobs froze. A sitting duck, still tethered to the bed by his legs. Surely his attempt at escape would earn him a severe punishment.

The door handle stopped moving.

Bobs strained to hear…thought he heard the guy moving off. He did not waste any time. Forgetting everything else, he desperately set to work freeing both legs. Once he had undone the straps, he swiveled his legs together and slid off the side of the bed. This new movement caused him to realize just how sore he was from being held in that awkward position. He looked around the room, picked up a dumbbell bar, and moved over to the door.

He wondered if, when the door opened, he would have what it took to hit another person. All he wanted to do was go home, but he had to remove the obstacle in his path. As he waited for the guy to return his thoughts again drifted back to the events that had led him here.

* * * *

After a night out with Marco, who had copped off with a fit guy and he had not, he went home alone. He was horny as hell, and as he had moved from his bedroom door he stripped off his clothes and got into bed, grabbing his laptop to find some porn to wank to. But just a straightforward wank would not cut it. Or maybe he had something to prove to his friend who could easily pull in the real world? Marco had warned him off, but once online Bobs went back into his old chat rooms. Even though it was late at night, the rooms were busy. Perhaps others were just getting in from an unsuccessful night out, or they had never been out at all and had spent the entire night in front of the screen, or any significant others were asleep, leaving them able to play.

Bobs had scanned through the rooms looking for someone to talk to, when a private message to him came up: *"Hello stranger"*. It was Martin, his trusted confidante, the first person he'd ever come out to.

He felt that he had been unfair towards Martin in the way he had stopped going online, never actually saying goodbye or explaining to him that he would not be chatting anymore. His actions had been driven by how he thought others perceived him, and how they were judging him. But he had fancied Martin from what he said, his personality and what he had seen physically of him. So Bobs decided to go for what he wanted to do from the moment they'd first started chatting.

"The folks took away my computer when they found out about me, but it's all sorted now. So did you miss me?" Bobs typed and then stared in the private message box for a reply— Hotstud25, Martin's username, was *"typing"*. He waited for the message but Martin obviously deleted it, as nothing came through and the box went back to its default, the process repeating itself. Bobs thought he had missed his chance, when the answer came in, *"Yes"*. It was just one word but it was all he needed.

Bobs did not want to waste more time. He quickly typed what he had wanted to type from the beginning of their online relationship. *"I missed you too, do you want to meet up?"*

"Awesome, but look I don't want to get you into more trouble. Don't want any trouble and your parents angrily banging down my

door."

"Don't worry they won't, I haven't told them or anyone about you like we originally agreed."

"Cool. So when were you thinking?"

"Tonight. I could really do with some cheering up."

"Seriously I want to meet you but think we should take things slowly, you're special. Let's get back to chatting and meet when you're ready."

"I'm ready now, soooo horny."

"You are making me horny too with all this talk but lets just chat, we will meet soon I promise. So tell me about what you been up to since you've been AWOL?"

So Bobs had filled Martin in on his night and everything he had been doing since they last spoke, including how he came out to a friend and they had slept together to try it out, but were just going to remain friends. The chat ended with the two having cybersex and giving Bobs the much-needed relief he craved.

This routine continued for a few weeks, progressing to phone sex where Martin would always be the caller, withholding his number. These sessions kept Bobs sated, and he stopped desiring schoolmates as the new year kicked into full swing with A-level module exams. He had started to consider Martin as his boyfriend because he was very caring, not putting pressure on him to meet up, rather wanting him to concentrate on doing well in his exams. Once these were over, Bobs would finally get to meet him. On the day of his final exam, there was just one thing he had left to do and that was to tell Marco, not because he felt he owed it to his friend after he was so negative about his faceless Internet lover before, but because he needed him to provide cover as he planned to spend the night out.

Bobs did not want to be judged again, so when he told Marco he said they had swapped a lot of pictures and talked regularly on the phone—the last fact being sort of true. "As it's the last exam and a Friday, my folks expect me to go out, so I told them I'm spending the night at your place."

"You can spend it at mine—he might just want sex and kick you out," Marco had said, sounding a lot harsher than he intended. "We could actually just both go out and find real people."

"Martin *is* real. And he doesn't just want sex, there are feelings there."

"Okay, I'm just trying to look out for you. So text me after you meet up so I know he's not a psycho. Then later, like the Saturday morning, so I know that everything's good. And if you need to, you can come and crash at my place anytime."

Bobs decided to let the "looking out for" him comment pass, feeling that actually, the opposite was true. Marco was wrapped up in the various guys he'd been seeing. "I promise I'll text you to let you know his picture does him justice, and the next morning I'll fill you in on all the gory details."

"I can come and meet him with you and then disappear when you give me the thumbs up."

"I'm meeting him at his place." Bobs instantly regretted telling Marco this, as he saw his friend's pupils dilate in disbelief.

"Look, he wanted to make me dinner after all the revising I've been doing. He lives in Nightingale Hall—

that really nice building by the common. It'll be fine."

* * * *

Standing naked by the door, Bobs knew it was not fine, and wondered why he hadn't listened to his friend or why his own judgment was so crap that he had trusted this good-looking guy, only to be rewarded with the worst twenty-four hours of his life. The anger in him rose.

Then suddenly the door opened.

Bobs saw his attacker before Martin saw him. Martin walked into the room, naturally looking towards the bed and not behind the door. With all his remaining strength, Bobs swung the weapon at Martin. The bar connected with the back of the guy's head with a heavy crunch, and he dropped to the floor almost instantly. Bobs looked at the body on the floor and hit it again flush across the back; he would have continued to hit him, but he just wanted to get the fuck out of there. He flung the bar down and ran out into the living room, made his way to the front door and started fumbling with the numerous locks on it. Opening the door, he stumbled out into the corridor.

He felt someone grab his shoulders and call his name.

"Bobby...Bobs! What have you been doing?"

A familiar voice roused him out of the shock he felt after his desperate escape. "Marco? Jeez, what are you doing here?"

"I came to find you after you didn't text or answer your phone," Marco responded as he supported his naked friend, who was leaning on him. "Your mum called my house asking what time you'd be back."

With no sort of explanation forthcoming, Marco led Bobs back into the apartment he'd seen him come out of.

"No! Not here!" Bobs said and pulled away from his friend. As he did so Marco noticed his friend was hurt.

"What the fuck has happened to you? Who did this to you?" Marco asked, pointing at the obvious bruises on his wrists.

"It was Martin." Saying the name hurt, not because of what had been done to him, but because of what he had just done to Martin.

"I'm calling the police." Marco took out his phone.

"No!" Bobs shut the door. "Look…you can't. I…think…I think I…killed him…" Bobs tried to justify his words, explaining what had happened to him. As he was talking, they moved back into the living room, where Bobs saw his clothes neatly folded by a roaring fire.

Bobs started to dress as he told his story, saying they'd had sex on the sofa, which was good. Then when they progressed into the bedroom things had started to get kinky, and he had allowed himself to be tied-up. Then events progressed to rough and he wanted it to stop, only then he could not do anything about it. He thought he was drugged maybe, and rough soon became torture, and Martin genuinely seemed to be getting off on subjecting him to various forms of abuse.

Between half-sobs, Bobs told how he'd managed to free himself, club Martin with a heavy object, and hit him again when he was down. "And then I ran out, and that's when you found me."

Marco let him finish telling his side of the story, and felt disgusted for his friend. "But that's more reason why we have to go to the police—he sounds like a right sicko."

"Sounded like. I hit him hard and he went down…I

9

don't think he's getting up. What are we going to tell the police? I killed my gay Internet friend in a lover's tiff? Can you imagine me telling my father that? You didn't tell anyone I was here?"

"No, I didn't tell anyone. After you didn't turn up back at my place and didn't respond to my phone calls, I came over here. I saw the apartment number for 'Fealy' on the mail boxes downstairs and made my way up, and I was going to knock when you burst out the door."

"So no one saw you?"

"No. But I don't think we can do what you're thinking."

Bobs looked at his friend and then looked at the fire in the fireplace, realized why his clothes had neatly been folded next to it. He picked up a poker and started prodding the fire. "Look, I think he was going to burn all my clothes and do who knows what to me."

Marco joined him by the fireplace. An industrial looking glass jar sat next to where the clothes were. Marco opened it, and the liquid in it was clear but the smell was strong and strangely familiar.

Bobs pleaded with him again. "Let's just go, and we won't tell anyone what happened here..."

His plea was interrupted by a sound from the bedroom.

They both looked in that direction. The door started to open. To keep the evil at bay, both Bobs and Marco instinctively threw what they had in their hands towards the opening door—the poker and the glass jar—and ran out of the apartment.

Neither of them looked back. They just ran, down the stairs—taking a couple at a time—and then out of the building. They ran all the way back to Marco's home. Once safely inside Bobs was able to catch his breath. "Shit! He wasn't dead. Christ, I didn't kill him. Thank fuck!"

"I know…look, call home and tell them you're going to stay here another night. Then go have a bath and tidy yourself up. Then we can work out what to do next, in case he comes after you."

* * * *

Bobs was starting to relax a little bit in the hot, soothing water. Martin did not know his name or address, so there was no way he could come after him, and even if he did, he could just go to the police without having to admit he was gay and what he was doing in a man's apartment.

Marco started banging on the door, shouting. "Bobs! You have to come with me! Now!"

Bobs got out of the bath, panicked at the thought they had been hunted down. He yanked open the door, searching Marco's face for some kind of clue as to what had happened.

"We have to go back to Nightingale Hall. The whole building is on fire! It's all over the news."

Even though he was still wet, Bobs put on his clothes and dashed out behind Marco. Arriving near Martin's building, he detected the smell of burning in the air. They approached the building from the common, and got the first look of the flames licking and destroying what remained of the French Renaissance building. Against the black night the scene ahead was incredible, with the fiery colors enhanced.

Marco spoke in a hushed tone. "I think that liquid I

threw was some sort of alcohol or acid, or something that I've smelt before in chemistry class. That, added to the red hot poker..."

Marco did not need to finish his sentence. "We started this," Bobs confirmed as he continued to watch the destruction ahead.

They moved closer to the barrier that had been set up, to try and see if anyone had been hurt or if the cause of the fire had been established. As the building burned, the devastation was seared onto both their minds permanently. They listened as a reporter next to them spoke on his phone relaying the information to someone else: "Find out everything you can about Martin Fealy, F-E-A-L-Y. The fire killed him. My fireman source said the fire started in his apartment and there were accelerants used. Yes, definitely sinister. Wait, I'll call you back. I think they're bringing out more bodies."

Marco stared ahead, wondering how he could live with himself in the future. Then and there, he made the decision that somehow he had to atone for his part in the fire. Further, he'd have to learn what are the signs and clues to recognize a person who was so deceptive and evil.

1

HE IS KIND

Today is my first day starting a new job, so I decided I would take the tube in to be on time and not arrive sweaty and needing a shower. Once I've established myself at the company I'll run or cycle in. These alternative methods of traveling are preferable to me because it will form part of my exercise routine while saving time, but more importantly it means I'll spare myself the displeasure of having to be squashed next to a bunch of degenerates.

Why do I think of the general population as degenerates? They are wasting away their lives, spending seventy percent of their week working in some dead-end ass of a job they hate just to pay the bills and scrape by. Every Monday they wake up, judging by the smell only some will shower, then get ready, and go to work involving some horrendous commute, which I'll get back to. They arrive at work, gorge themselves on food and caffeine drinks because they were too lazy to wake up thirty minutes beforehand and have breakfast at home, before settling down to their desk, counter, floor, site and starting their mundane routine of whatever they do, until they get to their first break of the day. Then it's a case of pretending to work again until lunchtime, for those lucky enough to get a lunch. Then they start the process again for the rest of the afternoon, deluding their bosses into thinking they give a crap while secretly just hoping they can make it through without having to off themselves. Then it's shit commute part two, back home to spend the last few hours of the day before going to bed, erasing all memories of work in order to wake up on Tuesday and repeat.

That is why I think of them as degenerates, which is actually quite kind of me. If they were insignificants, or nothings, there would be no hope of redemption. Whereas as degenerates are only diminished, there is the chance they can be more.

Am I not one of them too, following the same pattern, and playing by the rules society has set out? Worrying about getting into work on time, or by actually caring enough so that I bothered to get a new job? No, I am better because I know what I am, and the lies we are force-fed growing up to enable us to function under these conditions are transparent to me.

I am the brightest star in a dark night's sky, about to go supernova; my name is Sebastian Bowman. I am that stranger invited to a threesome. The one who is unknown but has been waited for. The mysterious guest that will be known intimately and in time, the guy who has the potential to be coveted, loved or hated by all others.

Today is my first day starting a new job; I've been transferred, at my request, to the London office from the New York one where I chose to live and work for a few years. Before that, I was out in Japan and the Far East. I need to be in different places, not from a desire to see the world; it's more that no one place holds my favor for too long—I tend to wake up one day and then think it's time to up and leave. So I do.

Why London? Did I blindly stick a pin in a spinning globe and get somewhere awful like Paris and see that London was close enough to cheat? Well, no. This is the homecoming leg of my world tour.

The office is based on Soho Square, so I can either go to Leicester Square or Tottenham Court Road from my temporary accommodation in Clapham—an area I like and hope to permanently move to. To that end, I've already started making plans to do so.

Walking down the tube escalator, there is no point in just standing there waiting for the automated stairs to carry me to the bottom. I can see how busy it is. My journey is only meant to be between eight to nine stops but I left extra early, because first I'll have to go in the opposite direction. Instead of joining the hordes of degenerates heading into town I take the tube heading towards the suburbs, the opposite way to my final destination, in effect going backwards to go forwards.

Arriving at the platform I avoid joining the majority, and accompany the ten others going south. I board the empty tube when it arrives, choosing to stand by the doors when I'm on it. This I don't mind because I'm not lazy but more importantly I don't have others next to me, touching me, stinking right beside me, breathing on me and sucking in my air.

Quickly we arrive at Clapham South. I stay on and head further south; from my observations it's best to head north from about the Tootings, safest at Colliers Wood. Definitely you need to head past Balham, or poor man's Clapham, where the locals think a lot more above their station than they should. To me, they have that look about them that says, "I think I earn a decent wage and live in a decent place, making me better than those around me," but they're just degenerates like the rest. They secretly wish they were Clapham but are too meek to do anything about it, so they pretend they are satisfied with their Balham lives.

I arrive at Tooting Broadway and decide for today this is south enough. I get off and cross over to the other platform for tubes heading into central London, which is sufficiently sparse for me. The trick is to stand where the "mind the gap" is splattered on the floor, the position at which the tube stops and the doors open. I wait; a woman with what can only be described as fluffy hair stands next to me. Having to stand next to that on a crowded tube is the reason why I come further south for my journey. Imagine standing there holding on to the hand rail with one hand and the other holding your bag, paper or whatever is being used to stop others touching you. Then it gets busier—you get surrounded by more commuters, including fluffy hair woman; more and more get on. You get a faceful of hair invading your personal space and tickling your nose, then suddenly you have to sneeze but your hands are not free to cover your nose. You don't want to do it in someone else's face but you can't hold it in, so you down your head and let the explosion out. You sneeze on yourself, managing to also get Fluffy Hair. She looks at you in disgust. You want to explain that it's all her fault; that if she washed, conditioned, used the appropriate anti-frizz products and routine, you would not have been forced to sneeze. You attempt to say you were a gentleman by turning away, so getting most of the sneeze on yourself, but she would not hear it through her "high barnet."

The tube pulls up, the doors opening right in front of me. I let Frizzy go ahead of me, having already ascertained, as the tube was slowing down, that there are plenty of free seats. She takes the seat nearest to the door, a classic schoolboy error. I take the seat in the middle, equidistant between the two doors and on the opposite side to where I got on, so I can look out at the idiots on the platforms for most of the journey. Tooting Bec is uneventful. A fat woman gets on and luckily does not sit next to me—I did *not* want to share my seat with her. She gets out a Kindle and starts to read. I find this annoying, as I would have much preferred she got out a paperback so I and everyone else could have judged her. Instead she is choosing to hide whatever self-help, chick romance or latest read based on a film-television crossover society deems worthy.

I'm not reading anything because I do not need to pretend to be immersed in a book or newspaper to escape the reality of the commute. As I've said, I prefer to watch the commuters. I've headphones in, so as not to look like a total freak just sitting there, death-staring everyone, but I'm currently not listening to anything. Balham, the usual suspects board and fill all the remaining empty seats; the self-importance emanating from this crowd is nauseating. The last seat is next to the fat woman, it is taken up by a man who does not look best pleased.

A heavily pregnant woman gets on at Clapham South. She looks down at the seat that should be hers. She then scans the rest of the carriage, and just by standing there announces she is pregnant. The rest of the commuters choose to ignore this and continue to read, sleep, listen to music or play games. Preggers turns back to her original plan and looks at the seats closest to the doors, the ones dedicated to those less able to stand, and says "excuse me." Frizzy looks up, her second mistake, for acknowledging Preggers forces her to give up the seat. Frizzy does this reluctantly, hoping that by making the amount of noise she does one of the two men in the four designated seats will be chivalrous and give up their own seat. Obviously paying men the same lack of attention she does her hair, she has failed to notice that these two guys both got on at Balham and would therefore be way too important to stand. She slings her large Mulberry bag over her shoulder and stands directly in front of me, facing me.

Ha-ha! She obviously thinks that as I let her go ahead of me, I might give her my seat. Actually, this is now a tempting option, as faced with her crotch I feel disturbed, imaging the massive unkempt steel wool pubes in close proximity to me. I brave it and leave her to stand, in the hope someone manages to get phlegm in her hair.

Clapham Common. A lot of commuters get on, leaving the platform still full. There are shouts of, "Can you move further down?!" Frizzy and the rest shuffle a minute step to make it look like they are trying, but judging by the crotch in my line of sight she does not go far. At Clapham North the same cries are reiterated.

Now here is a thought. Instead of shouting for them to move further down, why not try this? "Could all of you standing in the aisle turn to your side? Yes, that's right. Face forwards, or backwards if you prefer. This will save others from having to look at your crotch, but more importantly would mean, due to extremely simple laws of physics relating to packing, not requiring an in-depth understanding of the Kepler conjecture that more objects will be able to fit into the available space. And could all you women take the large bags off your shoulders and just put them between your legs? Because they also take up lots of room when held aloft." I'm sure this would prove to be more effective, even though there might be some initial resistance from the women to put their bags on the floor. Once it's explained to them that every other woman in the carriage has a Mulberry bag, obviously the current trend in London, they should see the light. Unless this starts a "mine is bigger than yours war", which could have its own entertainment value.

A new influx of commuters has now joined us as the tube departs from Stockwell. Here there is another tube-line, so an exchange of Northern liners moving to the Victoria line and vice-versa occur. The shuffling makes available a seat next to a woman taken up by the guy who was chatting non-stop to her since they had got on together. Fatty is still engrossed in her e-read, while Preggers is looking around, probably wanting someone to congratulate her for just being pregnant. If I pull the emergency alarm and shout in her ear, maybe the shock would cause her to go into labor and she can get the attention she obviously wants. Disappointingly, Frizzy got off the tube at Stockwell without getting anyone to sneeze on her. Maybe she left because the woman who stood side-to-side next to her, and not in the appropriately packed way, had a bigger Mulberry bag. The bigger bag would mean that the other woman earned more than

Frizzy, or was screwing someone that earned more than Frizzy. Realizing she'd lost the battle, Frizzy took the coward's way out and fled.

Oval, nothing to report, except a couple are co-reading the Metro. There are at least two other copies of the free newspaper behind them; just turn around and get one each. You can't be so much in love you need to read the same stories at the same time as each other. Actually, they both look so dull it might be all they have in common.

We arrive at Kennington where the line splits into two branches. I have to change here to go via the trendier branch, Charing Cross, and not the boring Bank branch. The latter goes via Bank station, which must be ironic since they moved the majority of the bankers to Canary Wharf. I'm joined by Fatty and the man from the annoying couple. He slurp-kissed the girlfriend goodbye three times. *Mate, you can't love her that much*, as I notice she is not wearing an engagement ring, and probably more importantly she does not have a Mulberry bag, not even a small one. I walk further down the platform to escape the man from the annoying couple who can't afford to buy a Mulberry bag for his unattractive girlfriend. If I have to look at his face, the temptation to punch it would be too great. In fact, he is probably crying at being separated from his shared brain cell.

Arriving at Leicester Square, I decide to get out and walk the rest of the way, as I have time and I just want to escape now. The Kennington to Leicester Square journey was uneventful, which further fueled my desire to bolt. This part of the journey was filled with a massive influx of new degenerates, who I tend to have even less regard for, getting on at Waterloo. They have to use both the train to get into Waterloo from some suburb and then the tube to complete the rest of their journey. Living further out from the city center, yes, they can get more for their money, but seriously, how much of their lives are they wasting by the longer commute? And for what? Working in a job they hate just to pay the bills like the rest of them. And believe me, the rush hour trains are no better than the tubes; in fact they're worse. The number of trains per hour can be few (dependent on the line), and they are reliant on schedules that are forever running late and are at the mercy of nature. Not in the sense of where a butterfly flapping its wings in London could cause the formation of storm clouds in Beijing, but more in the way a few leaves fall on the track and delay the train.

I decide to stand on the escalator and let it do the work of ascending me to freedom, as I've clocked Fatty standing about ten feet in front of me and I've no intention of brushing past that large, sweaty bulk. Not everyone has assessed the situation like I have. One brave guy is storming up the escalator to ultimately be confronted by the bulk. Now, I may have exaggerated the size, and he could get past Fatty if he turns to his side, but no, he shoulder-barges her quite aggressively. He must have boarded at Balham.

"I'm sorry," Fatty says to him as she rubs her left shoulder where impact was made.

"What did you say?" Balham man turns around and demands of her.

"I said I was sorry, you know, for colliding."

"Well, if you didn't take up the whole width of the

escalator I wouldn't have been nearly knocked down the stairs."

She responds again with another sorry from a trembling voice. She has her back to me, I can't see her face to see if she is near tears but his scolding is extremely harsh. I think she is genuinely sorry and not being ironic. In her apology was a sorry for being fat, for taking up too much room on the escalator, for not having any self-control or discipline to manage her weight appropriately, and for potentially imposing herself on the healthcare system, to which he contributes by paying taxes.

Balham man doesn't care what she has to say and continues, "I mean, look at you."

I walk up to join them. "Enough! What is your problem?" I cut in. "This woman apologized to you, even though you pushed into her. You should, in fact, say sorry to her twice—once for barging into her and the second for the way you're behaving."

He looks at me, sizing me up. He must work out to some extent, as his arms look quite muscled through his suit. Being that solid means that he could have actually hurt her when hitting into her. We all arrive at the top of the escalator.

"This lady is still waiting for your apology," I say as the three of us move to the side to finish our business and let those behind get past. They don't walk off, rather they loiter close by to stare and listen.

"Whatever," he replies and starts to walk off.

I place my hand on his shoulder, not in an aggressive manner but more in a way to say we need to finish talking. He looks down at my hand then into my face, trying to decide what to do next. Before he reacts, I know what will happen. He will apologize, not because he actually believes he is in the wrong, even though deep down he knows he has been a dick, but because he is not prepared to see how far I'll go. If he had some friends around to spur him on, to try and show off to, he might have considered it. Instead he has to go, to get to his little job and earn his little wage.

He looks at Fatty. "I'm sorry."

I remove my hand, letting him walk off. Fatty looks at me and says, "Thank you." I think, *don't worry about it because you're going to pay me back.*

2

HE PLAYS THE GAME

The company reception area looks like that of a boutique hotel. The two workers are sitting behind a minimalist glass table with a MacBook Air each. The guy informs me, after welcoming me to the public relations (PR) company, that this was a refreshed design as they wanted to give themselves an updated look. I decline the offer to sit on the rather comfortable-looking white leather sofa, where the newspapers for the day are spread out. Instead I walk away from the black walls illuminated with a hidden soft light from the green ceiling, and head to where I can see workers congregating.

They are all near a coffee bar, getting various free hot drinks and helping themselves to the selection of pastries and fruit on offer. Opposite the bar are tables scattered around, which are meant to resemble rocks and have a non-uniform surface. The brown-colored plastic has been cut away at various angles, making placing anything on them interesting. They are surrounded by red, yellow, and green plastic cylindrical stools. The lights dangling down from inconsistent heights are covered by different-sized spherical shades made of a white mesh.

All the walls are covered with flat screen televisions showing news from all around the world, typical of any company controlling the media like we do. The centerpiece of the room is a very impressive rug; it's perpendicular to the walls of the room, taking up a quarter of the floor. The design is not a repetitive pattern but something trying to tell a story, the four focal points being halfway between each of the corners. I'm upset I don't know the designer.

"Sebastian?"

"Hello." I extend my hand to shake that of the young woman who has come to greet me.

"It's lovely to meet you. I'm Louise," she chimes. Her accent is pleasant. While I can't place it, I can tell she has been brought up well. Maybe I'm out of touch with all things English, as accents and designers are now eluding me. "I see you were admiring our rug. It was a commissioned piece; those four parts are meant to represent the different places the square leads to."

"Oh," I respond feeling relieved. "It's charming." I decide to speak at the level her accent dictates.

"I heard that it cost them fifty thousand." She is staring at me. I'm not sure if this is to gauge my reaction or if she's checking me out. I'm sure once it was announced to the masses that a new team member would be joining them, they would have checked out Facebook, Twitter, LinkedIn, and the other social media outputs to see if I was hot or not. However, despite being in this industry, I've opted out of having any sort of online profile or presence.

"Were they going for a hotel look so that clients would feel easier about getting into bed with them?" I laugh, so that she thinks I am joking.

She smiles back with a sly grin. I can tell she is not disappointed in me. "I had better get you up to seventh where they are all waiting for you." She tells me that the main meeting rooms are all on the seventh floor, at the top of the building with its monumental views of London (including Big Ben, the London Eye and the recently finished Shard), where they tend to hold all client meetings. I would not go as far as saying my first impression of this Louise is that of liking her; but I definitely don't dislike her. In my head I've nicknamed her Bunty, after the character from a comic I used to read to my younger sister when we were growing up. This was the Bunty from the earlier days who used to ride ponies and was worried about watching the ballet on the television before she got more politically correct.

Bunty is taking me to meet my immediate team. Then I'll meet the wider group before going off to do human resources inductions and form-filling. She informs me that my boss is out for the morning, which explains why he did not originally come to meet me, and would be back before lunch to take me out. I don't really care about doing the face time with him but understand it has to be done. He would want to be seen acting as a good manager, but deep down he must be smarting that I was hired from above him without his ever being given the chance to assess and evaluate me.

There are only two others in the room. I presume along with Bunty that I'll be expected to manage the three of them. The first guy introduces himself as Jay, from Northern Ireland. Even though he is at least six feet tall and must spend a few hours a day in the gym, his accent is the best feature. He wears braces, both on his teeth and to hold up his trousers. I guess he has foregone wearing a belt in an attempt to try and exhibit his chest more with the two straps. Jay tells me he went to the University of Reading and completed an Economics degree after trying two years of dentistry at Cardiff. He has been at the company for over a year, and moved to London with his boyfriend. The second one is another gay male. That's the thing about PR companies—ninety percent of the male staff will be homosexuals. This guy is a lot less candid providing that information. His name is Raj, I'm guessing of Indian origin, he lives at home with parents in Wembley, and has a Master's degree in microbiology. He ended up working in communications for a research laboratory before starting here approximately six months ago.

While Jay wears being gay on his sleeve, Raj is a bit more discreet with the information. Why they both felt the need to share this information with me is beyond my comprehension. If I'm going to oversee this lot I'll have to tell them what information is acceptable to share when first meeting a business colleague. It does let me know that the boss must be quite lax with them. I tell them about my business experiences to date, the various places I've worked, the accounts and clients I've worked on, and with. I don't disclose anything about my personal life, even after a couple of probing questions from Jay as to why I decided to work in London and not stay in New York. I end the team meeting with a little motivational speech, letting them know I'm here for them and want to help them progress and fulfill any career aspirations they might have.

The human resources part is painful, Two women and another gay guy all flirt with me and intrusively ask about whom I live with, care about the most, my general health status—all under the pretense of required information. I stop short of challenging them as to whether this is really a three-human resources job, tell them that I've got to go meet my manager and that I will fill in the forms later and drop them off. I will not. Maybe in about six months after my probation when they go into my file they might ask again. Before I leave, I chuck in a few compliments to the most senior of the group to keep them onside. The guy tells me to keep Friday after work free for a drink in the office bar, a tradition with new starters. Joy.

"Nathan Lockwood."

I extend my hand to shake the one in front of me. His arm is heavily tattooed. I look at the detail of the tattoos and decide, unlike in many cases, these don't look crass or make the canvas tacky. Perhaps when he is sixty they would look bad on saggy, wrinkly skin, but maybe he doesn't plan on living that long. He has a smile that is very welcoming and doesn't appear to be a fake PR one. Well, technically he is not a "relationer" but is an in-house designer, so it could actually be genuine. His eyes seem alive at the moment, but behind them is something hidden. How I can tell this just from looking at this guy for less than a minute? One of my many skills lies in reading others, an art I'm highly trained in, and sometimes all I have to go by is the eyes. "Sebastian Bowman, but you can call me Seb."

"My friends call me Nat," he responds. I see he wants to be friends then, after knowing me for two minutes. Someone should tell him to choose his words more carefully or not to be so trusting. I smile back at him. "So you worked with this client before?"

My golden goose. I guess I'll be dining out on my knowledge of this account for at least the whole of my first month here. "Yes. Louise mentioned that you're designing some advertorials for the UK pitch and suggested my insight might be helpful."

"Thanks." He pulls out the chair next to him. "I've been through the company branding guidelines but they're too restrictive in allowing me to create anything that we would want to show to a prospective new client."

I sit down and look at the InDesign file on his computer screen. He's observed all the rules from the guidelines, which makes the document look as dry as a piece of toast. I start offering him my advice, things which the client in New York would like. Next I amend the text to incorporate the key messages instead of the standard Latin placeholder blurb. Hopefully, the UK counterpart has drunk from the same company water cooler and has the same vision. Nat starts to make the changes while casually chatting to me. Instead of the bombardment of questions the others kicked off with, he tells me about himself without revealing anything very deep or personal. The level of information is the kind you find on LinkedIn—the professional background without going into details about how many times a day he likes to ejaculate.

I offer similar information in return, when the topic of where I live comes up. Deciding I want to know more about Nat, I realize it's going to be a case of quid pro quo. "I'm staying with friends at the moment but am looking at getting my own place; actually I've got a viewing tonight.

An apartment in a building called Nightingale Hall in Clapham."

He looks at me, pausing from the keyboard while assessing this data, which either means nothing to him at all or my gut reaction is totally spot on. "Yes I know it. Do you?" he responds.

"Sure, good location and size. It has a gym and swimming pool. Probably a bit on the expensive side but it should represent a sound investment." I decide to play with him a bit.

"Are you moving in by yourself?" he asks, taking the bait but trying to find out what he wants to know subtly.

"Yes."

"Well if you can afford to live there, are you sure you need to be working?"

Nicely played, little Nathaniel. Instead of pushing the issue you really want to know, you changed the subject to something most find embarrassing, to put me at unease. You did it without being distasteful by talking about the money outright as I feel Jay would have done. But you gave away too much by letting me know you know a lot about the building, as it's not the sort of place that advertises the price on the Internet. "Well actually, I mean it's more an investment for my parents as they're the ones providing the cash." My controlling the information and letting him hear what he wants to makes him seem relieved. After all, he does not want to know that someone roughly his age is a multimillionaire.

Nat starts laughing. "Everyone that lives there seems to be parentally funded." He looks up at me to apologize if he offended me. My face was not that of offence but surprise, as he is proving to be a great source to explore.

"So do you think I'll fit in there?" I remember that he wants me to divulge first. "I mean it's not just a bunch of sad queens using it as a status symbol?"

"I knew two couples that used to live there and both were young professionals, so you should be fine." He looks distant, thinking whether to continue or not.

I decide to help him along, "I heard on the scene it's nicknamed the Phoenix." I say it as a statement, not a question.

That gets him to open up, a lot more than I expect, but he still maintains the non-gossipy dignity he started with. This is what I already know; Nightingale Hall is a French Renaissance Grade II building that had been destroyed by a fire. It was rebuilt with the inside getting a total makeover, which made it very desirable. The pink pound won out and a lot of gay men moved into the building, rebranding it the Phoenix among the community. More and more gay men coveted living there, pushing the prices up and making available apartments a rarity.

This is what I found out: one of the couples he knows is a guy and a girl. The girl's father bought the apartment for her and she has put it up for sale due to breaking up with the guy. This is the actual apartment for sale that I'll be viewing. Nat advises me to tone down any gayness with the estate agent in case they report back to the owner. The reason for this is because the guy, Ricky, cheated on her, Carmen, with another guy. And left her pregnant.

The other couple he knows is a gay couple and they lived next door to Carmen and Ricky, but they split up too. Their relationship had seemed to fizzle out, as they got together when they were quite young. Nat deliberately does not mention their names to me; I guess his logic is that the scene is a small place and he wants to protect their identities. The guy who "owns" that apartment, that is had his father buy it for him, went traveling after the break-up, and the other guy is still in the area but lives elsewhere. He then tells me that one of their mutual friends, visiting from Ibiza, is currently staying in the apartment and I should go and say hi. Nat says if I tell this guy, Joe, that he sent me, I'll be shown around the bigger apartment and may be able to get additional insider knowledge because Joe is always in the know.

Once Nat has finished telling me all of this I can sense what he's going to ask next, so I beat him to it. I ask that we keep this whole conversation between us as I don't want everyone in my new job to know all my personal life details. He laughs, saying that he was going to ask the same favor as he tries to keep his work and personal life apart somewhat.

We continue on the design and just talk about general stuff, mainly worst client moments. I feel he is holding a lot back from me, which makes him more interesting than an open-book sort of man. He's telling me a story involving a sports drink manufacturer. After all the efforts to design a suitable PR campaign they had to run around covering up the name of the product, because an actual event was going to be filmed at the venue and non-sponsored branding was not allowed on the field of play. The story is amusing to him; I guess you had to be there, but I laugh along. Suddenly, an old man interrupts us.

"What's so funny?" the old timer asks.

Nat goes a bit red in the face. "Oh nothing. Sorry, I seem to have stolen your new employee."

I get up to introduce myself to who I presume is my boss, but before I get a chance to say anything he cuts in.

"Well, I would have assumed a new associate director would have sought me out instead of wasting time." He turns and looks at me. If looks could kill..."We need you to hit the ground running. An account executive like Louise can handle design issues."

"Rod, it was my fault, there were some technicalities," Nat interjects.

The hostility I'm getting from my new boss is more than I originally anticipated. I knew he would have certain issues with me but he's being a total dickhead. "Rod, is it?"

"Roderick."

"Roderick, I should have come to find you after my HR inductions. I was just using my relationship with the client to help optimize current work, and I did not want to brief any other members of the team until I had spoken to you." I will not apologize to the twat. In fact, I never use the "S" word. "Shall we go and catch up properly? Patrick from New York spoke very highly of you and said I'll be able to learn a lot." Patrick had mentioned his name once and there was no qualification.

Nat is staring at him. Rod pipes up. "Sorry, I've had a busy morning. Why don't you go for lunch and I'll send you a diary invite for a meeting this afternoon."

"Great." I guess he is no longer taking me for lunch then. "It was nice meeting you, Nat."

"And you. Good luck with tonight."

Leaving the room, I smile at both of them. I stop by

my new desk just to show my face again before heading out. The desk is by a window; all the directors have a window seat. Opposite me is Jay's seat, next to him is Raj, and next to him is an empty desk. I am told the usual occupant is a freelance consultant who works part-time and is not in today. Next to me is Bunty's seat, and next to her is an intern who is on annual leave for a couple of weeks. My work Blackberry is next to my keyboard with a post-it note stuck on it letting me know the password is London. I scoop it up and head to the elevators, when Bunty appears.

"Did Rod not see you? I told him where you were."

"We met briefly. He's quite busy so we will meet properly this afternoon."

"Is he not taking you out for lunch?" She giggles. "I'll show you around. Wait here while I get my bag."

"Super." My response is a word I believe would be in Bunty's vocabulary.

She returns carrying a large white, blue, and brown leather bag. I look at the label: it's a Massimo Dutti. If it were Mulberry, I would have come up with an excuse not to go out with her. She catches me looking at it, smiles and starts telling me the story behind it. She has joined an on-line dating agency, one of the more up-market ones where a friend writes a profile for the client. She has been on multiple dates including a hostage negotiator (she found him to be too old), the founder of a major Internet selling site (she found him to be too boring, but dated him a few times just to make sure, including sleeping with him in the hope things got better), a nuclear decommissioner (she found him to be too camp and ginger but accepted the bag as a present on the third date). Now she's trying a scaffolder from Essex. She says she's had loads of offers and only tries the exceptional guys as a girl has to eat, and on a poor salary in London needs must. All the unique ones turned out to be nothing special, so she thought she would try normal. And she likes him.

I'm starting to like her more. I respect the fact that she turned down the money, probably because she has enough family wealth herself. However, I don't think she'll stay with normal; she needs some level of excitement or drama in her life. I tell her she's acting like a gay man, which must be very liberal for a young woman like herself. She likes this, and tells me to check out the site because whatever I prefer, there would be attractive ones on there.

At lunch, after half a bottle of wine, I start probing her about Nat. She tells me that he is gay but he is not out at work. She knows this because he told the old intern, a girl named Erica, who told her. Bunty then tells me the very interesting fact that Nat shagged Erica because he wanted to try it with a woman. He went on to date the love of his life and become a bit freer about his sexuality. Then the guy and Nat went on a massive drug binge and the guy died, and Nat became depressed. This information is all based on rumors she heard, and she says she is not sure how much is true because Nat doesn't seem like the drug taking type.

The information I was fishing for comes out when she reveals that Rod is gay, and he has been lusting after Nat for ages. She heard that after Nat killed the love of his life with the drug binge, Rod took care of him and sort of nursed him back to health, making sure that he kept his job when he was just a zombie. Now the two are a couple but Nat still wants to keep it a secret. She laughed when she told me that, adding, "If you had that wrinkly ass on top of you every night, wouldn't you want to make sure no one else found out?"

This actually amused me, but more importantly told me about what she thinks of Rod. Obviously, Rod is not being as discreet as Nat would want, as the rumors must have started from somewhere. This gossip explains why Rod was hostile with me; it was nothing to do with work, just raw jealous emotion coming through. Now that I know what buttons to push for him, I no longer see him being a problem.

3

HE DOES WHAT IT TAKES

The man seems to have the perfect proportion, where the shoulder-to-waist ratio is just right and his firm buttocks stick out just the right amount to be inviting, unlike a flat ass or a big fat one. His legs seem long and like the rest of him are adequately sized. He's one of those guys that works out everything—not just his upper body while leaving his legs like sticks. I can't see his face, which I find frustrating, as for completion I want to know what he looks like. I guess the purpose of this is that anyone looking conjures up the image of the face they want. A body in decent shape can be recognized by all; while some may say it's too skinny or there's too much definition, they will still have to agree that a level of dedication has been put in and to a certain extent that is attractive. Now, a face is more subjective, with the options being yes, no, or maybe (depending on alcohol consumption). This individual aspect of attraction is deeply personal. By not including the face in the picture, everyone can fantasize that it's whatever immaculate is to the individual. I, on the other hand, am not thinking in the same way as the majority and believe this is a cheap get-out. I am left exhibiting feelings of being cheated.

"Bloody Adonis."

I turn and look at the estate agent. She continues

talking, unaware that I want to headbutt her in her face to make her stop.

"The picture. It's called '*Bloody Adonis*'. The Adonis part is obvious, I mean look at him. And the bloody part must be to do with the red stuff. It's really pretty, isn't it?"

Looking at the picture, I take in the glorious red blood on the black and white backdrop of the rest of the print. It runs down one side of the faceless Adonis. I want to take the picture in more, as even though it cheated me something about it still draws me in. But she has ruined the moment with her small opinion.

"You know the seller could be persuaded to throw it in. It's a limited edition and was all the rage in Clapham when it first came out. The artist used to live here and he gave the first copy to the seller." She is going on a full-on sales spiel. I feel like asking her if that was before or after he started taking it up the ass. But I remember I must play nicely with her.

With this knowledge at front of mind, I remember the strategy I devised on coming to the Phoenix after work. "It is intriguing, but not really my cup of tea. I would prefer to hang a family portrait over the mantelpiece."

She raises an eyebrow and says it will obviously not be a problem for the seller to remove the picture. After this exchange, I walk off to look around the apartment again. She follows, breaking the boundary of my interpersonal space and telling me all about the individual features as we pass them. The urge to strike is returning; why can't she just remain quiet? I decide she wants to pretend she is a knowledgeable estate agent. So I might as well have some fun with her.

"Was it this flat where those victims died in that fire?" I emphasize the word *flat*.

Her face goes paler. "That was over ten years ago; and no, it wasn't this apartment." She emphasizes the word *apartment*.

"How do you know? The Internet does not give the exact details of the fire. I don't want to live in a place so morbid if it was this flat."

"Well, the whole inside was remodeled, so it's all different. I'm pretty sure nothing bad happened in this particular apartment."

So she has gone from an absolute "no" to an uncertain "pretty sure" after one question. This makes me grin, which she sees and assumes she has satisfactorily deflected the question. I could continue, but I do want the place and don't want to spend any more time in her company. "Okay."

"Good," she exclaims. "So, if you are done here, let me show you the swimming pool, sauna, and gym."

"So do you live locally?" I'm not making small talk but trying to find out anything that might help me when I put in my sealed bid for the property.

"I live in Balham with my boyfriend. We come out to Clapham tons, so can confirm it's a very vibrant area with lots of great restaurants and bars." Obviously she is a Balhamite. Why did I not see that?

"Has there been much interest in the place?" *Just tell me you fucking bitch what I should offer to get it without overspending.* The money is not the issue, but I don't want her commission to be any bigger than it has to be.

"I shouldn't be telling you this but there has been a

lot."

You shouldn't tell me, as in you swore an oath as an estate agent to always be so honest? I don't think so, sweetheart! But I know she's not lying, as this place would generate so much interest.

"The previous owner really loved the home. You can tell by the way she cared for it. With every bid placed she has asked to know a bit about the buyers putting it in."

"Well, please tell her I think she really looked after the place well and I think that picture is nice but not really to my taste, so she doesn't need to throw it in." That should get the correct message across to Carmen and get me the apartment. Anyway if it doesn't, once I finish with the second phase of my plan the apartment will be as good as mine.

Having shown me the "leisure facilities" available in the Phoenix, we leave via the main reception so I could see the twenty-four hour concierge facility. We then re-enter the building through the underground car park, so that she could pick up her car and drop us back at the office. I watch her key in the entry code. During that time I tell her I liked the place, and make an offer. She explains to me how a place like this was to be sold via sealed bids. I know this, but her reaction to the figure I quote tells me what I need to know. I'll put in a lower offer and continue with my plan.

Now I'm standing outside the Phoenix watching the coming and goings.

When the moment is right and no one else is around I walk back into the building via the car park. Maybe once I am a resident I should complain that while the area where the cars arrive and exit have security cameras, the door where someone can enter does not. Earlier today on a half-reconnaissance mission, I determined the route I should take to get upstairs without being detected.

I take the erratic path to the service door to avoid the cameras in the car park, and open the door. Expressing my fire safety concerns earlier, I had made sure I was shown whether the building had a suitable fire exit; then it was just a case of making sure the door did not close properly.

Now I'm outside my soon-to-be neighbor's apartment hoping Nat's friend Joe is in so I don't have to break into the place. The door swings open and I'm greeted with a "what now" from a very camp little man. Some guys and girls just scream out "I'm gay" from every orifice, and he is one of those guys. He is skinny and probably lives off a diet of cigarettes and wine. Scanning his face for signs he might be a frequent drug user, based on what is rumored about Nat's friends, I disappointingly (it would make things easier) don't find any. It does look like he may have been crying. He has a natural tan, the healthiest thing about him. However, if he continues being a sun-worshipper, it looks like his skin will not be forgiving and he will become very leathery and heavily wrinkled. It's a good thing I'm here to put him back on the correct path.

"I'm Seb, a friend of Nat's. I was just viewing the place next door and he told me to pop by and say hi." I extend the bottle of wine I bought after leaving the estate agent and heading back here. "You look like you could do with a glass of this, and I actually need your help." I make him feel needed. He has probably never been in his life, so he'll want to give this new emotion a test drive.

"Oh! Sorry for being rude. I thought you were someone else. Come on in." He opens the door to let me in. It's a good thing I'm not a vampire. "So how do you know Nat?"

"We work together." Well, we started working together earlier today. "I'm looking to buy Carmen and Ricky's place. I had my second viewing just now." Drop a few names that he might know, indicate second viewing because isn't that what regulars would do if buying a place? After all, he doesn't need to know the clarity of mind I have, that a second viewing would be redundant to me. And pretend that the estate agent knows I came here. But to be honest I don't think I'm dealing with an overly complicated individual here; I think I had him at wine.

This thought is confirmed when he literally runs off and reappears in seconds with two wine glasses. I re-open the screw-top wine bottle and pour us both a drink, making sure to give the flamboyant guy in front of me a very large glass. "You look like you need this. Is everything okay? Would you like me to call Nat or someone else?"

"Oh, it's nothing, just a horrible blast from my past," he tells me, gulping down the wine. I top up his glass even before he's finished. "Anyway, tall, dark and handsome, how can I help you? In fact, where has Nat been hiding you away?"

"It's not like that, we're just friends. Maybe he didn't say anything out of respect for Rod."

"Oh yes, the mighty Rod."

"Nat never actually goes into much detail about their particular relationship."

"I know. Even though I live in Ibiza I would have

expected more gossip from one of my oldest friends. You know, he's never been the same since Jas and his overdose. Sometimes I think it would've been a lot easier for all of us if he'd passed away. But being a vegetable, with some machine just keeping him alive, makes it impossible for Nat to let him go." He starts to tear up. Maybe he's not really distressed, just cries at anything.

I move over next to him and put my arm around him. He looks surprised. "I have a boyfriend," he says quickly.

"Don't worry, I'm not the sort of man to put out after five minutes of meeting a guy," I say in a camp voice not quite matching his own, so he knows it's all in jest. He laughs and I realize I should put him at ease. "So I've viewed the apartment next door and I was wondering if you know anything that might help my bid. I mean, you know the guys who used to live there. Are you still in contact with them? Have you seen many potential buyers coming and going, overheard anything in the elevators or corridors?"

"She has a problem with gay men at the moment, and I don't think she would let her dad sell the place to a gay man, just to spite us all. I haven't heard or seen many of the people viewing the place as I just got here yesterday. I could try my friend Benita. She's still friends with Carmen."

"No, no. Don't put yourself out. It was more wishful thinking on my part. So tell me about your boyfriend and Ibiza." I think it best to make it about him because I don't want him involving anyone else.

A massive grin appears on his face. I guess by the goofiness that he's in love. "His name is Jesus and he is absolutely gorgeous! He's a DJ and has been playing the clubs in Ibiza all summer." He finishes his wine and jumps up and sort of skips off. In his absence, I pour my wine into his glass and top it off from the bottle. I add some more to my glass and move it to my mouth in time for his return. He hands me his phone and I look at pictures of a Spanish man. I can see that generally he would be attractive to most. I scroll through the pictures and see ones of them hugging, posing together and being coupley. The guy Jesus has the same goofy expression on his face. I pity both of them.

With black hair, tanned skin, a decent body and his chosen job, Jesus must have lots of suitors; it would be intriguing to meet him and ascertain why he's picked Joe for his mate. It's not a relationship meant to last, of course. When it ends, Jesus will move on before Joe does; Joe will just go into mourning, take years to get over it—though he never truly will. I feel my plan is actually a good thing for both of them, not that that is any concern for me. But this secondary benefit can only be a good thing.

"He is lovely. You guys make such a sweet couple. So what brings you back to sunny London and the Phoenix?" *Did he want you to piss off for a while so he can fuck all those other guys he has lined up?*

"It's my dad's birthday in a couple of days, so I thought I would surprise him for it. Since I moved out of the country I actually miss my family lots, including my annoying twin brother."

"So they live around here?"

"Hell, no! They are all in deepest, darkest Essex. I'll go up on his actual birthday. I promised my friend who owns this place I would check in on it, but I needn't have bothered." He has a gulp of wine, as if going for dramatic effect.

He doesn't continue, needs more encouragement. If he persists drinking at the rate he is, this could be a very short night. "So where is your friend now?"

"He visited me for a while in Ibiza. He went through a bad break-up and wanted to escape everything. Now he's planning on doing an around-the-world tour. I think he said he'll go to Australia first, basically so he can have some of those yummy blond surfers. Then he's going to work his way through Asia doing volunteer work and helping people."

What a humanitarian, I think, but I don't interrupt with my comments.

"Then he said he'll head on to Africa and continue assisting where he can." I might actually throw up. "But he hasn't booked any flights or anything, apart from Australia. So who knows where he'll end up?"

He's going to shag his way around Sydney; once he gets bored, he might go and bang his cock in Bangkok, follow some gap yearers around and have them. Then return home when daddy's money runs out. "Wow, that sounds amazing."

"I know! If I weren't with Jesus, I'd be going with him. But I think I'll miss all my friends too much. I miss them just being in Spain. I saw my best friend Ben, then Nat yesterday; this morning I went to the hospital to see Jas for a bit, but that was too hard. I love those guys; it was so great seeing them and it seems they missed me too. I guess it's only in a situation like this you get to know who your real friends are. There was one guy, Marco, I was really close with. In fact, before Jesus, I thought he was my life. After I left, he didn't bother contacting me, see how I'm doing, or attempt to even bother coming out to see me. I guess he never really cared."

"Joe, everything seems like it's nearly perfect for you with your great boyfriend, family and friends. Can I ask why you were so upset earlier, was it this Marco guy?"

He stares at me, feeling what I doubt he has ever felt before. "I can't tell you. I can't tell anyone." He remains stoic.

"Sometimes it helps to tell a stranger. Your secret will be safe with me, and it looks like you really need to get whatever it is off your chest." *This is going to be your last chance, you should use it.*

"I'm just so ashamed." The tears start.

I pour him the rest of the wine. "We've all done things we're ashamed of, but you have to let it go. Otherwise it will tear you apart and consume you. Did you cheat on Jesus?"

"No, it's nothing like that. It's all in the past and I don't really care about it anymore…but there was this one man and I saw him again today, and he made me feel cheap and dirty."

"Well, maybe one day you'll be able to exorcise him and no longer let him win."

He has more to drink, lets out a massive sigh and starts talking. He tells me that when he was younger he used to sleep with lots of men, though not in an "I'm young and want to sleep around" kind of way. Apparently these men used to seek him out when he worked at a cinema, the one just down the road from here; he never approached them.

46

The men tended to be a lot older. Some actually had girlfriends or wives with them at the cinema, while some just wore rings on their third finger. He never understood what their fascination with him was. The first guy who flirted with him at the cinema, he went with because he was at an especially low point in his life. He wanted companionship and to feel loved, because at that point in his life he didn't have much. Joe ended up sucking him off in the toilets. When they were done, a side effect of the sexual act was that the man left him money—which he never asked for or wanted. Joe really emphasized this point as he told me about it.

After that first incident, there seemed to be a string of men lining up. He did it for the fleeting moment of intimacy, which made him feel better about himself. The money they left him was just a welcome bonus. The punters (my word, not his; even as he is telling me the stories he has a sort of affection for the men, using the word "companions") included minor TV personalities. I think in his head he's trying to tell himself that his prostitution was acceptable because he got to bang someone sort of famous. But for every one he enjoyed "being with" there was always a "tosser".

One man is described to me as a particularly nasty piece of work. When Joe first met him he was attracted to him, and he looked like a "hunky," albeit, "older gentleman," with something weirdly familiar about him. To take care of the needs of this special companion, Joe told him to hang back after all the films had finished showing, and he would be able to give him the attention he needed in one of the empty seating areas. When they were alone together on the floor of screen three, he got Joe to completely strip while he remained clothed, and then suck him off while he called him a dirty, queer bastard. Joe didn't mind this; after all, everyone has a personal fantasy. The man then started gently pinching Joe's nipples. But any tenderness soon disappeared and he became rough—pinching became tugging aggressively, licking became biting to the point where blood was drawn. When the man's mouth was free, the obscenities would continue—how the sluttish faggot needed to be punished and how Daddy was going to teach his pussy a lesson. Then he forced himself inside of Joe, and when Joe tried to protest got a punch to shut him up for his troubles. As the rape continued, Joe realized he was being fucked bareback. Again he said no, but the man choked him until he was quiet; he'd thought he was about to pass out.

This abuse was the most extreme Joe had suffered, but he could not help but involuntarily cum as his prostate was being banged. Once he had cum, the guy came inside him and quickly whipped himself out of Joe. Then he shoved himself in Joe's mouth and demanded Joe clean him up. A beaten Joe complied, and was subjected to the taste of a mixture of the man's cum and his own ass. When the man felt suitably 'cleaned', he zipped up and patted Joe on his head. He told Joe he was an obedient filthy queer, threw three hundred pounds on the floor, then walked off. Joe wanted to report the incident but thought he would be in too much trouble for using the cinema as a "whorehouse". He thought he would just have to deal with it alone. He tells me he would have been okay if he never saw the man again, but he found out later that the guy was in fact his best friend's dad, the friend who owned this apartment.

There is still loads I could find out about from him. The wealth of information he has on Nat, his twisted old lover and junkie ex; how he managed to land and keep his boyfriend; the owners of this flat, the gay-hating neighbors; any names of punters he used to escort for. But I fear time is running out for us.

He had spent the past few years avoiding the dad, which was difficult for him because it meant missing special occasions for his friend. Then suddenly the dad appeared to check in on the place and recognized him straight away. Joe says the guy felt no shame or remorse at what he did, and then tried it again. He said he'd said no, and the dad looked at him crossly, and something about the look scared him.

When he answered the door to me he thought it was the dad who had returned, and he was glad that I was here. After his tragic story is told, he tells me this is the freest he has felt in a very long time. I tell him if he wants to be relieved of this burden he should write a letter to his friend telling him exactly what he told me—including how scared he is that the dad might return, so he can't keep checking up on this place. He looks at me, and I tell him he doesn't have to ever send the letter but the act of doing it will truly liberate him.

I watch as he's frantically writing away, helping with a bit of dictation when he looks lost for words; he is tired, he's been through a lot. He finishes the letter and asks me to read it. I leave it on the table where he put it and read it standing up. It's hardly James Joyce, but it catches the essence and gets the message across. When I turn back to him, he is fast asleep on the sofa. I scoop him up and carry him to the bedroom; he weighs next to nothing. It's a hot night so I gently remove his clothes—we are past being coy with each other after all that he's shared. I look at him lying there totally naked, sleeping on the bed with his chest moving up and down as he breathes. He looks so innocent. He stirs a little bit. I kiss him lightly on the forehead goodbye.

4

HE CAREFULLY SELECTS THE GUY

The act of dating—a prearranged social appointment, engagement or occasion with another—has always intrigued me. It is something that the majority engages in to find a lover, partner, and ultimately a soul mate. Why? At which point in our lives did we lose the ability to be self-sufficient? When did we say, "I must find this 'significant other' to complete myself?" I totally understand the physical urges, which seem to drive most, so by all means go and fuck around. But this would make us seem like the animals we evolved from. So we are led to believe that we fuck until we find that one, perfect being that we can live with, commit to, and have a family with. This is bullshit. It's actually another sanction passed down to control the masses. When settled with another, your actions can be monitored. It becomes harder to rise up against the machine. By conforming you can fly under the radar without detection, you get a pat on the back and can go on living the lie. It's another sign of being a degenerate, of being weak.

If I think this, then why am I currently on my way to go sort of dating? Yes, I have the physical desires which need satisfying, but I have other needs which can only be fulfilled by contact with others. However, I know why I do these acts, and they're not to conform to the path laid for me but for my own personal gain; I'm not like the degenerates. I'm actually vastly superior to the others, including those in power who try and control society, because I'm beyond them and their plans. I have my own plan.

So what "other" does it for me? Firstly, am I heterosexual or homosexual? I guess my strong desire to move into the Phoenix presumes the answer to this. The presumption, though, while correct, is based on false evidence. I'm a bender, shirt-lifting fairy, fudge-packing poof, gay, faggot, queer. But do I think of myself in those terms? Not at all. They are just the labels that are thrown at someone of my persuasion. Do I care about being called these derogatory terms? No. Others seem to have the need to label the exotic, to categorize the unknown into an acceptable box in an attempt to understand it. Another example of how society attempts to dictate what is "normal." As I said before, I'm dating to fulfill a need— not because I'm on some ridiculous quest to find a suitable mate to love for life.

I arrive at a bar called Twilight, which is holding a speed-dating night. Yes, I understand this very act in itself may seem pathetic and cause me to be judged negatively, but feeling the need to please others is not something I strive to do. Before I get the chance to go over to the man by the bar holding a clipboard, he is on me. He sizes me up, probably wishing employees could participate in the night's festivities.

"We have a special speed-dating night on here." *No really, I thought all the posters outside and in were just decoration.* He continues rather too keenly, "So are you participating?"

"Sure."

"Oh, that's fabulous. There are tons of cute guys here already. So do you want to be a sitter or mover?"

"Mover." *Do I look like the sort to just sit there?*

He places his hand on my left pec, sticking a label with the number fourteen written on it there but leaving his hand longer than required to affix the white stamp. "So you move around to each guy sitting when the bell rings, every three minutes..." I stop listening. Others have arrived, wanting to participate; I use this as my opportunity to walk off. I go to the bar and order a double vodka, neat, half-tempted to use it as rubbing alcohol on the place he touched me. Instead, I drink it and order another as I start to scan the room, sizing up the prey. Number seventeen joins me at the bar, ordering a gin and Slimline tonic. The barman makes his drink using my vodka measure to quantify the gin. This is highly annoying. I wonder what other drinks my vodka would have been contaminated with beforehand. Is it too much to ask that they have enough measurers for each drink? Even washing them out in between use causes water to remain and dilute the actual drink. I contemplate leaving, but number seventeen starts telling me we have to go over there, as they're starting. I don't "have to" do anything, but I find myself going along, thinking that I'll have to just drink bottled drinks from this place in future.

The first man has a self-importance beyond belief, spending the first two and a half minutes talking about himself and how much money he earns. Because of that he is too busy to find someone, but all his friends begged him to come to this. At least with this man I don't have to make up a pack of lies to tell. When he finally realizes he should probably ask the guy sitting across from him something, he turns the tables and says, "So, over to you." In the remaining twenty seconds generously left to me I tell him in Japanese that I can't speak English, and sit there smiling. I don't get to savor the bewildered look on his face for too long as the bell sounds and I just get up and leave.

The second date conducts the whole thing like a question and answer session, telling me a fact about himself, and then asking the same from me. He's being keen to make up for the fact that he's damn ugly. I want to tell him he should save his breath for when someone twenty years older than him sits down, but I just sit there lying to his questions, occasionally feigning interest in his responses.

Guy three is boring. He must think himself too attractive to even bother to try and say anything to make himself seem intelligent. He plays with his floppy brown hair. I'm tempted to fuck him, and then when he sleeps cut it off. But I doubt even that pleasure could persuade me to sleep with such a dullard. I tell him he should give number one a go. After all, who am I to stand in the way of true love?

Four and five are nondescript. Six is a university student. How bland he must be not to be able to meet another guy at the university where it's just a hotbed of youth, horniness, alcohol and experiments. He's a timid sort but I'm nice to him, asking him about his degree and getting him to open up. I tell him some lies about me to spark his interest. When our time is up, he is disappointed.

At the end of the night, I know he'll be one of the ones to mark number fourteen down for another three minutes of time together. If I do the same, he'll get his request.

* * * *

Speed dating was a couple nights ago. Tonight I just want to go out and have sex. In the past this would have meant having to go to a bar or club, having a few drinks and dancing to show how great you are. In this day and age, you can just use your own personal phone and various applications to find a fuck. I can even start this process towards the end of the working day, unlike when people had to use the Internet on their company computers and would be scared of all the urban legends about the IT department tracking what sites they visit. These phone apps use your location and tell you where men close to you are. Being in Soho, if I switch it on I'll be bombarded with others in a very close radius, including co-workers, as the office is full of gay men. I opt for the aptly named "FAF"—"Find-A-Friend." "Friend" really stands for "Fuck," though they're not allowed to call it that. No faff with pretending that you're looking for a friend, gym buddy, to go on a date or start a relationship. This is purely for men who want to meet to fuck.

I quickly scan the distance of the bloke nearest to me. It's far enough for him to not be working in the same building as I am. I didn't think the gay guys who work here would really use this app; they would go for the more mainstream ones with romantic inclinations, not this one used to satisfy carnal desires. The types of men who use this one are married straight men in denial and living a lie, gay guys already in a relationship but looking for that extra-curricular activity to validate that they're still desirable, men just looking for a quick bunk-up to kill time after a business meeting before catching their train or plane out of here, or tourists bold enough to want to try and get free accommodation for the night. The latter is my personal favorite, because after the act they will soon be departing the country and there'll be no awkward future encounters.

I've received private messages from three guys so far; *Top or btm? Where u at? Accom?* Perfect directness to my torso picture, which on an app like this, after a cock picture, is mostly what the users care about. Not something as trivial as your name, whether you are a potential crazy, or even whether you are HIV negative; no, the main concern is whether you have a nice trim body and work out. Fat gays just don't have as much sex as their toned compadres. Of course, they can get it on "fuck a bear" or chub services, but these are niche markets.

I don't like the looks of any of the three guys who have contacted me after being visible for all of ten seconds. I have a hankering for something European today. A Spaniard would hit the spot nicely. I'm scrolling through the thumbnail-sized pictures, looking for a nice tanned body. It's rare a guy would have his face up for the initial point of contact. One bloke has taken up three of the one hundred available positions. This is highly frustrating and selfish. I refuse to buy this app out of principal, not wanting to line the pocket of the twat creator who created something with so many flaws, so I'm limited to the free version. My choices are limited to the one hundred closest to me, so it's thoughtless taking up three spaces. Nor has he made any effort to hide what he's doing, as all the profiles are next to each other and have the same location. He also has left the same weight and height in all of them. This desperate fucker is sitting at home with his personal mobile, tablet device, and laptop or desktop on FAF thinking somehow that will increase his chances of getting laid.

One guy ticks all my current criteria; he is a visitor to the country, unfortunately French and not Spanish. I'll have to keep his mouth busy so he doesn't talk. He does have a slim, dark body with black hair, though. Being French, I know he will love it up his ass, as they all do. I mean why else would they take most of their medications via suppositories? Our chat is brief, along the lines of; *What are you looking for? NSA (no strings attached) fun. What are you into? Kiss, lick, suck, wank, fuck. Cool, position?* He's versatile, but is looking to bottom now. *How hung?* I send him the necessary picture, to which he responds with one of his hole. *Where are you at and can you accommodate?* He says he's a tourist, but I doubt that. He must be here on business, as he's staying in a central London hotel by himself. He sends his location, then we swap face pictures, having already seen body shots, including my cock and his ass. He is keen to meet up. Once I've met him, I'll delete him from my FAF, which will subsequently erase our whole conversation and anything we've shared.

Twenty minutes later, I find myself standing outside the door to his hotel room, knocking. I listen to him approach. He takes a moment, presumably to verify through the distorted little peephole that my picture he saw on FAF is a true likeness. He must be happy that it is, as he opens the door and stands there in his pants with a visible hard-on. All the anticipation and buildup to our meeting must have gotten him excited.

I enter the room and start kissing him, groping his package. I push him further in the room and gently kick shut the door behind me. Even though it's his hotel room, my actions let us both know who is in charge. I slip my hand into his pants; he is already pre-cummy. I push him towards the bathroom. He takes the hint, strips off his underwear and hops into the shower while I undress.

* * * *

Bunty's recommended website is one where a friend writes a profile for you in an attempt to be more humorous, which offers a unique selling point over other sites. I like this because you don't actually have to give away anything about yourself. The profiles all seem formulaic, and the friends are trying to be funny while saying my friend likes to travel (he likes to fuck foreign men, not just English men), likes to be the life and soul of the party (he is a selfish queen who goes clubbing all the time), but also likes to cuddle on the sofa with a nice guy and bottle of wine (when he has spent all his money or he is on a comedown, he has to stay in but he can't do this alone). He is as happy being outdoors as he is indoors (he likes to fuck in park bushes too), he is a great listener (he has been around the block enough to have an opinion on everything), he is nice on the eyes—just look at his pictures (he works out to compensate for having an ugly face), and I just can't fathom for the life of me why he is still single (he likes sleeping around too much to settle, but now he's getting older he has had a rethink, as he doesn't want to be alone).

My profile, a sort of alibi, has been up and running for a couple of days now and I'm scrolling through the messages I've received. These guys, while wanting to fuck as much as the FAF guys, are under the pretense of looking for love. Maybe they're not as direct in asking how big your penis is, but ultimately that is what they want to know, and will try and find out by the wining and dining method. The first message is from a guy who seems like a complete douche, who says my profile was so interesting that he had to just contact me. There is nothing personal about his message and it seems like a standard one he has probably sent out to every guy he likes the profile picture of. He has no redeeming qualities; I block him. The next guy is a lot older. Maybe Rod has a slightly younger (but not by much) brother. No thanks. The third message is actually quite insulting because the guy is so ugly. How could he ever think he was in my league that he could even contact me? Fourth is talking all about himself. Seriously, these guys are clueless at how to find someone—no wonder they're stuck on the Internet. Five, six and seven's profile pictures are just bland; I don't read the messages. The next message is from an average-looking guy. It has some charm to it, so I reply with a more charming message suggesting we meet up.

I decide one is not enough, and do my own search looking for a compatible guy. Being the searcher, I can quickly put in some parameters to cull undesirable members. I put in the age limits, entering under thirty. There is a weight and height category but I'm generally not that bothered if the guy is tall or short, so therefore I won't restrict the weight. Next, I select non-smoker because I don't like the taste of a smoker, and I'm not just talking about the kissing—it seems to affect other bodily fluids. The other options, none of which interest me, include education level, religion, location, and the keywords that the friend first entered when creating the initial profile, such as trustworthy, dependable and marriage material. I'm still left with lots of profiles to scroll through. Maybe I should have tasked this to Bunty.

I decide to not bother looking at the profiles of anyone who looks like they're using a professionally taken photograph of themselves because I can't be bothered with a guy like that—one who loves himself too much. It would be too much hard work. In ignoring a lot of these pictures I notice a little logo in the corner of them; sometimes it's cropped out or only partially visible, but I can piece it together. It says Dick C.

Eventually a guy stands out. He has innocence in his eyes, something that says there has been vulnerability in the past. He's not overly physically attractive to me, but his purity draws me in. I start emailing him hello, paying him a compliment based on his profile information, and then subtly convey how great I am and would like to get to know him better. The ball is now in his court. After I finish sending the email, I notice I've got a reply from average-looking guy, suggesting we meet for dinner. He'll do, as I wait for Haunted to get back to me.

* * * *

Last week I spent my time setting up the dates, which was a chore in itself. This week, I actually have to go on them, which will be another mission. Having to sit there and pander to a guy's needs or his whimsical behavior makes me think at times it's really not worth it, but I persist. First up is average-looking guy from the website. Out of the dates I've lined up, he's the best looking. We go out for dinner. He's actually normal and is trying to be charming. I think he likes me.

There is no fussy eating, or being overly bitchy about exes or work colleagues. He seems happy in his job and with his friends and family. Perhaps in a different world I would, but I don't see this making it past the night. I give him back as much as he has given me; no point wasting an opportunity to hone one's skills. Towards the end of the dinner, he stretches out his hand further to touch mine and says, "I would really like to see you again."

I still have it! "I think I've jumped the gun slightly by joining that website. Just moving back to London and all, I don't think I'm ready to settle into a relationship. It was more of a case of looking for friends. I just wanted to be honest and not lead you on, because I've been lonely since my return."

"That's a shame, but friends would be cool."

I re-establish the hand contact and thank him for being so understanding. Knowing that I've said no to dating him, he picks up on my loneliness comment and offers to help in that department. The French Connection was a week ago and I have needs. So I say yes, comfortable in the knowledge that when we get into the bedroom he will be so keen to please me in an attempt to get me to change my mind that I'll be in for an experimental night.

* * * *

The next day I'm actually tired; my predictions came

through. I'm meeting Six from the speed dating for a lunchtime coffee. He tells me how lucky I am to work in Soho and it must be so much fun being in the gay capital of the world. I'm not sure what he thinks happens at work; that everyone in Soho just bunks off and has a mass orgy or something. He is self-depreciating, saying he doesn't think he'll get such an amazing job as mine; he thinks I work in the film industry as an agent. He is very passive and weak. I expect the same from Haunted, one of the guys from the dating website—we are going on a date tomorrow night. I try to be a bit positive to get him out of his lull, and he does seem to perk up a bit before saying something negative about himself or his life.

He keeps looking at his watch, so I ask him if he has another place to be. He goes red. "Oh, not me! I keep checking for you. I know you'll have to go back to work soon, but I don't want this date to end."

"Yes, I'll have to go soon." I watch the disappointment register on his face. I wait for him to ask what he is dying to ask, but doubt he will—he doesn't have it in him.

"So are you going to see any of the other guys from the speed dating?" I ask.

He hesitates, like he's trying to style the answer out. "No." He smiles and accidentally spills the remainder of his hot chocolate. Considering we're at the end of our time together, there is a lot of drink left. I sit back so as not to get any on me. He apologizes to me about twenty times before a woman comes over to clean it up. Then he starts apologizing to her.

If Six was on a date, well, just a coffee, with anyone else, they would have run away by now, knocking his confidence even further down; luckily, he has me to help him find his way. When she has finished cleaning up and giving him dirty looks and has moved off I say, "You're a great guy." To which he looks surprised but happy. "But you really aren't my type." You can't give it all on a plate. "That said, we could have something here. I feel some sort of connection between us."

"I feel it too. I'm shy when someone first meets me, but once guys get to know me they see how great I am." He smiles meekly. "I would love to see you again. You'll see; I'll become your type."

Of that I'll make sure.

5

HE CAN FAKE IT

It's coming on to the end of my second week at work, which all in all has gone a lot better than I could have expected. Was I lucky? No, I'm in control of my life, so things happen the way they do for me because of my impact on the external factors that could influence me. To do this is not difficult; to a certain extent I'm shocked that the degenerates have not picked up this art yet. Then again, they are what they are, the pawns in the game of life.

Part of my enjoyable time or good fortune (if you believe in that kind of thing) has been due to the noticeable absence of Roderdick. Don't worry, I've not killed him or anything like that. Shortly after I started, he emailed saying due to family issues he would be working from home for the next couple of weeks, but he is fully contactable. This was quite restrained coming from someone working in PR. Usually an employee, no matter what level they are, sends a detailed description of anything that might stop them from "working." Because, let's face it, the work we do is so important and God forbid the clients have to wipe their own asses.

Some classic examples include: I'll be in training from ten a.m. to one p.m.—my manager thinks I'm underdeveloped in this particular skill set and is sending me to learn about it from someone equally lacking in the skill. My transportation is delayed but I am working on BB (a favorite of Jay's)—I could not be troubled to wake up or leave on time to make it into work at the correct hour, but if anything should come my way work-wise I'll just forward the email for someone else to handle. The worst examples are the blow-by-blow diary descriptions: I'm at a client meeting on Monday; Tuesday working from home on the follow-up from said meeting but contactable if needed; Wednesday am taking a comp day for working a weekend five years ago.

Bunty informs me privately that our illustrious leader is away because of Nat issues. She comes across as very likeable, so I guess others trust her and tell her information. But she shares her own news just as freely, probably to facilitate the exchange of gossip. This morning our whole work pod was treated to a scaffolder-family update. She found out last night her boyfriend's dad is a right psycho who beats the mother, argues with the son and is doing questionable business deals hiring out garages to "unsavories" (her word, not mine). Well, last night she had to go around to their house, a three-minute walk from where the scaffolder resides, to drop a dish back off, and then the dad started on her.

She thanked them for the food they had sent, and he smirked as he told her that when he was a young lad off to work his wife stayed at home and cooked and cleaned so he could provide for the family. Bunty says that after his comment he stared at the wife, and she backed him up. She puts on her best Essex accent and mimics what the wife said.

"Lou, my darling, in my day my job was to make sure

Brad senior had all his washing done, his food prepared and came home to a tidy house. Then when little Bradley came along, I made sure I could do the same for him. I don't mind him bringing his clothes to me to wash and iron but you really need to start doing this for him." The mum had looked up at the dad before continuing. "Why do you have to work in London? Why not get a local job if you must work? And all these weekends: Bradley says you're out with friends and not here. What's with that? It's not fair that you leave Bradley by himself so much."

The husband stood there agreeing with her and kept telling her more examples of how Bunty had let them down. They told her that before she goes to work she should do the washing up, she should only spend one weekend a month away from Bradley, and her parents should not visit again as they think her mum drinks too much.

Now Bunty, not one to back down, answered them on all the points, and it soon became a slanging match. Both parents ended up shouting her down while she stood there trying to hold her own. It finally ended when she felt herself about to cry, so she left—but not before thanking them for their insightful advice in her calmest voice. When she arrived at Brad Junior's, she cried and told him everything that happened. She had to stop him from going over there and punching his father one, and that's when Bradley broke down. He told her all about his dad's colorful past, and that he did not want her to ever be alone with the man. His mother used to turn up at school plays with a black eye; when she'd mentioned she thought his work associates were doing illegal activities his father had dragged her by the hair out of the house on the way to one of the criminals so the mum could confront said colleague herself.

Finally I get her relationship. She loves the drama. If he had "normal" parents who liked her, there would be no excitement for her. It's histrionics that she gets off on, and keeps her with the scaffolder for now.

Jay had moved over next to her, and is hugging her for the entire trauma she's been through. Raj advises her to leave the bloke, as he'll turn out to be just like the dad. Cindy, the intern who was absent in my first week, is trying to get the attention back onto her by giving examples of all the men she's dated who turned out to be like the scaffolder. I'm wondering what the problem with Nat is. Perhaps Roderdick has pulled the plug on his comatosed ex because he can't handle the competition, even if it is from a vegetable. This is unlikely, though; he doesn't come across as a man of action, more of a whisperer in the ear. If I were ever in that situation, which is practically impossible, I wouldn't pull the plug either. Instead, I would have made sure no coma predicament ever occurred by doing a proper job in the first place.

The downside of this is that any budding friendship I was planning on developing with Nathan will have to wait. For now I'll make do with Bunty and the others who are tolerable. While I'm not the sort of person who needs friends in work or out of it, I prefer to keep some allies. At work, having them means the time can be whiled away with irrelevant discussions, emails and instant messaging; and should the need arise, they can have my back. Outside of work, it's not because I want an active social life, but rather because they have something I need.

"Guys, if you just turn it down for a minute I'm going to call Roderick." I use his full name to emphasize the "ick" part, hoping one of them will add the "d" like I do.

"Tell him we miss him," Raj pipes up.

This amuses Cindy, and she teases him by calling him a little suck-up. I guess she's not bothered by Roderdick, as her charms are useless on him. She is young and attractive, which she uses as her main asset. When she walks, it's actually a slink—but predatory too. She thrusts her pelvis forward with her shoulders back so her pussy is the first thing anyone encounters. My fountain of knowledge has informed me that she'd regularly fucked one of the directors, Ben, a guy more senior and older than Roderdick. They were heard to be at in the toilets, with her screaming her head off how she loved Big Ben. He left the company soon after that, either because all the women and gay men stared at his crotch looking to see if he was that big, or because his wife made him. Cindy wasn't bothered and merely moved on to the next guy who could give her what she wanted. I'm still trying to determine if that's a big cock, career advancement, a father figure, or if she just gets off on destroying families. I hope the latter.

"Cindy, don't tease Raj. You know he has a soft spot for Roderick!" She grins, thinking I've taken her side, but my comment was meant as a dig at both of them. "I think I'll make the call from his office."

In the office I check my phones. A couple of missed calls and a few texts from Six, the "boyfriend" who wants to confirm lunch today. Even though we've only met up once after the speed dating, he is being too needy;

obviously, playing it cool is not something he's aware of. I can't be bothered to speak to him, so I text back that I have to meet a client for lunch and will need to postpone. No sooner has the message been sent than my phone starts to ring.

"Hey."

I don't respond.

"Can't we even meet for a coffee?"

He's getting on my nerves.

"Can you not do a drink after lunch with your client? I've been looking forward to this since we last saw each other."

"The client requested to see me. Do you think I want to hang around with this suited and booted city jock instead of you?" I describe a guy who is everything Six is not, just to wind him up.

"I might just come into town anyway, to do some shopping."

"You should."

"Can we meet after work?"

"I need to see how this meeting goes. I might have to go out for dinner with him. Look, I've got to go. Bye."

I listen to the voicemails; none are from him because he's too nervous to leave a message. He probably knows that he would just babble on and come across even more desperate than he is, and so doesn't bother. The messages are interesting. I listen again to one of them…it ends asking me to call him back.

I use the office phone to call the number I memorized. "Hello, can I speak to Detective Morgan?" I get transferred, and a gruff-sounding man starts explaining the situation and asking me questions. I reply as best as I can. I behave in the appropriate way to the selected information he is telling me, acting surprised, shocked, a little bit concerned. He is vague with his responses, so while we talk I start looking at porn on my phone, not to get off on it, but because I think it's funny for this dead serious policeman to have a potential witness not listening to what he's saying and who's watching some twink take it up the bum.

After that call, I decide to call Roderdick to check how he is and ask if there is anything I can do for him, if he wants me to pass on any instructions to the team, and basically report back on what everyone is doing. He seems genuinely touched at how caring I'm being, and lets slip what the tragedy was without mentioning any names. He is hardly being subtle to his secret lover; even Jay would have been able to decrypt his blasé innuendoes.

My next call is one that I've been looking forward to making. I return the numerous calls from Balham Bitch.

"Good news. The seller has accepted your offer," she informs me.

"Really?" I act surprised. "You said you thought my offer was way too low." *Why are you such a dumb bitch who knows nothing about real estate?*

"The circumstances have changed."

"Oh."

"In the interest of full disclosure, I need to tell you about a little incident that's happened."

I interrupt her. "Is there anything structurally wrong with the apartment?"

"No. It's to do with some of the other people who live

in the building."

"I don't care. Get a pen and paper ready to take down my lawyer's details. I'll proceed with the purchase. I want it done quickly."

"Great…" she's hesitating. "The seller wants a quick sale too. But I really do need to tell you about the incident, as it could put you off and decrease the price of your new place. And the police will—"

"Okay then, go on."

* * * *

Today for lunch I'm meeting Fatty, the woman I stepped in to save from abuse from a fellow tube commuter. As I said, I have uses for acquaintances in my life. Do I want to abuse her myself? No. Well, maybe to some extent. Instead, though, I've got bigger plans for her. Being the caring individual that I am, I insisted we swap numbers so I can check up on her. After all, I'm guessing it can't have been pleasant having a stranger pick on you. Initially she seemed reluctant, but once I let it be known that I am gay and new to the area, wanting to make new friends, I had her. In her head that was believable, and she could see herself playing the role of my big fat straight female friend. We would share stories about men while drinking bottles of wine, and she would be just fabulous pointing out men for me to date. However, that is not her use; she is wrong.

Before leaving to meet her, I ate at my desk—well, Roderdick's desk—so now, when she wants to go on a feeding frenzy in front of me, when I order only a salad or soup it might cause her to show some self-restraint.

She is patiently waiting for me outside of my building;

she looks happy. I kiss her on the cheek and say hello. She doesn't smell of fried food, the type you get in those yellow boxes. I'm disappointed and relieved at the same time. She actually smells quite flowery. I give her a subtle once-over, which tells me she's made a bit of an effort. She must really want to be friends. I'm not surprised, and a little part of me is flattered.

"How much cock have you noshed off since we last saw each other?"

"Huh?"

"I was asking how things have been for you since we last saw each other," Fatty responds.

In my head I heard, and had wanted to hear, the question about noshing off cock—that would have been a far superior question for her to have asked. We are both sober, meeting each other for the second time after exchanging some texts and emails, and she decides to ask the normal question, that anyone would have asked. She could have excelled herself and impressed me by cutting to the chase, but I guess she thinks impressing me would be effectively achieved by normalcy. I extend my arm so she can link hers in it, and without any words she gratefully accepts this invitation.

She is soft and warm. I make a mental note to get drunk and sleep with a fat guy. I couldn't fuck one, though, as the thought of having to get through all that flab to get to his hole repulses me. Nor could I suck one off, as I don't want to head-butt the big fat gut in the process, but to lie down with one and have the soft mass warm me would be nice. It would make a pleasant change from sleeping with guys who are hard and solid. Plus, do they not say fat ones are grateful in bed because they have to be? So I could let him suck me off and see how true the saying is.

"My boss doesn't like me," I tell her. I need to move our dynamic on to why she's been chosen. She is my sounding board, my platform to vent. I can tell her all my frustrations and she will metaphorically suck me off and make me feel better. So, I want to test her. "I think he's jealous because he knows I can easily do his job and that I'm younger than him. And his boyfriend was flirting with me."

"Of course he'd be jealous of you. Everyone feels a bit insecure when someone new starts, especially if the newbie is as great as you."

I give her a look to tell her to continue.

"I mean, look how you helped me out. I was a stranger and you were so kind."

I let her continue singing my praises; I do deserve it, after all. I really did help her. I'm walking her to Selfridges, which is probably farther than she's used to walking. I need to inform her that our lunch plans have changed and we're not actually going to eat. But I feel a bit guilty about upsetting her when she's been so nice.

"Do you mind if we quickly pop into Selfridges? I need to buy something and I could do with a second opinion on it."

After hearing we won't eat straightaway, she doesn't start devouring her arm on the spot. Instead she informs me that it's okay. I guess she probably ate a chicken for a pre-lunch snack.

"It shouldn't take too long, then we can eat

73

something," I tell her.

Her smile says she's dying of hunger but will persevere. To prevent her from fainting on me, I concede to eating in Selfridges before the shopping. Once seated, I quickly order a salad with the dressing on the side and some green tea to set the bar. Disappointingly, she orders chicken and couscous and a diet coke. So much for following my lead. During lunch I don't touch the tea and have still mineral water to drink; the salad is so-so. Fatty doesn't wolf down her chow, eating sparsely as I do while she entertains me with stories of her workplace. I turn the conversation to diets and how I hear the Dukan is the way forward, hoping that she'll take the hint. She continues to eat, and does not appear guilty. More complex a being this fat one is, I think, while trying to will her to do something I would associate with someone of her size.

Eventually, we finish our food and get to the kitchenware part of the store. I casually walk around with her instead of making a beeline for the beautiful metal. When we finally arrive at what I want, I act slightly coupley with her. A couple buying such instruments is a lot less suspicious than a single man, especially one as good-looking as me. We will not be remembered. Everyone fancying me will be put off by my large companion, will quickly move on and not register us.

She picks up the most expensive knife and asks me who would pay so much for a knife. She's right. The Global G Series is a great chef blade, but it doesn't have the flexibility in handling one would want. Aesthetically the Joseph range, another high priced model, is pleasing but it's not as sharp. My knife of choice is the Zyliss. It's a thing of pure beauty—light, sharp, practical and very sexy. I pick the ones with the baby blue rubber handle and casing, just small enough to be very convenient but with enough precision to remove a rat's kidney in one quick flick of the wrist. I select the set and hand them to Fatty to carry for me. I know it won't be long before I get to use them.

* * * *

When I return to the pod after my long lunch, the "children" are talking about Christmas, how it's only September but already some shops and advertisements have started the hype. Apparently the start to Christmas begins in the UK with the return of a "reality" search for a pop-star show which has just begun. Judging by the excitement level in the conversation, I don't believe that will be all we hear about the show. Surprise, surprise—Jay loves the holiday season and can't wait. Raj, who I'm not sure celebrates the holiday in the "traditional" way, says he's looking forward to all the parties. Cindy purrs that she is too, and that's the best part of the season. Bunty is just smiling along, but I guess she's trying to decide if she will take the scaffolder home to play lord and lady of the manor. My take on the season is that it's another manufactured piece of crap to control the masses and introduce an element of separation across the globe for those who do and those that don't celebrate the event.

In a way, though, it's a very clever scheme. Give the degenerates something to look forward to, something they feel they will need to work hard for. If every one of them questioned why they bothered with the tedious routine of life laid out for them, they would look at Christmas and see it as a milestone. Must capitulate to earn a salary to buy presents to please those around me, or to just impress others by how much I've spent on shit. Must buy nice clothes and take care of myself to try and get some action at the Christmas party when others who would never give me the time of day would be in an induced trance-like state of niceness.

Ever since I was a young boy at an age when I should have been excited by the receiving of presents and the general buzz around, I knew it was all bollocks. Ultimately, this told me I was different. Even though the whole Santa Claus thing was so far-fetched, I had decided to test the theory. Deep down I knew it would be a waste of time, but I was just an innocent toddler so maybe a small part of me wanted to be proven wrong. My hypothesis was that if I did something really bad, would I still be rewarded come Christmastime? That was the Year of Beginnings.

I was proven right. In the Christmas of the Year of Beginnings I was actually given more gifts. What could I do? Tell all others what I had found out to be true and hope that I could save them? A part of me knew that I had to stay quiet and keep what I knew to be real from those I came into contact with. So I pretended to enjoy Christmas and all the irrelevant other occasions that the suppressors dictate to us to dominate us. Some were easier to enjoy than others, like Alex's birthdays where I had a mission to make sure that she was especially happy. Because my little sister was special, others did not appreciate her in the way I did. Her tenth birthday heralded not only a milestone for her, but another significant period for me. Another memorable year: the Year of Death.

6

HE HAS THE MOVES

Five in the morning and I'm awake. I decide to get out of bed instead of waiting for my alarm to go off at five thirty-two. I don't need much sleep. I've adjusted to my new temporary accommodation over the past two weeks. I guess I've always been used to traveling around and making my home wherever it needs to be. My Clapham stopover I still visit when necessity dictates, but I've decided that I need to put some distance between myself and that place, as things are about to come to an end there.

Picking up the phone by the bed, I hit the number for the reception and tell them that I'll have breakfast this morning. After my first day staying here I gave them very strict instructions on how I want my food prepared, so now I can just say "the usual" and get precisely what I want. I'm not worried about them spitting in my food for being a tosser—this is a hotel where they're used to a lot more diva demands than the ones I make. The types of clients who stay here order their coffee at a specific temperature, and that is what they get. This level of service is why people like me stay here, the professionalism of the staff is why we come back. Besides, to make sure they're being honorable, I had checked.

Getting out of bed, I admire my naked body and know I look good for my age. I could easily pass for mid-to-late twenties instead of the early thirties that I am. I stretch my five-foot-eleven frame as I make my way to the bathroom. I'm glad that I never grew that extra inch because six feet is too round a number. If I need to be taller, I can achieve the look with appropriate shoes.

My erection has gone down, so I pull back my foreskin and wee. I wonder about those guys who've been circumcised. Always being exposed means they lose sensation. I've been with cut guys before, and they definitely take a lot longer to finish—not in a good way but in a "my hand or mouth is getting bored" way. Do they feel mutilated? Do they feel incomplete? Or do they not care, not ever fully appreciating what they never had? It's another example of society dictatorship. Your parents are a certain religion or have a set of beliefs, and you do not get a say and have that cut made for you based on what they think. In Africa, where certain practices regarding female genitalia are rife, you hear all these stories from humanitarian groups saying that it's an abuse and not right. Is "developed" world circumcision so different from that? Or is it, in fact, the same thing—a violation by that society?

While brushing my teeth with my sonic toothbrush I examine myself closer in the bathroom mirrors. My face has no wrinkles, probably because I hardly ever smile, frown, laugh or show any emotions. I've been told that I'm too pale, but I like my complexion. I'm not so fair that I would burn if exposed to any sunlight, nor do I look like I'm the least bit concerned about tanning. My dark brown hair sets off the whiteness of my skin perfectly. When I was a boy my hair was platinum blond, but over time it darkened, which I'm grateful for. A blond would stick out in situations; I don't. I manage to blend in, and this is what I like.

I have a light dusting of this hair on my chest and forearms, not enough to make me look too hairy but adequate so I look like I've passed puberty. I trim my pubes down to a blade three, not to make myself look bigger—it doesn't need that—but I prefer the tidier look, as do my bedfellows. My legs are hairy, which I like. Men with smooth legs feel weird. Even those who shave for professional reasons, like sportsmen or dancers, lack a certain manliness.

I wash my hands, dry them on one of the larger towels and wrap this around myself, as I presume breakfast will arrive shortly. Thinking about the uncut versus cut men I've encountered has started to give me a semi. Part of me thinks about answering the door naked and letting the person bringing up my food finish me off. However, I have standards, and I need to keep the hotel staff sweet until I can move into the Phoenix.

Breakfast is brought up by a young, plain-looking teenager. I guess she's too unattractive to turn a trick to earn her university fees, so she has to work. She tries not to stare at my toned body. It's not over muscley or too skinny—it's just right, and I realize I could get her to do the deed if I want. I ask her where and what she is studying. When her response is business management at a nondescript university, the University of Westminster, I tip her too generously. She is obviously poor and is trying to better herself, so I appreciate that. When she becomes a society-slag, playing along to the song, then I'll wish her dead.

I take a sip of my chilled, freshly pressed apple juice with enough lime in it to take away any overly sweet taste. I then take a small Gucci wash-bag from a drawer next to the bed; the contents are condoms, lube and various pharmaceuticals. I find the blister pack I'm looking for, take out the off-pink octagonal tablet and swallow it. I wash it down with some more juice. I stare at the near-empty drug packet, realizing I'll need to get some more. If I miss a few days it's not a problem, I could miss more and nothing will happen. I take the synthetic enzyme inhibitor as a preventative measure, not to cure anything wrong with me.

I consider the finasteride tablet I've just taken to be a vitamin. It blocks the conversion of testosterone to dihydrotestosterone, thereby stopping the shrinking of hair follicles and reducing the potential to go bald. My hair is not thinning or receding but I don't want to risk that happening later in life, so I take the supplement. I don't bother with any other vitamins as I make sure my diet provides me with all the essential nutritional intake I need.

I sit down to eat my breakfast, put on the television and watch the news. Working for a media company, I know that most of the stories are planted to control the masses in some way, but I watch to gain clues as to what THEY have planned. I lightly butter the warm wholemeal rolls, watching as the yellow spread melts away and changes form. On the news they're showing pictures of soldiers having to use inadequate kit in the Afghanistan war—jackets unable to protect them from the shots and explosions they face. Next up, they show a solider with a bandage around his head covering his right eye. I cut into the poached egg nearest to my knife and look as the yolk oozes out onto the plate. I dab a cut of the pink freshly smoked salmon, from the Pacific Northwest and not Scotland like they originally tried to peddle to me, into the yolk. Pink fleshy burn wounds are now being shown on the soldiers. It's getting too depressing, even for me, so I switch over to watch cartoons while I finish my breakfast.

Watching Hong Kong Phooey is just the light entertainment I need as I finish eating. I let my food digest while I get the clothes I want to wear later ready. I do the motions of the martial arts moves that I know, not wanting to hit anything but to keep myself flexible. To top it off, I do one hundred press-ups, balancing myself on alternative legs while I draw the knee of the other leg to my side as far as it will go. As I do this I wear my Slendertone, which works my abdominal muscles, giving me my perfect six-pack by sending electric waves to the muscles, causing them to contract.

* * * *

I'm running around Hyde Park, as it's near the hotel I'm staying at, and from there I'll continue the jog into work. I decide not to listen to music but instead savor the surroundings by having all my senses fully alert. If it was later in the day, when the place is full of tourists, there would be nothing worthwhile to savor, so that would be a headphones moment. Even though I'm only lightly jogging, I feel the wind in my hair. This is because before leaving I had rinsed my hair to give it a damp look; I don't like to run with bed hair. I haven't bothered with a shower, as I'll do that once I get into work.

This means the routine will have to wait until the after-work gym session or before bed. The routine is nothing exciting, just a series of products I apply to help maintain my stunning good looks. I admit I use the odd body scrub, exfoliant, moisturizer, toning cream, and concealer when necessary to combat the extra pressure put on us, but I'm not a queen needing to apply fake tan and shave my body. I do believe in helping myself detoxify against the unnatural environment we are forced to live in but I don't believe the marketing of the major brands; I'm sure Vaseline would be as good as any other product to lock water in, but there is the look and feel factor. Plus, I don't have to do anything cheaply so I stick to the big brands.

Usually, I would aim to do a five-kilometer run like this comfortably, in less than twenty minutes, but I'll go to the gym later to work on my muscles so I'll take this run slower. Running at this reduced pace enables another random runner to synchronize with me. He's using me to keep pace. I could just bolt off, but I'm feeling sociable this morning so I drop to his level. I guess because I'm not wearing headphones and have joined him, he sees it as an invitation to start a conversation.

He tells me, "Talking while running is meant to help with breathing technique; and you look like you want some company."

He gives me the once-over; it is clear which team he bats for and what technique he really wants to work out. "I'm training for the marathon," I reply.

"I figured as much. We're the only ones stupid enough to be up at this hour! I've got my first half one coming up soon in Amsterdam."

His accent draws me in. It's Northern Irish, but a lot more diluted than Jay. He was probably born there and then moved to England in his early teens. When he sees his remaining family there on the holidays that necessitate a visit, only then will he revert back to the familiar programming. "You didn't fancy going the whole hog then?"

"No, I thought I would ease myself in. Then I'll progress on to the full thing."

"Sometimes it's easier to just throw yourself in at the deep end. The body can handle extremes if the mind is strong enough."

"I'm Bryan, by the way."

"John." I use the most nondescript name I can think of.

He stops so I do too, and extends his hand. I take up the offer and look into his eyes. I barely hear him say "Pleased to meet you, John."

We are showering together in my hotel room, kissing and touching each other. When we finally make it to the bed, the sex is amazing. The dates we go on I always seem to be laughing; I must be in love. What used to matter no longer does. We are in matching morning suits with different colored ties—his is blue, matching his eyes, and mine is gold. His parents and siblings are there, as is Matt, Fatty and Bunty. Our honeymoon is spent on a deserted beach making love, drinking cocktails and eating local produce. Our home is magnificent—a gorgeous detached house in Putney next to the Thames. For our one-year wedding anniversary I buy him a dog like the one he had as a child. Bryan's eyes still sparkle like the day we first met. We adopt a baby girl and call her Alexandra after my sister. I love her as much as Bryan. We are old men, we have a couple of grandchildren, our lives seem so happy...

I snap my hand away—quickly—like pulling it away from the flames when you get too close to the fire. He asks me if everything is okay. I wonder if he saw our whole lives together flash past in that moment when we first touched like I did. It doesn't matter if he did or not, nor does it matter what my feelings are. Happy-ever-after is not the path that has been chosen for me to walk. I can't deviate from my life, my plan, my destiny. I must be strong.

The kiss is perfect, just the right amount of pressure. When we start using our tongues, I feel myself getting lost. My response to his question if I was all right was to kiss him, just to know. When we finally pull away he is smiling. There is nothing else left to say or do, so I take one last look at him and take off. He calls out "John!" repeatedly, but doesn't pursue me.

I keep running as fast as I can.

* * * *

I'm taking the day's frustrations out by beating the shit out of a punching bag. I look at the sign that says no kicking and start throwing in a few kicks to the punching rhythm I've built up. I know I'm being watched by other guys in the gym. It's a chain well-known as a gay pick-up, and we are in Clapham after all. They can all look; I'll not soil the memories of the day by being with anyone today.

"Nice moves."

I turn around and see a guy wearing the gym uniform—well, sports vest. If he says anything to me about kicking the bag I'll have him fired.

"I feel sorry for your ultimate fighting opponent."

This comment actually relaxes me. I look at his badge. His name is Tim and he is a personal trainer. He sees where I'm looking, probably thinks I'm checking him out, and blushes.

"I'm Timothy Douglas, Tim for short." He extends his hand and continues, "I've just started working here."

I rip off my boxing gloves and shake his hand. "John Henry." There's no need to tell him anything real about myself, as this place is more like a male sauna with gym equipment. There's the option to just pay each time you use the place, which is what I do so they have no record of me. Not many places have a record of me. "So, Timothy— Tim—Douglas, what pointers are you going to give me to make sure I finish off the opponent?"

He hesitates. "You looked like you knew what you were doing. My area of expertise is building muscle mass. If you strengthen your muscles, your hits would be more effective."

"Well, I guess you better show me then." His company is a nice distraction, so I go along with him. I don't bother telling him I would hate to be as stacked as he is.

After the quick show and tell on the machines and a mini-session, he is buying me one of those protein shakes, telling me that protein intake is important for building muscle mass. I don't like the taste of these drinks. I don't tell him this, take just a couple of sips as he downs his with gusto.

The reason for my niceness is that by really looking at him I can tell he's another tortured soul. He spent our session asking me all about myself, so now I turn the tables on him. His pupils dilate and he looks away. He tells me that he recently came out of a long-term relationship, and when he was just getting over it something terrible happened that brought it all back. Then he changes the subject. Based on how much I have on my plate at the moment, I decide Tim here will have to be a slow-burning project. I sign him up as my personal trainer.

* * * *

The housing estate is quite seedy. When they decided to stop building those god-awful tower blocks they must have thought these were a vast improvement. They were wrong. I guess their thinking was to stop the dwellers literally living on top of each other. By opening up the concrete monstrosities, it would give a more aesthetic look and feeling of a real home. The sacrifice to do this means a lot more space is used up. The further away from the city center you geographically move, where this space sacrifice was acceptable, fewer of the high-rises were built. So in Clapham you get these housing estates that no longer physically look like their predecessor buildings, but in essence are exactly the same.

In the surrounding area including Oval, Stockwell, Vauxhall, Battersea, Kennington the human-tiered pens reign supreme. By having the very poor next to the rich, but not the "very" rich because they would not tolerate it, THEY have created a perfect parody. The poor get to see what their lives could become if they work hard and play by the rules, and they get to climb the social ladder. The ones beyond retribution get to mug and steal from "not their own," thus keeping them content and themselves in funds to keep any illicit activities on the go, basically the darkness of life at the forefront of society. The rich wanting to be in the very rich category and move away from the eyesores, muggings and the bottom of the barrel types work even harder to escape the area. They also get to indulge in cheap drugs and prostitutes due to local availability.

THEY are happy that life over here appears to function better than in other countries where the rich-poor divide is much greater. In places like the United States, where the divide is so great that a wrong turn and ten minutes down that route can get you shot, the division exists to a much greater extent. Over here THEY-UK can say, "Look. We have the rich and the poor living as neighbors in a somewhat harmonious relationship, and we can control them."

Ultimately making them the superior overseers.

Why am I here on a housing estate? Well, being in the area I thought I should check in on the Clapham stopover and make sure everything is fine. I just need to take care of a last few remaining items before cutting all ties to the place.

Unlike the tower blocks, the homes are only four floors high. There are no lifts, but that just means there are lots more stairs to piss and graffiti on. There are meant to be green communal areas but these are overrun with groups of adolescents, making it impossible for a young professional couple looking to spend time together barbecuing and picnicking on a green area to do so. These couples are the types who bought into this crap based on the area, and it being all they could afford.

Some of the kids are just that, kids, innocently playing with their friends after school. It does make you wonder where the parents are and why are they letting their pre-teenage offspring roam around this housing estate at nine thirty-eight. The older ones hang out by the bins—the bin gang—probably because the sheds offer some kind of shelter and they can smoke and work on repopulating the estate with the next generation. Judging by all the pram-faces I've seen in my time here, they're doing a bang-up job. Then there is a new type to me, the late teen–early twenties bored Eastern European male adult.

I've never noticed this breed before, but I do now, as there are four of them and a dog directly in front of me as I turn a corner on my way to leave the development. I recognize them as Eastern European because they're all wearing extremely pale blue denim jeans and drinking Tyskie beer. The dog starts barking at me, brandishing its saliva-dripping teeth. I think it's a bull terrier or a Staffordshire type.

The men stop talking among themselves and stare at me. In broken English, one of them asks me what I'm staring at.

"Both your fucking balls because I can see exactly where they're hanging in those jeans." I say that in my head but decide not to say it aloud. Instead, I simply reply, "Nothing."

"He look scared from Brutus," the best-looking of the group says. With his muscular body and shaved head he should have taken a job at Eurocreme.

The fattest of the group, holding the chain leash, lets go of it and the dog runs at me growling before he grabs it again. "I save you not to get your throat rip open. You owe me."

"How much money you have?" the leader of the pack asks.

Now, three options are open to me: give them the two hundred and something pounds in my wallet, stand my ground and be prepared to fight it out, or run away.

So for the second time today, I decide to run away. As I take off, a beer can is thrown at me—it misses, hitting the ground. Then Brutus is set after me.

I'm not going to be able to outrun a dog, but I can easily outsmart one. I head to the nearest bin shed, where as I thought, there is a bin gang just hanging out. Sometimes some of them have their own pets, but there's no other dog present this time. I linger around them...they're trying to work out what is going on when Brutus appears. He goes for one of them—probably one who has his own dog and smells of it.

I slope off.

Leaving the estate, I assess why it was necessary to run: I couldn't afford to get caught in a situation here. This makes me feel no better—I hate having to act like a coward. My mind wanders back to earlier. Was that cowardice that made me run, too? I vow to myself I need to make amends, and when the time is right I'll definitely return to one of the things I've run away from today. To right the wrong.

7

HE HAS MANY FACES

Most parties are shit. Having to make small talk with the guests you know and pretending to like them. Having to interact with strangers who are trying to act cooler than they actually are. Then there are the cliques that develop because the degenerates can't handle insecurity and being alone. And the desperate attempts by anyone single trying to mingle with a potential sex partner. Then there is the purpose of the party—to celebrate a birthday, moving house or occupation or country, engagement, some sort of special occasion that means something to the host(s) but absolutely fuck-all to anyone else. Why do I care if it's Adrian's twenty-seventh, that Pauline has decided to keep her legs shut to all other men apart from James, that Luke is going travelling for a year? I don't give a toss, and I'm certain ninety percent of the guests don't care either. Partygoers have their own reasons for attending: they feel they should because the host is a close friend or relative, they want to get laid, they have nothing better to do, they need something to tell others they did or they need to put in some face time with the other guests.

As this party goes, it's no exception, being equally as dire as any other. The occasion is worse than anything I could have imagined. Raj is going to climb—well, walk up—Mount Kilimanjaro for some charity supporting diabetes, because his father was recently diagnosed with the disease. This party is in the work bar and is meant to help raise funds for him. I'm utterly disgusted. Why the F do I have to pay money for him to have a holiday or do something fun in the name of charity? Seriously, if someone wants to skydive, go trekking, swim with sharks, run a marathon or any other activity they ultimately want to do, they should save up their own money to do so.

I would never do something like this in the name of charity—I give generously to those charities close to my heart, but I don't advertise the fact or ask those that know me to support my cause and pretend it's for the betterment of humanity when really, deep down, I'm being a selfish tight cock. Come on, do something that would really warrant someone having to give you money. Starve yourself for a week, don't speak for a month, sleep in a buried coffin every Friday night for a year. These might deserve some form of sponsorship, not a trip to Africa and a trek up a nice picturesque mountain.

Six would have enjoyed it here, not because he is a social butterfly and would have been able to mingle or integrate with anyone. He would have liked to have seen where I work and have a night out in Soho; the atmosphere would have been enough for him. Plus, all these queens would have been so nice to him. But he doesn't know my real name, occupation or anything true about me, so I didn't invite him.

The date I have brought seems to be holding his own.

Plus with Six I don't like to give him everything on a plate; he needs to work for things in life, and the sooner he realizes that the better it will be for him.

* * * *

Six and I met up for lunch earlier today. It has been one month since we first met at speed dating. I know this because he gave me a one-month anniversary gift—a pair of Hackett socks, which was something I would actually use. This made me realize he listens to every word I say, but I wonder if he listens to the ones I don't. We have never had the discussion about whether we are actually a couple. I did agree to date him, but never said it was exclusive.

I think our lunch went something like this.

"It's great seeing you."

"Hmm."

"Do you know what day it is?"

"Friday?"

"Ha-ha, yes." He then handed me the gift. "It's our one-month anniversary."

I stared at him in utter disbelief.

"We met each other a month ago at that speed dating. I'm so glad my friend forced me to go there and we met each other."

I opened the present and was pleasantly surprised. "Thanks."

"I was thinking that we should try and take our relationship to the next level."

"Yeah, I would like that, but you live with your parents, I with my aunt. Anyway, isn't it better to wait and make sure we are in love before we make love?" He's a virgin, so I thought I'd make him wait; then he'd be willing to do anything once I'm ready for him.

"I know how I feel about you. I just want to show

you."

"You have, with these socks."

"You don't like them? I kept the receipt so you can change them."

"They're fine." If I didn't like them I'd just chuck them. I gave him a kiss on the cheek to feign appreciation. "I didn't get you anything. I'll pay for lunch."

"You don't have to."

"I really want to." No, honestly I prefer to. That way he'll not have anything physical from me to make a shrine to.

"I've got another surprise for you. I've applied to stay in a hall of residence for my final year, and I stand a good chance of getting in, as I haven't stayed in them before. So we won't have to wait much longer."

"I'm an adult and I am not going to sleep with anyone on a single, crummy bed."

"I just thought..."

"It's my fault. I should've realized you're still very immature." I know I'll lose him once he's in halls, and by diffusion he will pick up some friends who he'll be able to go out with. With a wider social circle, he'll gain confidence and move on. Maybe I should just let him, but I hate to leave something unfinished once I've started on it.

He looked like he wanted to cry, but silently ate his food.

"Sorry, I'm just frustrated. I want our first time together to be special, but it won't be in University of Surrey halls of residence."

"At this rate, I'll still be a virgin when I'm twenty-five."

He said it as a joke, though I caught a hint of defiance in his voice.

"How about I book us a little weekend away?"

"Oh yes! I'd love that."

"Amsterdam?"

"Oh my God! Really?"

"Yes."

Reality sets in and he realizes he can't afford a trip away. "Only..."

"I'll pay for the flights. Consider it a late one-month anniversary present. We might have to go halves on the hotel as I wouldn't be able to afford your share of that too."

"Okay. I can use my student loan and some of the halls money."

He should have offered to pay for his own flight—that will be the cheapest thing on our weekend away. The hotel I'm going to choose will basically mean he'll be stuck at home for the entire year.

I changed the subject to my work event tonight. It makes the monotony of being with him bearable when I get to extract these little nuggets of pain.

"What shall I wear?"

"If only you could come."

"Why can't I? It would be nice to meet some of your friends."

"Work colleagues are not my friends, they're just associates. Plus I haven't met any of your friends yet."

"You asked me not to tell them about you."

"Have you?"

"No. But my best friend Roxy will keep your secret. I'd

love you to meet her."

Your only friend. "I'll let you know when you can tell others about us. Anyway this party will bore you; it'll bore me."

He has a look on his face which I've not seen on him before—determination…

* * * *

Raj interrupts my thoughts of which Amsterdam hotel I should book, my own version of escapism to save my mind from the dullness of his party.

"Your boyfriend is great."

"Thanks." *Like I need your validation.* "So how far off your target are you?"

"Two thousand."

"Don't tell the rest, and make sure you put it down as anonymous," I tell him as I hand him fifty pounds for the cause. "I don't want to be seen playing favorites, okay?"

"Wow, thanks. That's double what Rod gave."

"Oh, is it?" I ask innocently, knowing it's actually two and a half times as much. "Well, he still seems disturbed by his family emergency."

We both look over at him. He's talking to my plus one, so I decide to go over to them. As I get nearer I hear Roderdick talking to him, and it sounds like he's flirting with him. I guess this is payback for my behavior with Nat. But what he doesn't realize is that I don't give a toss.

"Do you mind giving Roderick and I a minute?"

"No, not at all."

"What a lovely fellow you have there," Roderdick tells me.

"Thanks." I watch as Haunted saunters off. He is the

perfect date to bring to an event like this. "I just wanted to see if you're all right. You still seem a bit distracted. I wanted to say this outside of office hours so we could talk more freely and you'd know I'm asking as a friend."

"That's good of you."

Since meeting Haunted tonight and thinking that as I have my own boyfriend I'm not after his secret boyfriend, Nat, the dick is being a lot more pleasant to me.

"It'd be great if we could be friends. I don't know many like-minded guys in London, and all the twenty year olds just want to party and go out all the time. You know I met him online."

"He did mention that. It must be difficult moving to a different country."

"It is, yes. I only came back as my father is ill and I thought I should be close by." That will seal the deal. Now he won't think that I came over here to steal his job.

"Well, you have a friend in me."

"And you in me. If you need me to take on any more accounts while you recover from your crisis, I'd be glad to help."

"I might need to take you up on that. The problem might continuously raise issues, and I think it's going to take a while before it's resolved."

"Ouch, it sounds bad. You sure you don't need to take some vacation? Get some nice rest and relaxation?"

He examines my face and thinks I'm being genuine. "It's not me." He lowers his voice. "My partner is going through some stuff. It's mainly to do with friends. He's physically fine but he feels betrayed, and it's really messed with his head."

"He's lucky to have you." As I say it I gently tap his shoulder to reassure him that I care about him and our new budding friendship.

I tell him I better go check up on my boyfriend, but scan the room looking for Nat. I saw him earlier, briefly, but not doing much socializing. He's in a corner with another guy. They look close, not in an intimate way but a way that says they have history together. If he was an ex or potential, I'm sure that the dick would be on it, preventing Nat from ever being allowed to be in the guy's presence. It must be platonic.

I wait for the guy to get up and leave Nat alone, before going over. When the guy gets up I notice him picking up a fancy camera and a bag that looks like it contains camera stuff. The guy catches me looking in his direction and takes my picture before I have a chance to turn away. Then the photographer starts snapping other guests.

On my way over to Nat I see Bunty, the fountain of all knowledge, so I ask her about the photographer. She looks at him and informs me that they used to use him a lot when she first started, but then he became really big and only does occasional shoots like this. She has a devilish look in her eye, and says maybe someone called in a favor to get him to do this. She glances over to Raj. I know Raj doesn't have that in him, he's here because of Nat. The last thing she tells me is the photographer's name, Richard Clarke, which she remembers as she had to sort out his invoicing back in the day.

Haunted intercepts me on my way to Nat, asking if we're going to go out clubbing with Jay and Raj and some others. Looking at him, I remember the website and some of the pictures of some of the other guys that I had to scroll through, and that signature on them, and wonder if I've just seen Dick C. I've had my fill of socializing and don't want to continue the night with these guys. I think about what else I could be doing, and tell Haunted that I'm tired and he should go clubbing, but come to my hotel afterwards so we can have our own private party. He tries to tell me he'll go with me now, but I insist he go and have some fun, as that is what I intend to go and do.

* * * *

Luckily there is no queue, otherwise I would have just barged to the front and bribed the bouncer. They must just let the few that want to enter come straight in, as this is not the sort of place guys want to be seen to be hanging around, even if they were out. If you were a British guy on holiday in Europe in somewhere like Berlin, you and your group of friends would all enter a place like this, it would be a laugh. However, on a degenerate's own doorstep they feel it is sleazy. I get security-searched on my way in; I presume they're looking for drugs—not on some moral crusade to wipe out illegal substances, but because if you were to use under their roof you should buy from one of their sanctioned dealers. The search is hardly extensive. If a guy wanted to smuggle anything in he could just shove it down his boot or up his ass.

After paying the admittance fee I pass the cloakroom where a sign encourages you to leave as much as you like behind. On the counter there is a vast supply of condoms and lube. At least these sex clubs are thinking about safety, but if they cared so much you'd think they would have security cameras everywhere to make sure everyone was safe. They have them on the tills to make sure the staff doesn't steal, but nowhere else—the punters value their privacy. And I'm not exactly sure if "sex club" is the right term for the place. It seems more like a glorified sauna with dance music and full bars. Plus you don't have to take all your clothes off.

It would be nice to think society had progressed to allow a place like this to exist where horny men could just go and hook up. Unlike a regular club—where you go with friends, listen to the latest chart hits, wearing your fanciest and tightest clothes, and cruise guys you hope to pull and then date and introduce to your friends, then eventually take home to Mummy and Daddy—this place exists for the sole purpose of getting a very discreet fuck. You don't even bother taking the fuck home or going to theirs—it's all done in the club. THEY let these places exist on their doorstep in Vauxhall because they love to wet their heads and indulge too. Obviously, the club pretends to be a regular club—it wouldn't survive long under its own guise.

If one is in any doubt as to the sort of place this is, the clues are plentiful. On entering the place, the strong aroma of the legal "room odorizer" amyl nitrate hits you and starts loosening your smooth muscles for you as you just breathe normally. The screens scattered around the place are showing full-on hard-core gay porn—not the twinky frat-boy kind of stuff but the hairy older man engaging in bondage, barebacking, and general rough sex. The screens are providing most of the illumination for the entire club. The music is pounding with a heavy beat, though the dance floor is empty. The three barmen are all wearing different types of leather underwear and nothing else.

I buy a bottle of beer and am asked if I would like anything else. The emphasis placed on the "else" suggests not another drink for a friend but something entirely different. Perhaps some narcotics, or maybe him. Men come here for sex and you're guaranteed to get something, depending on how fussy your standards are. The barmen are probably the youngest guys in here, so some of the fussier, richer clientele might indeed want something else.

In this room, there is a sparse scattering of men all by themselves scanning the new meat joining the party. Off the main room are two corridors, excluding the one I entered. I go wandering. The corridor I'm nearest and venture down first splits off to stairs leading to a floor above me with the toilets that smell shitty and are home to fucking—going on now—and to a room cordoned off by a black heavyset curtain. I pull back the curtain and find the dark room. I hear panting, breathing and the sounds of fucking. I don't enter. The only appeal would be no one would be able to see me, but I like to know my surroundings and a pitch black room with faceless souls does nothing for me.

Now I'm upstairs, the layout of which is maze-like. Around each corner is a sofa, table, or stool, inhabited by various guys in states of copulation. In the middle of this floor is another bar with two dancers on the specially adapted counter. The tiny underwear worn by the dancers shows off the shape of their excitement, which I presume is chemically driven. The dancers have a few admirers lusting after them. I decide to leave and head back downstairs. I go down the other corridor, which opens out on to a wider one made to look outdoorsy like an alleyway.

Here, most of the guys are. Everyone is watching all the live sex between strangers who have just met. Some are just watching, others are initiating similar acts with like-minded guys or are trying to join in with those already engaged; most are touching themselves.

Watching the sex is turning me on. Getting hornier, I stay here and finish my second beer. A guy moves to stand next to me, not saying anything but letting his arm touch mine. I move off, ignoring him, and go to another section of the club, the last part I've not ventured to yet but the area I came here for.

I enter the cubicle. It's painted purple and is larger than that of a toilet one, and it's completely empty. A short man in his mid-twenties enters after me, before I have the chance to lock the door. He's smiling, and produces his erection; it's also short. I laugh, open the door and leave. Walking down the row of cubicles I pick an empty one far away from my original one, which looks to be occupied on both sides. This time I lock the door straight after me.

Closing the hole in the wall to my right side, I move to the open one on the left and stand next to it. This way, when the tenant next door looks in he will see my jeans and nothing more. The guy in the right cubicle to this one will not be able to look in until I reopen the slot, which I might do depending on how the left goes. The stranger has realized my presence, and shoves his finger through the hole and motions me to come with him.

What I can see of his finger looks clean, and it's not that of an old man. I unbutton my jeans and pull down the front of them and my boxers, and shove my erection through the glory-hole. He gasps in delight and instantly takes it in his mouth. The anonymous stranger is an expert cock sucker and I'm super turned on already from everything I've seen and thought about since entering the club. I've bent my knees slightly to get the best angle to penetrate the hole. Now my whole body is splattered against the wall, my arms and hands spread out wide to support me as I give as much of me as I can to the hole.

Images of the blank canvas sucking next door enter my head…I see both Nat and Bryan. He's enjoying himself and making sounds to say so. Before I know it I've started to grunt along with him. As I start shooting my load his mouth tightens around my cock. He is determined not to spill a drop of cum and starts swallowing the whole lot down while I continue to supply him with more.

When he can take no more or I'm completely spent, I don't know which, he lets go. As I pull up my pants and jeans and tuck myself away I notice he has shoved his shiny cock through the hole and is expecting the favor to be returned. The cock is not as big as mine but it's not an unattractive one. He is gently thrusting it in and out. He did a good job bringing me off so expertly and quickly, so maybe I should. Instead of placing it in my mouth I grab hold of it tightly, which he likes. He moans louder, which starts me thinking, wondering who the fuck does this guy think he is that I would want his cock in my mouth? I wanted satisfaction, which he provided, but never once alluded to returning the favor. Why the fuck would I want to do that? What pleasure would be in it for me? My thoughts and free hand then drift to the baby blue nine-inch razor sharp Zyliss in my boot.

I give his cock a few tugs and he starts his moaning

again, begging me to start sucking. I really should give him something to beg about, I think. I'm certain that the knife will be able to cut his penis off, but I'm wondering if I'll be able to do it in one quick slice—or would it involve a series of hacking? At which point would he know something is wrong? Once the penis is completely off and he falls back into his cubicle with blood gushing out from the stump that is left? Or would he somehow manage to remain at the hole and a hot spray of blood would jet out at me where the cum should have spurted from? Would the loud music drown out his screams or would he just pass out from the sudden trauma and loss of blood? What would I do with his penis? Feed it to an animal, chuck it back to him to give him hope of a reattachment, stick it in the right glory-hole and let the friend at that side have a little suck before realizing something is up—well actually not up—or chuck it on the floor in here and stomp on it, mashing it down with the heel of my boot until it's a fleshy pile of unsalvageable mess?

Decisions, decisions.

8

HE IS HELPFUL

THEY let everyone believe that money is the main motivator, the driver of life. That money makes the world go around, that if you had it all your dreams would come true, so you must work to obtain it. Be a good degenerate, go to work and pay us handsomely with all those taxes. Then buy goods and services to keep the economy going. This lie, and the belief in it, really gets to me. The number one driver of life, more important than money, what everyone wants above all else, the engineer of the universe is—opportunity.

It is opportunity that the masses truly desire. Sure, money allows you the chance to realize the opportunity to live in a grand house, own nice material objects, go to exotic locations, eat in the fanciest restaurants, and afford to start a family. But the misconception of money being the essence is just propagation. It is what the money can buy, and that is the opportunity in all its various forms, that everyone wants.

If those without money had the same opportunities as those with it, would the world be a utopia? Everyone existing not to gain wealth to fulfill their desires but being equal as all others, with nothing left to strive for but personal development. Everyone working together to do some good, to solve famine, drought and environmental issues, and by default, eradicate inequality, poverty and war. THEY do not want this though, preferring everyone to slave, fight and kill for money. Because THEY have taught society to falsely believe money is what is desired, a nice metric, so that THEY can control everything.

Just imagine if someone worked an hour doing whatever they were able to for the good of all society, be it a doctor, teacher, rubbish collector, and as payment they equally have earned the ability to choose the same reward. All work is seen as equal and is paid for by time. Every child is afforded the same level of education, with no privileged education for the elite, no matter what their parents do. All services are equal for everyone. Then this would be a fairer place.

My Tramp would not exist if the world was fair and THEY did not exert their controls on society, and if the majority did not buy into their propaganda. However, THEY do, and until I stop them the world will remain disjointed and out of control. So, homeless degenerates do exist. I do my bit and try and improve the life of one. Since I have been in Clapham, I've noticed various homeless types that hang around outside a bank by the cash machine. I selected one of them and whenever I see him I give him money, usually a note; he is My Tramp. Our relationship, like most of mine, started very slowly and is built on me lying to the other and then gaining their trust. I see My Tramp and others like Six and Haunted as ones to be saved from THEM.

It is not necessarily my duty to help them but it is part of my destiny, this destiny I have always believed in. Sometimes I see another path for myself. Like the time I started to waver when I met Bryan, thinking maybe a standard life was an option. My momentary lapse caused me to have some doubts and I decided I should visit the House of the Departed. SHE will know, SHE will see if I still have to save others or if I have paid my dues and this particular path has ended for me. I have contacted the number and am now waiting to hear back. The House of the Departed is busy, but I had hoped once SHE realized it was me and I was back in the UK I would have been bumped up the list somewhat.

Since the first couple of pounds, altogether now I must have given My Tramp over a hundred quid. He looks like he has put on some weight; maybe he is able to afford proper alcohol to waste his life on instead of using mouthwash. Maybe the drugs he gets for himself are of a better quality, no longer cut with industrial cleaners. Or maybe with my aid he is getting real sustenance and is able to sleep somewhere dry and safe without having to fight off the other homeless or opportunistic non-homeless ones. I guess where he goes does not offer him a shower or bath, the chance to have his clothes cleaned or more appropriately destroyed and given something more pleasant to wear. As soon as he spots me he starts blubbering on; I don't think it is to me or to anyone in particular. I vaguely hear that I am a good man, sir, so helpful, please, he needs to eat, thanks.

No one else is close enough to hear us. "I am sorry but I do not have any money on me today." He looks absolutely gutted, after becoming reliant on my hand-outs to fuel whatever it is that gets him through his life.

"Yawe soooo k-ind."

"I feel really bad. As I've told you previously, you remind me of a friend of mine. I want to help you get back on your feet."

"P-p-p-lease."

"I have money back at my flat; you could have a meal, a bath and some clean clothes. It's not far." He is staring at me in disbelief, wondering how would be the best way to properly fleece me. In case the look is one of cautiousness I add, "Maybe you could bring along a friend."

"Noooo. It's juzz me." Typically, he does not want to share his new found cash cow, and by me mentioning potentially assisting another, he has gotten on the defensive.

I give him directions to the housing estate. He knows it, I'm guessing after spending many a night in the bin sheds. I tell him which bin shed to go to, where I will meet him. It takes him a good five minutes to gather up what possessions he has and he looks reluctant to leave his spot. I figure he thinks he is in a prime begging position outside this bank and getting the numerous high street passers-by. Not that he could get that much from them; I must at least double his daily earnings on the days I see him.

When he eventually sets off he has a gait to his walk. I am about a hundred meters behind and finding it very difficult to walk this slowly to keep pace with him. From my distance I watch to make sure he is going the right way. He stops at a few bins along the way to pick up any cigarette ends littered on top. Why he is being so him is beyond belief when here he is on a promise of food, clothing, hygiene, but he insists on staying true to his nature. It must be difficult to break from what you know. I should have told him he would be able to have all the fag butts he wants back at the flat.

He is at the rendezvous point at the bin shed and the bin gang is ignoring him, they are probably too scared to be their obnoxious selves. Actually, after he starts looking through the bin they all disperse, I guess to another bin shed with no random smelly man rummaging around chucking rubbish about. I was close enough to hear one of the gang say, "Man, you need to wash," and sniggering about My Tramp's reply. Quite a brave move on his part, considering there was five of them and they were already moving away from the hobo.

He seems distracted when I approach him; such a wealth of resources he cannot let go without a throughout investigation. It is funny how the waste, the undesirable crap for those living on this housing estate, is complete rubbish to them, while to My Tramp that stuff represents the difference between starving, dehydration and hypothermia or not—basically between his life and death. Recycling does not seem to be a priority here. I guess it is more difficult to do that environmental kindness, as the refuse collectors will not go outside every door to just collect purple or green boxes on different floors. For those living in houses where the binmen already have to go door-to-door to collect the regular bins, it is viable for them to also individually collect any recycling.

The quality of leftovers My Tramp has includes dregs of liquids inside bottles, something that must be harder to come by nowadays. Part of me feels pity for him, but witnessing this strengthens my resolve to continue to liberate this man.

I approach the animal guarding his prey cautiously because I do not want to anger or scare it away. When he first sees me he seems confused, as though he has forgotten that I was the one who invited him here.

"Kind sir," he murmurs.

"Hello, remember I was going to give you some money and some hot food and drink?" I over-pronounce the last word and smile at him.

"Drunks?"

I motion with my hand the drinking sign of knocking back a few. I then point out the entrance to the staircase he must go through and tell him to walk to the top floor, the fourth one, hoping that he has enough in him to do so. I finish the directions, telling him it is the end flat; I point out the red door to him, the top of which is visible to us, and check that he understands where his destination is. I let him know to come in his own time; after all, he should be allowed a last scavenge.

The place is very tidy; I have had a big clean up since it will be my last time here. Not being a sentimental sort I do not care. It is truly the opposite, as I much prefer to move on from place to place. The first property I will actually own will be my apartment in the Phoenix. The thought of moving there fills me with varied emotions—everything from excitement, trepidation, longing, to a sense of finality. Moving back to London I have found myself becoming somewhat an emotional sort over things that would have never before elicited any sort of response in my being. It's weird. The things I should care about still do not matter to me, and degenerate things like moving into my own place and a chance encounter with the Running Man, I shall not use his name anymore, have gripped me in new sensations.

The House of the Departed will see me right, if only one of her minions told her it was me that requested a meeting. I am sure SHE would expedite my visit.

I scan around to make sure nothing is out of sorts and prepare My Tramp a drink, not that I think he would be fussy but I decide he is a scotch sort of man. He can finish off the rest of a Black Label Jonnie Walker, much better than what he must be used to and not something that would go near my lips. I am thinking about what to put in it; not being a fan, I am not sure if some ice would make it more pleasant. Thinking it might not be good if he got totally drunk—after all this is about his rehabilitation—I dilute it with some Coke.

He will show up in his own time. I sit patiently looking at the drink, watching. After a while the condensation builds up and slowly trickles down the glass onto the table. I did not bother with a coaster. The water will leave its mark on the table; the table will feel the presence of the water invading and penetrating it but unable to do anything about it. Who is really in the wrong: the defenseless, being passive and allowing things to happen, or the invader, seeking to do and take as he or she pleases?

Looking beyond the drink and all it represents reminds me of the owner of this place. When I first returned to London, to celebrate I went to a club, not a sex club, just a regular run-of-the mill gay club to check out the scene. It was a weeknight and over the academic summer holidays. The place was not very busy but there were enough around. That night all I wanted to do was have a drink and a dance, basically a night off.

I was not even bothered about hooking up and spurned the advances of many suitors. So there I was, literally minding my own business, when a guy fell off the stage and landed at my feet. The body lying on the floor looked decent enough from behind, slim with just the right amount of muscle. I looked up on the stage to see if he had any friends to come and assist him but it was apparent he was there by himself. As I bent over to help him up, he started up saying that he was all right. Rather disappointingly, his face was below even average; his chin was small and awkwardly shaped, and even though he looked too old to have acne, his skin showed a different story. His eyes were small and nondescript.

He was in fact pissed as a fart, and stumbled on to me. Instead of apologizing he acted like it was my fault. Now, this type of behavior is usually rewarded by a quick sharp knee to the stomach, but as it was my first night out I thought I should behave. He then started drunk dancing next to me. When he finally took the time to look at me he obviously liked what he saw. Alcohol overriding the good sense he had telling him I was way out of his league, he started talking to me.

Now, I am not sure if we were being watched the whole time, but a bouncer came over and said he thought I should take my friend home. In some sort of admiration for the bouncer and his technique of totally managing to pass all the responsibility for the drunk on to me, I decided to play along. The club would shut in about forty minutes and I thought I might as well extend my night and see this stranger home.

It turned out he lives in Clapham, the area I was

thinking of moving to, so I ended up accompanying him in the taxi. Also, because no taxi driver would take him alone in case he threw up, they needed someone to pay the extra fifty pounds and clean it up. As we approached the address he'd told the driver before shutting down to a catatonic state, he woke up again. Somehow programmed to know he was near home, his instincts aroused him. Or, he had been in the situation so many times before so he subconsciously knew how long he could sleep before being awakened. I was surprised that he did not throw up.

He forgot, or was never aware of, the fact that someone else was in the cab with him. When finally aware, he tried to cozy up to me, I think more to shock the driver than anything else. I rejected him and he acted like he did not care. He asked the driver to stop at the main road intersection to the housing estate entrance. Once outside he started fumbling around for his wallet. I paid the driver and got out too, and the driver took this as a good sign and hurtled off. The second guy that night to run away from the Drunk, leaving him in my care.

"What are you all fucking looking at?"

There was no one else around.

"You are going to wake your neighbors," I warned him.

"Those bastards can sleep through anything. Like when some of them were mugging me and broke my leg. No one managed to hear my screams then."

I was going to leave him there until his rant, but this guy seemed to have a very self-destructive element. Part of me was tempted to watch from the sidelines and see what happened next, how he would really handle any trouble that arose. I did not want to give some chumps the chance to gay-bash this guy, even though I thought a little slap might do him the world of good.

"Maybe they did it because you were being so loud."

He was staring at me, unsure if I was joking or not.

"Well..."

"Look, let us go inside."

"You want to fuck me?"

Not really, mate. "Let's get a drink, of water, inside, and see what happens."

"I'm a great fuck. I've lost count of the number of men I've slept with. It's in triple figures." He was telling me all of this as he led the way to his place. On the stairwell he tried to kiss me again, but I managed to turn my face in time. In such close proximity to his neck I smelt his aftershave, the original Diesel. He must really hate himself to feel the need to douse himself in a fragrance thinking that would get a man to love him. It was apparent that he wanted love, desperately sleeping around to try and find it, hiding the pain with copious amounts of alcohol and wearing a giant target on his chest saying he is a victim so come beat him some more.

Inside the flat (it looked bigger than it did from the outside), he saw me looking around and proudly told me that he owned it. That he bought it about ten years ago and the mortgage is really cheap. I believe this is all he has in his life. He offered to make me a martini; I neither accepted nor declined. I just sat and watched him. He started playing around with a cocktail shaker and after a while he gave me a drink. It tasted strong, he downed his and topped up his glass.

"So were you really mugged outside?"

"I was." He was speaking slowly and I do not think it was just because of the alcohol. "It wasn't in this housing estate but the one next to it. I was taking a shortcut home after a night out and these bastards asked for my phone. I didn't give it to them and they attacked me. When I was down they stomped on my leg and broke it."

"You wouldn't know, looking at you on the dance floor." I felt he deserved some level of respect for not being a coward like I would have pegged him for. However, he was not clever enough to know which battles to choose and which to walk away from.

"It was over two years ago. But it still hurts at times, and I still have to have physical therapy."

Once the second martini was finished, taking approximately the same time as his knocking back the first, he left the room. I guessed that was the end of the night for him but five minutes later he was calling out, "Oi, bloke. Bloke. Come here."

I investigated the commotion and followed the sound of his voice; he was stark bollock naked on all fours on top of his bed with his ass facing the door.

"Fuck me," he demanded.

The offer was tempting, only because the way he was presenting himself would have meant zero contact with his face. I thought about his statement earlier and did not really fancy going where a hundred men had been before. He was getting frustrated and made his demand again, and this time he opened his ass cheeks wide apart with his hands. I wondered if I should slip a finger in to see if he was tight enough to make it enjoyable but decided not to. Speaking to his ass, which he was waving about in the air in an ironically off-putting way, I told him no.

He did not seem bothered, and just climbed under the covers and proceeded to go to sleep. I headed back to the living room and looked at his DVD collection skipping the *Tenko* and *Sex and the City* box sets he had. Unexpectedly I spotted something that I really wanted to watch and opted for *Dungeons and Dragons,* the cartoon series. I made myself comfortable and settled down on the sofa to spend the rest of the early hours of the morning.

I must have dozed off towards the end of the second DVD, which was now playing the home screen, and must have done so repeatedly as I knew what the words coming up next would be. My awakening to the lost children trying to find themselves a way home was because of the Drunk now sucking me off. I was not sure how long he had been doing it, or if the horny cavalier had got me going, but I felt myself close to climaxing. I could not stop him, even though under normal circumstances I would have halted this violation. I came, he swallowed.

Afterwards he got up and went into the kitchen. I went into the bathroom, which was full of products, and helped myself to a shower. In there I considered my options: to put this down to experience and call it a day, or finish what he had started...

There is a bang at the door, interrupting my thoughts. I get up and answer it. My Tramp is standing outside with his new haul. I usher him in and glance around to make sure no one has really paid much attention to him. Once inside, I tell him to make this place like his own; I pick the drink off the table and offer it to him. He sniffs at it and then gulps it down.

"You must have been thirsty," I tell him and fix him another. "You might want to drink the next one slower. You don't want to make yourself sick." He is not listening to me. Instead he is busy playing with the object near the fake fireplace.

"Guud, guud, boi." He is mumbling away something in his incoherent way.

The object has him fixated; he does not quite get it. I hand him the next drink, which becomes his new focal point; alcohol trumps object. He has some of the scotch and then drops the glass and shouts out, "Weir dur ed?" continuously.

Guessing he is tired, I decide to show him where the bed is. As I approach him he seems to withdraw. I hold my hands up and tell him I am his friend, here to help him. I take out my wallet and give him ten pounds and tell him there is more in the bedroom. He seems reluctant and keeps glancing back at the fireplace. I go over to him and put the money in his hand. Luckily I have been wearing gloves since being in the flat, so there is no skin-to-skin contact. I gently take his hand, which is clasping the money, and lead him; he follows. I open the door to the bedroom. He sees the invitation of something he has not had for as long as he can remember, and makes his way to the warm bed.

9

HE LISTENS

My Tramp has been in the bedroom for about ten minutes before the guttural noises of him enjoying himself start. The sounds of the bed shaking accompany his racket. He really starts going for it and the moaning coming from the room becomes very loud. Maybe I should shut the bedroom door and give him complete privacy, but he is obviously not being shy about the pleasurable gift I have given him. He starts to cum (I presume); there is no religious name calling, just grunts and groans. Followed by whimpering. I wonder when he will be ready to go again. After all, the tadalafil I put in his drink is meant to be the weekend-pill of the erectile dysfunction drugs, so it should have him raring to go again soon. There is further disquiet from the room, and from what I hear I guess he is going to sleep in the wonderland I have given him.

Even though he must have months of dirt and filth on him and has just added sweat and cum to this, washing does not seem to be a priority for him. I wonder if I should run him a bath, but I think even though he would feel comfortable stewing in his own dregs in a warm bath it would probably not be best for him. A shower would be the more hygienic option but would he stand there and clean himself? I doubt it...

The water is spraying down; the shower pressure is

average, not like that from the hotels I am used to, but it has to suffice after my falling asleep on the sofa. He has a mint and tea tree shower gel, which I quite like for a cheap product because it makes my cock tingle in a nice way. My cock feels good after the blow job and the Drunk draining me off. When I am done I go back to the living room to collect my remaining clothes and notice he has set the table. He enters the room with a pot of filter coffee and tells me he is making us breakfast, and I should continue watching the rest of D&D as the series just gets better and better.

In the shower I'd decided to let it go, and that the Drunk and I should just part company. Even though he was the usual type I would go for, albeit an uglier version, it was not the time to start anything new. So I go into the kitchen to tell him I would not be able to stay, and there he is making a full English breakfast. The quality of the ingredients looks good. I pick up the empty packet that had the sausages in and he chimes in to say he got everything from Borough market the day before, as he works at Guy's Hospital. He is grilling most of the food, as he is on a healthy eating gig. I decide to stay as the smell is making me hungry. He offers me a drink. I take a five hundred milliliter bottle of still water and head back to D&D and Hank, Eric and Co.

Eventually when we are seated and eating I notice he eats extremely slowly because he is talking non-stop. His conversation is all about him and how great he is: owning his own place, how he has all these fabulous friends including some in Chicago who he was going to see very soon, his job (injecting patients with radioisotopes before an x-ray) depended on him because he is so great and is the only one able to do such a meaningful task properly. Listening to him trying to validate himself is in some way endearing. He never once stops to ask me anything about myself so I do not even need to bother with the usual lies. I could spend our time together absorbing all his bullshit, which he needs to say out aloud to believe it himself. But where would the fun be in that?

"Are you happy being single?"

"I'm just so busy, going out with my friends all the time, so I don't have time for a boyfriend."

"Like last night."

The irony being totally lost on him, he continues; maybe because he needs to hear his own whiney voice some more. "I was out with some friends but they all had to go home early and I just wanted to dance."

"And dance you did; you fell off the stage."

"I was wondering why my leg was hurting more than usual."

"How much of last night do you remember?"

"Bits and pieces. It's whenever I drink gin I seem to forget parts of the night."

You could try not drinking gin. "Well, you were telling me about being mugged; maybe for your own safety you should not drink so much."

"I can look after myself."

"Can you? If I didn't bring you home, what would have happened to you?"

"I would have met someone, gone home with them and had a much better time."

"What if the guy was weird?"

This has him stumped, he goes quiet. Result. However, it did not last long. "I've been raped twice."

Looking into his eyes I know he is telling me the truth. He has said it for the shock value and to try and get the last word in because he is that type of guy, but I am me. "Well isn't that more reason to try and not be assaulted a third time? You know last night you were begging for a fuck but I was too much of a gentleman to take advantage of such a pissed guy." *Plus I do not want you, you are far too easy.*

"Well, I'm sober now."

"After the sucking off you gave me this morning, I'm spent." *Your face, your voice, slow eating and slow talking are major turn-offs.* "Plus, I think we would be better friends."

My Tramp is awake or he is having a nightmare, as he is back to making noises. I decide some music might settle him. I try and guess his age, put him in his forties and start scanning through the collection to find him something. The Drunk's tastes are very Kylie, Steps and general stereotypical camp gay man songs. My Tramp deserves better so I go into the Drunk's iTunes account and resume the search on his pretty shitty laptop—another thing I inherited when this place and all the contents became mine.

My backhanded compliment pleases the Drunk and after finishing breakfast, which he does very slowly, he tells me to continue watching D&D. He loves having company, that is apparent to me, and with the DVD on he actually does not speak so I am okay in the situation. His rape story, his weakness in needing to find love by fucking anyone that would go with him, his delusions of grandeur thinking his job and flat were great, his general patheticness mean I change my mind. I would be his savior.

When it comes time to swap DVDs over, he begins telling me more about his fantastic life. I think surely he is not deluded enough to fool himself to think that this would make me jump into bed with him. His self-hatred is evident, as he is just a hole for hundreds of men to use. He never was a top, he says he does not like it; more probably he sees himself as forever passive, not just sexually but in every aspect of his persona. I guess he was one of those kids so bullied and victimized growing up that this is all he knows. That said, circumstances in his adult life had made him bitter and that gives him a dangerous arrogance, which kept unchecked would land him in serious trouble.

He is having a lunchtime vodka martini. No matter what difficulties or pleasures he is going through in life he still has a life-long friend to help him through them— alcohol. I am sipping a weak screwdriver. He continues blabbering on so I just listen. He tells me about these great friends he has in Chicago. There are three of them: he had met one of the guys in a club over here and then slept with him. The guy probably wanted free accommodation for whenever he visited the UK again, and struck up a friendship with the Drunk. Chicago bloke introduced him to his other friends to dilute the agony of having to spend alone time with the Drunk. This obviously means the Drunk fully expects to have free accommodation if he goes to Chicago. This bizarre relationship has existed for a couple of years now. Well, each to their own.

It means that when the Drunk is due in the States in a

month no one, not that there could be many, would miss him from over here. And if he were not to show up for some reason, a quick email to the Chicago lot explaining something came up would bring them the relief of not having to put up with him…

I open up the Drunk's emails; there are a lot from play.com suggesting other box-sets he might like. One from a girl named Felicity who is meant to be his best friend, asking for a catch-up when he gets back from Chicago and asking what has happened to his Facebook account, which seems to have disappeared. I return to the matter at hand and continue looking for a song for My Tramp, who sounds to really be going for it this second time around. I search Seventies music and find the perfect song, which I download and set up to play continuously.

Such a feeling is coming over me. I am really pleased by my song choice, which as it plays out across the flat seems so suitable on many levels. There is wonder in almost everything I see as I take one of my last looks around the place. After the night this place will no longer be mine. It was never mine to begin with, only borrowed.

Karen Carpenter continues to belt out her number; it is a jolly song to an outsider but to me I hear this truth behind the lyrics. Dear Karen was a true role model to women all over the world. She highlighted the fact that fat was not good. Showing everyone that anorexia exists should have given hope to millions of fatties. "Look, you have let yourself go but there is redemption. Just stop eating. The celebrities are doing it so you can too." Oh, Karen, you were a true trailblazer. If only everyone had the courage and willpower you did to starve, the world would be a much skinnier place.

She was one of the first high-profile cases of a fat cure that nowadays are everywhere. Where models size zero are deemed too fat, where clothes manufacturers refuse to make sizes too big to stop larger ladies tainting their products, where every magazine picture is touched up to remove fat, where celebrities share their diets with everyone via social media, where those larger than most say they are happy with their bodies but attempt some diet nevertheless, where the gym is actually full of athletic types and no one is overweight.

As Karen gets on top on the world looking down on creation, I know this is not because of love, as the song would try and have us believe. No, this is about death: starved, with no energy to carry on, or going to a dark place and not wanting to carry on. The character in the song is looking down at the mortal world. It is about an out-of-body experience, one you get when death touches you. From what we have been led to believe, your soul ascends to heaven. At this point, yes, you would see all of creation. The something in the wind that knows your name is perhaps your angel leading you to meet your true maker. It tells you "things are not the same because they are not, you are dying." Everything you know and believe in is about to change forever.

I guess the true meaning of the song was hidden to the masses because the degenerates do not want to hear about death. They need to believe in happy thoughts and ideas, and the illusion that the world is perfect. So it is sung supposedly about love, but the word is interchangeable with death and dying.

After three full rounds of "Top Of The World" by the Carpenters I have had a chance to absorb the lyrics and the true meaning, and I decide it is time to check in on our guest. The song continues to play in the background so we can all listen to it. I think this is comforting and should help the transition.

The Drunk and I left our first encounter with him trying to blow me again; he'd said he wanted to thank me for being such a gentleman and not taking advantage of him, but I had stopped him because it was not something I could consciously let happen. I said I would prefer to be friends, a concept new to him. In my first couple of weeks settling back into London life I would come around to this place, basically treating it like my own. Yes, he was very possessive about his possessions and told me not to wear his clothes. He said it was because he did not want them to lose their shape in case he wore them, but I know it was due to the fact even though he had an older sister, he could not share. Or it could have been his inability to handle the jealousy of his things looking better on me. This was obviously not a problem for me, as I did not wear the shit he had in his closest, apart from when I realized it wound him up.

The thought enters my head that maybe Sissy used to mess with him when he was younger, and that is why he is the way he is. That would have definitely made our time together more interesting, instead of hearing about all his wonderful friends he never gets to see as he is so busy, even though he is always home when I call. I could have heard how his sister made him take his little willy out and strum it in front of her and her friends. Did they even go as far as shoving something up his ass? I am a bit upset that I never thought of it at the time and that it is too late to find out from him.

I go into the bedroom to check up on My Tramp. While in there I can feel the Drunk's eyes on me. Maybe he is so drunk that he is on top of the world looking down at me, unable to speak in his drunken stupor, asking with his expression, "Why have you let a homeless man into my flat? Why are you allowing said homeless man to pleasure himself in the bedroom? Why did you not at least make him shower so that his soiled clothes and naked body would not be in contact with the things in the room? And what is on that plate you are carrying that smells so good?"

Being the sort of guy I am, trying to be a good host and live up to my original invitation, I am bringing My Tramp a meal. Everyone, well, those not on the Karen plan, deserves a nice dinner. The meat I obtained for the dinner was very tough, and even though it was lean and all muscle, it needed to be cooked properly. I have had it cooking in the slow cooker all day with beef stock, onions, turnips and bacon bits. I have not over-seasoned the dish with pepper and garlic as I figured My Tramp would have a delicate palate. Once I fished the one piece of meat out of the cooker I skinned it, recommended for this particular cut, so he would get the best of it. I spooned some of the extra contents, the stock and vegetables, over the meat before serving.

He snatches the held-out plate from me—it is amazing what confidence blowing your wad a couple of times gives you—and retires to a corner of the bedroom. My Tramp does not bother with the knife and fork, he uses his hands to pick up the food and scarf it down. At this rate he will make himself sick. He seems to like it. It must be his first taste of this rare meat ever. Even I have not sampled the delicacy before, because the chance to do so has never come up. And now I thought it would be rude to deprive my guest of it, so did not even have a nibble. The juices from the plate and from his mouth are dribbling down onto his body. His body appears to be covered in rashes and sores. Between his legs is a thick black bush and his mangled cock, which looks to be getting hard again as he refuels himself.

With a finger I stroke the naked flesh underneath me. I cannot really feel it because of the leather gloves I am still wearing but I imagine it to be silky soft like yesterday, when I shaved off all the body hair. I continue up the leg and stop at the ass.

I hear a whimpering sound, and lean further up the bed so my head is by the pillows. I do not fully lie down, but perch myself along the edge of the bed. I stare back at the eyes looking at me with such hatred.

"Did you enjoy that?" I ask, pausing between each question.

There is a little moan.

"Not very talkative anymore, are you?"

"So did you enjoy yourself?"

"What would you like to do next?"

"You are looking very dirty, perhaps a bath?"

I continue to trace my finger along the buttocks and up his back; when I reach the hairline I grab a handful. I yank up the Drunk's head and lower mine so I can whisper in his ear.

"I think this is what constitutes a violation, you pathetic little thing. Me keeping you a prisoner in your own flat, which by the way is a shithole, would be something to really complain about. If you could, that is. Did you know no one has missed you? Not your coworkers, who believe you have extended your holiday for longer. Your Chicago 'friends' were happy they did not have to put up with you and totally believed that you ditched them because you found love. They might get a shock when they see what a strange bedfellow you have chosen. But I think everyone who knew you would know that you are just desperate."

He coughs up some blood as if to protest, once again always having to have all the attention. The red juice adds to the pool where his head was lying.

"You don't really know when to shut up, do you? That's why I cut your tongue out; no one should have to suffer listening to your voice again or have you abuse them when they sleep on your sofa, or put up with your painfully slow eating. Speaking of eating, pardon the pun, your new boyfriend." I turn his head so that for the first time he can fully see My Tramp in all his horrific glory. "Just ate your tongue. If it's any consolation, he seemed to like it."

The Drunk tries to struggle, I think not because he has heard his tongue has been eaten but from the revulsion of seeing the beast I brought back for him. When he was being fucked face down with his arms tied he was oblivious to the stranger doing the deed. Of course he would have smelt the guy, and felt the patches of dead skin rough and flaking on to him, and the beard and unkempt body hair, but there was always the option to pretend it was someone good looking. Now the reality is with him and he got to learn what rape truly is, not the drunken sob stories he told me. I free one hand and flip him over so that he is on his back. My Tramp, who was not paying us any attention before, has now got up and is pointing at the Drunk's penis, freaking out.

"I don't know what your problem is. So you fucked a guy. You can't be that stupid to have not known. Yes, from behind and with his shaved body he could be a good bitch, but deep down you knew. Look how hard your cock was for it. You must have remembered the difference between an ass and a pussy. Even if you did prefer women and used to take them up the back passage, you should have checked, you sadistic pig. Is that why you are a homeless nobody, you just used to fuck anything at will?"

I stand next to My Tramp now and I easily fling him back on to the bed. He does not quite land on the Drunk but I am quickly standing over the bed. I pick him up by his neck and one leg and dump him exactly on top of the Drunk. The Drunk is recoiling in horror at being face to face with what can only be described as his worst nightmare. Out of nowhere, My Tramp starts vomiting. Maybe it was the food, the alcohol, realizing what he had been screwing, or having the Drunk thrashing around under him, but this is a perfect end to the session. The look of absolute disgust on the Drunk's face is priceless and has made this whole endeavor worthwhile.

After letting them stew in the vomit for a while, I cut the Drunk's remaining hand free and leave the not-so-happy couple to it. As I brought them together, I feel it is only right that things work out between them, so I stay and watch over them, intervening when necessary.

My work here is now done. I silence Karen and make sure there is no trace that I was ever here. In the silence I can only wait, for there is one last thing I have to hear. It might be better to go outside and wait for this but I do not want to be seen skulking around this estate. After about ten minutes the commotion starts outside. I leave the flat and dart across the balcony; I take up a position on the stairs where I can see and hear everything but remain hidden. The Polish gang that I was forced to run away from last time are shouting, I cannot understand what though. There seems to be a couple of "fucks" thrown in the mix. Three of them have formed a sort of square around a blue duffle bag, formerly belonging to the Drunk. The fourth is kneeling facing away from the bag and is throwing up. Two of them start shoving each other as the shouting and screaming continue. The remaining guy is looking around everywhere searching for an answer. His face says that he is in shock but he is still being rational, trying to see if a rival gang is watching, anticipating something else to follow. He says something to the others, which sounded like "push off," and they pick up their fallen comrade and leave. They leave the heavily stained blue bag, now practically purple, behind. I leave this place with a smile on my face as I keep hearing the words My Tramp mumbled back at the fireplace, "Where's its head?"

10

HE DOES NOT DISCRIMINATE

Times like this I wish my sanctuary was up and running and I could escape somewhere private, giving myself a chance to re-evaluate the situation. I think I could be free if I got rid of her. It would not be a case of killing just her, I would have to wipe out her entire family and destroy her home. These actions are not beyond me and every ounce of my being says I should just do it, but part of me knows I still need her. Well, the knowledge she possesses. Then there is the question of whether or not she would see the attack coming and finish me off beforehand. These thoughts and decisions are not ones to be made in a hotel room, which is why I am wishing I had my apartment already. Instead, I am craving solitude in the apartment next door.

Breaking in was easy enough. For some reason, despite the history of the Phoenix, there is a major security flaw in the underground car park. Perhaps it is deliberate so that all the illicit affairs, concubines, dealers, rent boys and other assortments of men that need to visit the occupants can do so in the shadows, exactly how the elite owners want it. Trying to get into my soon-to-be apartment would have been a lot riskier as the owner could return anytime, or as a vacant property it might be under some sort of security scrutiny. The adjacent one, which I knew to be empty from my last visit, represented an easier target, one where I am unlikely to be interrupted.

So here I stand, completely naked in front of the large windows looking out across the common. I feel confident in this place; it has a good aura about it, which is what I need now. I have had to take in a lot today, and need to think through my actions. I think about what I am doing, what I have done and what I will do. For every scenario, I think about all the possible options and the consequences of each alternative.

The mind boggles when I think, what if by choosing option A, it never leads to result 1? What if B was chosen, influenced by factors C and D, giving a new result, 2? I have always believed in destiny and the chosen path, so by doing something differently, E all the way to Z, you might get a different result, 3. But will that result in feedback into the loop, maybe not requiring option A but F, G and H, all ultimately ending up in result 1?

I prefer the direct approach and do not have time to waste, so I decide to follow my chosen path.

It sounds like something a computer program would be able to work out, or at least map out the possible scenarios. Maybe I should speak to Matthew about it. Thinking about him alleviates my thoughts and what I am really trying to see past.

For me it always returns to the Year of Death and, "What if Alex did not die?" What sort of life would she have had, what we would have had? Would I have continued to be her protector, would that have given me a different purpose, would there have been love in my life? Or would she have died in some horrible way subsequently because that was the path laid out for her?

I need to think about happier thoughts, so I think about the incident with My Tramp stroking and trying to play with the lifeless object by the fireplace all those weeks ago. The quality moment was when he realized Brutus was not quite altogether there. Even though the alcohol and drugs had hit his system, he'd lived many years as a hobo and no longer possessed the ability to have a coherent thought, he looked fully in control of all his senses and had his first moment of clarity in decades when he realized the dog was missing his head.

His mutterings asking where the head was seemed to take him back to hobo random thoughts. I smile again at his reaction: it was priceless. It was even better than the Polish gang's reaction, and it was their dog. But they had it coming. My preference would have been to exact physical pain on them, but due to the situation developing in Flat 95 I did not want to draw attention to myself being tied to the estate. So their pain had to be of a different sort—emotional. I just hope they were close to that damn dog.

From a young age I learnt not to be discriminatory with my actions. In the game of life you must slay whomever or whatever stands in your way. It is not ideal if the victim happens to be an animal, but one cannot start growing a conscience the moment what is to be killed is cute and fluffy. If it was any consolation, his last days with me were better than he had with his owners. I did not make him go out and fight unnecessarily, open to attacks and hurt. He was well-fed and seemed to be enjoying his new lifestyle. Then when he was asleep, warm and contented, boy Alex, my sword came out and lopped his head off in one clean swoop.

It was a humane death; he never saw or felt it coming. His part in this was now over. He had been used as an instrument of intimidation by his masters, so it was only just that he was used as a tool to return the favor to them. To instill some level of fear in them and send them a message.

"Nothing should divert or distract you from your chosen path. Do whatever it takes to accomplish the mission." That statement was said to me earlier, and it rings true with what I did to the dog. This is why I stand here contemplating everything, because once you leave the House of the Departed that is how you feel.

The actual house is nothing special; in fact, it is below anything I would want to ever live in or anyone with worldly desires would choose. It is not the house that SHE lived in when I first knew her. It is just another degenerate house in the deep dark southeast. I guess the area is still classed as London, but I would not think so. There are lots of fields that surround the place, making the location seem more rural than it is. When I asked about this once, on my first trip, I was told that SHE preferred it this way. Her gifts worked better without lots of earthed electricity to disturb the force.

Her gifts enable her to glimpse the future, and these insights passed on to her customers can be a valuable commodity. Your general degenerate would go to see her to ask about starting a new career, or if they will ever find love, and random nonsense like that. To these, I am sure she lies and tells them the tale most likely to please them and convince them to come back. In that sense she is more like a counselor or advisor. Other degenerates, those thinking they are better than the majority (think Balhamites), might say she is a con-artist, that only those vulnerable or stupid would be taken in by her cheap tricks.

Why the fuck do I believe in this crap? Well, I do not consider it to be crap. Alex was born with the call and saw things too. Things that her little mind could not comprehend, that made her scared, things that disturbed her immensely. When she tried to tell anyone, they always just said she was a difficult child because of her Down's syndrome. I was the only one she could turn to, the only one who believed her and supported her. So I am a believer.

Then there is the fact that SHE and I have a history. SHE has seen things in my past that I had never told anyone, SHE predicted things that would happen to me and eventually did, and SHE never judges my actions. I trust the information SHE receives from glimpsing the future is what SHE has seen, that SHE does not lie. But I do not trust her; I would prefer her dead. But I am stuck with her until I can find, if one exists, another clairvoyant who has such accuracy. I close my eyes and remember our earlier consultation.

* * * *

After knocking on the door (there was no bell), I waited until SHE opened it. SHE gave me the once-over, as I did her. SHE looked well for fifty-plus, with short dyed hair and decent clothes covering her healthy plump frame. I guess charging sixty pounds for a reading lasting about an hour was lucrative work. As SHE led me through the house, a chill ran down my spine...her homes were always cold. SHE took me to the kitchen, which was warmer, and told me to wait while SHE finished off the previous appointment. I was told to help myself to a drink, as SHE left the room. Now this was the stage where the con artist leaves the room to go through their files and find the notes from a previous time to refresh their memory and keep to the same lies. And the customer is oblivious, and makes themself a hot drink. Neither of those things happened.

I'd started casually rifling through the drawers knowing there would be nothing of interest, while SHE had left probably to finish off the previous customer as SHE said. The kitchen was decked out more as a kitchen-living room, with a forty-two inch television and Sky box in the corner. I reached a drawer, two under the cutlery one; it was full of bills, receipts and take-away menus. As I poked around in this drawer I touched a cold, hard glass surface. I pulled it out from under the paper junk, hiding it away, and felt very excited.

When I looked at the picture, disappointment briefly entered my heart—it was not what I sought. I cast aside that useless emotion and studied the picture further. It could still be relevant. I committed the faces of the two teenage lads to memory. Her sons are no longer hidden from me—her mistake. As an insurance policy, and also for completeness, I took a photo of the picture with my phone and took a seat on the sofa. One: nil, me.

While I waited for my reading I started thinking of my own family. Maybe the bitch had wanted me to find the picture after all, so that those feelings were brought up in me. One–one, the bitch pulls one back. The only family member I ever cared about, correction—my only family, was Alex. Growing up, it was only us. The man whose sperm created me was a cheating cock, and when he was around he never paid us any attention. In the Year of Beginnings I highlighted his cheating ways by inviting his mistress over to our house, to accidentally meet the woman who gave birth to me. She was not bothered; she would have accepted the situation and let him stay as a cheat. I guess she always knew, but like how she treated everything else in her life, she had been apathetic. The man took the revelation as something good and moved out, seeing his chance to run far away from his Down's daughter.

I should have hated him for leaving us, but I never cared; maybe I picked up more traits from the woman who gave birth to me than I'd realized. He actually became more attentive to us once he had moved out; perhaps it was guilt, or overwhelming relief to be well rid of the situation. Birthday and Christmas presents were always plentiful, but these did not matter to Alex and me; we had each other for company and we loved each other. Yes, she had her problems, but it never really mattered until she grew older.

* * * *

It was her tenth birthday. I was fourteen and decided I would take her to London Zoo, as she loved animals. And I loved her smile and how animated she became when she was happy. The man had sent presents over but was busy with his new family to bother to be around. The woman was busy doing whatever she used to do, so as not to have to bother to be around. So it was just us, which was just fine. That morning I laid out her favorite dress on the bed for her while she had the bath I had drawn for her. The warm water (she did not like it too hot) was not filled very high. But the lack of water in the bath was made up for with lots of bubbles and her plastic duck she loved to play with in the bath.

I stood outside, the door ajar, talking to her while she bathed. She was not really bothering with what I was saying, concentrating on quacking at the duck. I remember the conversation we had when I eventually managed to get her attention. In fact, the whole day is seared onto my memory, which in some respects is good, as that way I know it was real. That she was real, and no one will ever be able to take that away from me.

"You're going get to see real ducks later; and elephants, tigers and scary snakes."

"Big ones?"

"Ducks or elephants?"

"Snakes."

"Don't worry, I'll be there to protect you. As long as I'm around, nothing will happen to you."

"Fanks, Seb-web."

"No worries, Xandi."

"I don't like that name."

"What shall I call you then?"

"Princess."

"Why do you want to be a princess? You are far prettier than the real ones. Xandi is special and unique, like both of us."

"Alex."

"Okay, my favorite person in the whole world. Finish

your bath, dry off and put your pretty pink dressing robe on. Then come downstairs for breakfast, I'm going to make pancakes. This will be the start of a birthday you'll never forget."

Little did I know it would be me unable to forget the day.

* * * *

"You look lost. It is a good job you have come to see me." SHE interrupted my thoughts, as if SHE knew somehow that I was happy again.

"Are you ready for me?"

"That depends if you are ready to hear."

"Born ready."

SHE led me to the back of the house to a conservatory, a new addition to the place since I was last here. SHE let me enter the glassed room first. In it there was nothing except a simple wooden table and matching chairs. On the table were some unlit candles, some stones and a well-worn-through tarot deck. SHE took her seat and I took mine.

"Usually my customers like a recording of their sessions so that they can refer back to it at a later date. Sometimes it can all be a bit overwhelming." SHE whipped out a recording device and placed it on the table. "But with you I think it is better for both of us if no recording is made." SHE smiled. "Anyway, you have a good memory; you will remember all that you have to."

"That is how we have done it in the past, so why change now?" I responded, picking up the device and making sure it was off.

"So what do you want from this reading? Do you have

a specific question you want to ask or do you just want a general one?"

"General." I tried not to tell her too much, to give anything away.

"Good. Now try not to think of anything and give the cards a good shuffle. When you feel you are done, cut the deck into three piles using your left hand." The temptation to use my right hand was ever-present but I did not. SHE took the middle pile and formed a grid on the table, with some cards placed on top, another to form a cross. SHE flipped over the card in the corner, furthest away from her and closest to me. We had begun...

* * * *

Sat at the table, Alex was eating her pancakes. She was a slow eater but it was sweet watching her. It gave me a warm feeling knowing that she was enjoying something I made for her. The television was on, and she was watching Pokémon. I thought it was too advanced for her but at that time she had to decide for herself what she wanted to watch.

"Come on, Jigglypuff," a name just mentioned on the television, "I'm going to brush your hair and put this ribbon in it."

Alex clapped when she saw the purple ribbon, as it was her favorite color and matched the purple polka dots on her white dress that she was looking forward to wearing. I took her glasses off, which she complained about, and brushed her hair. It seemed very delicate—like her—to me. The brown strands were fairer than my own.

"You know you have the nicest hair in the family."

She giggled and repeated what she just heard. "Squirt,

squirt." It was those damn Pokémon that had her. When I finished brushing her hair, I let her put her glasses back on so she could enjoy the show. I then attempted to tie the ribbon in her hair as a bow; it took me five attempts to get it to a stage where I was happy that it did her justice.

* * * *

In the present, back at the Phoenix, I move towards my pile of clothes and hunt around for my phone. When I pull it out from my jacket pocket I begin searching the music directory for our song. I hit play and crank it up as high as it will go. These apartments are soundproof. They were even when the place was known more commonly as Nightingale Hall, so no one will be able to hear the music, not that phone speakers generate enough noise to bother neighbors. It is the Jeff Buckley version of "Hallelujah," in my opinion the best one. At the time I had a major crush on him, which intensified once I found out that he was gay too. But his version is definitely the best. Whereas Cohen murmured along, the super-hot Buckley careened between the sadness and the glory. Even though the degenerates overuse this song in films and television shows, I have not let that ruin it for me as I just avoid watching or listening to anything that uses it.

I thought the song written for me to you, thinking my soul, when I was young and naive, was the "Hallelujah." It was more special as you really seemed to like the melody and instruments used in the song. And the lyrics were the truth for us, like the time I let you cut my hair sitting on the kitchen chair because you said I always looked after your hair, so you wanted to do mine. It was that night, the birthday, that you looked more beautiful than ever with the moonlight bathing down on you. That moment answered any questions about God and purpose and being. Everything I knew about love was from you, Alex; and this resolved me to what had to be done. So I had to outdraw…

* * * *

SHE turned over the first few cards and studied them. "The Knight of Pentacles represents you, the world is obvious, and death means the end."

Boring.

"Yes, I see it clearly. You, the worldly traveler, plodding along from place to place because you have to. Well, this is to end now." SHE continued flipping more cards over, holding two of the stones in her hand as SHE did so. "There is a property on the horizon, you shall settle there. No more travelling for a while."

Maybe you just did your homework on me and are just a con artist after all. This was dull information.

"This card, the Six of Pentacles, shows that it is a good-value purchase. You will always have money, it is not something you have to worry about."

That must just eat you up, you bitch; you in your little squalid house. I smiled at her. SHE continued turning the cards from the first pile on the table.

"Your career is going from strength to strength, you are good at it. But I am getting the feeling you do not actually care about it. You do it because, even though you strive to be on your own, you do not like being by yourself."

You whore.

"Stay with this job for now, but never let it distract you

MARK LAKERAM

from what is truly important, your real work. That is when you are really happy and what you are good at. All these cards show you must continue this vital legacy."

SHE had finished reading this first pile of cards and very carefully stacked them back up. Once SHE was done, SHE picked up the pile on her right and dealt it out on the table, forming a circular pattern this time. SHE turned over the first few innermost cards of the circle, and started "tutting" and shaking her head.

"You still dwell on the past too much. Everything that has happened has happened for a reason to make you who you are today. To prepare you for what is to come."

If you had my past you would probably think back on it too.

"Sometimes at night, you have very cold feet." SHE watched me looking for a response; I did not give her one. "It is because a little girl sits at the end of the bed, watching over you."

Cunt.

"This card, The Fool, represents her; she was a family member. Someone you were close to. I am seeing her as your sister. As once you were her protector, she now is that for you. She loves you very much and is proud of everything you have done."

Really? She does not mind that I kill to rescue those who would suffer from this cruel world?

"You must continue with your extracurricular work; she says it is more vital than you know."

Apparently not, then. Sweet Alex, you always had the ability to see the best in others.

"The Devil, followed by the Five of Swords shows doubt. That you still won't accept your path."

142

A path full of destruction and death: sure, what's not to doubt?

"Let go and become what is your destiny."

"What is that?" Crap. I was doing so well not to say anything to her.

"You know. It has not changed since your sister left this world to enter the next. She is so happy there; she is at peace. She says one day in the future you will be reunited, but you are not to follow her until you have completed what you set out to do. Oh, one more thing: she does not blame you for it and she knows it had to be done."

So my dear sweet Alex understands.

She understands why.

Why I had to deliberately kill her.

To set her free.

11

HE CAN BE VULNERABLE

All the fun of the fair was to be had. But we were at the Zoo, and the trip turned into anything but fun. We went from one animal enclosure to another. Alex was in awe of the various creatures she had seen on television or in picture books and was now getting to see for real. She was excited by the bigger ones, like the elephants and the giraffes, amazed by the "prettiness" of the more exotic, brightly-colored ones—this was mainly in the bird section. In that part of the zoo there was an entertainer who was giving out paper and colored pencils and asking all the children around to draw an animal. It did not have to be a bird; it could be from any part of the zoo. Everyone would hand their drawing in later and the pictures would go on a board they had to be displayed, there would be prizes and it would be "fun."

Alex wanted to stay and draw a toucan; she did not want it to be left out, as everyone ran off from that section to draw something else. So we found a bench close by and she drew that bird so its feelings would not be hurt. The look of concentration on her face as she attempted to capture every detail of the member of the Ramphastidae family showed me how determined she was. I was reading the blurb the zoo had included about all its captives. Earlier, the only animal that stood out to me was a

144

Panthera Tigris, not because I was in awe of the powerful cat but because I felt sorry for it. Caged and removed from its natural habitat, the tiger might have been born in captivity or be part of some conservation issue, but it was wrong. I knew it and so did the tiger; it paced up and down, snarling at the gaping pointing idiots. Alex did not want to spend too much time there, as it was obvious the animal was not happy. You could see the pissed-off nature of the tiger on its face, and to me it looked like it would have preferred to die than live how it was.

Two boys, my age or a bit younger, who were well-dressed and spoke with posh accents came over to the toucan and started calling it an ugly creature. One of them started banging on the mesh, scaring the bird.

"Hey!" Alex cried out.

"What?" the perpetrator shouted out.

"Leave it alone," she told them.

That is when they turned and took a good look at her.

"She's as ugly as the bird. In fact, more ugly."

"Stupid spastic."

They both had spoken simultaneously, managing to get out a derogatory comment each before I piled into them. I was trying to hit anything I could, not bothered about placing my blows where they would do the most damage. I did not know how to fight but I wanted them to hurt.

"Seb...Seb!" Alex yelled as she started crying.

Hearing her cry I knew I had to get back to her; otherwise I would have stayed there beating them or getting beaten until the end. When I finally managed to break free, there was a crowd standing there watching two teenagers attack another one next to an autistic child bawling her eyes out. Watching, doing nothing to stop the attack or help the girl in distress. That is the life lesson: you do not get help when you need it.

I went to Alex to comfort her, to tell her I was all right, though my battered face and bloody nose said otherwise. Whenever anything bad happened she always presumed it was because of her, and I tried to tell her it was not her fault. I hated those boys so much, and if my sister hadn't needed me I would have continued until they were dead. Or I was. I had to be the adult and pretend everything was okay, and that it was friends from school I knew and we were just mucking about. Now that the action was over, the crowd dissipated along with the boys, the cowards.

We went for a hot dog for lunch but her heart was no longer in it, and I knew our special day had come to an abrupt end due to the ignorance of others, an ignorance that would perpetuate. We were on the bus heading home when two rude boys sat at the back and started being loud and rowdy with other passengers. Then they saw Alex and turned their attention to her, daring each other to say the word "Mong" louder and louder. I looked down at Alex's lap and the drawing she was tightly clutching, the half-finished toucan. I talked to her, asking which animals she liked, to distract her from them. It worked, and she did not seem to understand that the abuse was meant for her. If I dared look at those boys I would not have been able to stop myself, so every line and detail of the toucan picture was burnt into my memory.

I could not distract myself from their tormenting, though and pushed the button to get off at the next stop.

"Seb, we aren't near to home."

The laughing at the back of the bus intensified.

"I thought we could walk and get some sweets."

"But I'm tired."

"I need some fresh air, this bus is filthy. We can catch the next one."

When we finally got home, Alex was indeed tired so I put her to bed. But this rest was short-lived; she woke up screaming. When I went to comfort her she told me she had a bad dream. When I finally coaxed it out of her, she said she saw strangers and lots of red, blood, and then I died. By the time I managed to convince her nothing bad would happen to me through a series of cuddling, telling her how much I loved her and singing to her, I think she passed out mostly due to exhaustion. She fell asleep in my arms. I looked down at her and realized no matter what happened in her life, she would always be bullied, always be a victim, always live in fear and have to overcome prejudice. I could try my damnedest to protect her…But what if I was not around?

She was too sweet and innocent. Whatever I did would not be enough. Her visions were also becoming more regular and fierce as she grew up; it took a longer time to calm her down as she became more aware. I removed my arm from under her and laid her out delicately. She stirred ever so lightly. I tucked her favorite cuddly toy, a polar bear, under her arm. We did not even get to see a real one due to our trip being cut short. The thought that every joy she deserved to have would be taken away from her strengthened my resolve. I picked up the spare pillow, and held it tightly between both hands, my knuckles turning white. I looked down at the sleeping angel, so contented and at peace, and gave her a kiss goodbye on her cheek.

I was crying now but something in me made me continue. I put the pillow over her face and held down as hard as I could. There was no great struggle; her body shook a bit under the covers until it was completely still. I held the pillow there long after the stillness, crying my eyes out. When I finally moved it, an eternity had passed and a man, unlike anything known, was born.

* * * *

SHE finished with my reading. What had started off with the mundane soon became very interesting and not something I'd experienced before. Maybe SHE sensed my boredom in hearing about the fact I travelled a lot and should buy property, things that degenerates would want to hear, and so upped her game. So accordingly the third pile revealed a lot, much more than either of us was prepared for.

"There is a lover coming, one who has already been."

"What do you mean?" Damn that tricky cow. I do not have exes that are alive, so I was not desperate to know if one of them was going to resurface. There was the bloke I met in the park…Now that it has been reconfirmed that I did right by Alex, maybe it is time I had a bit of happiness, if only for a fleeting moment.

"The cards shown do not tell me any more than that. Besides your sister, the Departed do not come to me when I read for you, it is like you have offended them in some way."

"I was not close enough to anyone else who has died for them to bother visiting me."

"Yet you are clouded in death."

"The joys of being an undertaker."

SHE watched me carefully and decided not to comment. SHE continued to flip over cards, now arranged in a star shape heading to the middle. "He, your lover, is more important than you know. He will lead the way."

"The way to what?"

"You want love?" SHE was not reading the cards anymore but me. This was off-base questioning for her, something one who cared for another would ask.

"No. I learnt from a very young age not to believe or trust in feelings and emotions."

"Who taught you such things?"

"The woman who spread her legs twice for me."

"She must have done more for you than that if she gave you life lessons."

"I was self-taught from example."

"Do you want to know about her?"

"No."

"I did not think you did. But part of me senses you still want something from this woman, you still cling on looking for answers to something. Why else would you visit me? I shall tell you this: she is a wise woman, and did what she did to you to prepare you for your destiny."

"I do not want anything from her, to know anything about her. That woman would probably want some of my wealth for her and her new family. It would mean they would be set for life and want for nothing."

"I am sure all she wants from you is for you to follow your destiny."

Bollocks. That whore would love some of my millions, no matter what you say. Bollocks to that destiny shit. All that bitch wanted was Alex and me out of her life to pursue her own pathetic dreams and desires. I doubt the woman had any dreams or desires beyond spreading her legs again to any random stranger who would put it in there. "Yes, I'm sure. That sounds like her."

SHE worked her way down another leg of the star. "The lover is like you, yet he is the complete opposite to you. You must be careful to never give yourself totally to him or anybody. You are a loner and must do what you do to this man, otherwise he will be the end of you."

"So we won't be lovers then?"

"He will be like nothing you have known before, which will mean it will be harder for you to allow your real nature to shine through. The consequences of not being true to yourself will be your undoing."

Same old story. I can have an amazing love and be happy, but it is not allowed. The powers that be, those that govern my life, do not allow it otherwise it will destroy me. Nice and absolute.

"What is this?" SHE said that more to herself but I heard it.

"What?"

"Fear. The reversed Nine of Swords amplified like I have never seen it before."

At last she knows me. I smiled.

"Great fear."

SHE was turning the cards on the third leg and was looking worried.

"It is your fear. That which you fear the most is coming."

"I don't fear anything."

"Maybe you don't know what it is. But there is something and it is coming for you."

"How can fear seek me out?"

"The cards are open to interpretation but they are telling me your greatest fear will soon be realized. What it is, they do not tell me. What this fear will do to you is unknown."

Great. Sounds charming. I was not sure if SHE was playing me now because nothing scares me, and I think SHE knew that so wanted to have her little mind games.

"Fuck."

I had never heard her swear before.

"What?" SHE said, turning over all the remaining cards. Suddenly SHE jumped up, knocking over her chair, and looked all around. "This can't be!"

The panicked look on her face amused me more than anything else. I guess SHE wanted to go for dramatic effect, give her customers value for money, and had included this new trick in her armamentarium. SHE walked away from the table, leaving behind her pebbles, and went to one of the conservatory panes. I hoped SHE would just shove her head through it. Alas no, SHE touched the glass and stood there for a couple of minutes. I did not want to pander to her whims so I remained seated, looking at the cards on the table that meant nothing to me.

"This is the last time we can meet," SHE informed me.

Suits me, I am bored with you.

"I have seen Departed."

Well, this is meant to be the House of the Departed.

"These were different. They...they..."

Come on, what does this have to do with me?

SHE left the room, leaving me alone. From what I knew of her, this behavior was highly erratic. Perhaps it was for the best if we no longer met, as SHE seemed to be losing it. At that moment I contemplated stealing a couple of cards; that would be funny. It could be a little experiment to see if I could change the future of her customers by removing this card marked the Wheel of Fortune laid on the table. Meaning SHE would never see their Wheel of Fortune and whatever it means would never apply to them. Fifty readings later SHE would be like, "No one has a Wheel of Fortune, what is wrong with the balance of the world, where is the Wheel! Why can I not see the fortune?" Or the bonus effect might be that SHE thinks SHE is losing her abilities, and fucks off for good.

My hand was on the table about to swipe the card when SHE reappeared. The glass of water, or it could have been gin or vodka for all I knew, that SHE was holding was shaking. SHE put the glass down, picked up her upturned chair from the floor and righted it. SHE sat and looked me in the eye; her eyes are the same color as Alex's were. SHE took hold of my hand and there was no warmth, just a coldness.

"Look, son."

Do not call me that. I hate it when those older patronize those younger by calling them "son" or "child." My intelligence is far beyond hers; SHE should say "look, sir."

"I saw a sandy place. Not a beach...more like a desert. You were there and there were Departed."

"I thought the Departed don't like me, and stay away."

"These were not your regular ones from your," SHE

paused for the word, "undertaking. These were different because they are not yet Departed. It was a sign of what is to come."

"So there will be a few more deaths around me, but if you knew me you would not have to be psychic to know that."

"It was not a few, there were lots of them. If I had to guess I would say there were thousands of them."

"Oh."

"As you can see, our time together has now come to a permanent end. Don't worry about paying me for this session. Contrary to what you believe, I don't need the money. Now go forth, my little Seb-Web warrior."

I got up to leave, and placed a hundred pounds on the table. I will never owe anyone anything. Everything that had to be said between us had been said, if what SHE saw was real; or if SHE was just fucking with, me I did not care. *Be emotionless now, think on these events later in your private sanctuary, do not show anyone weakness.*

SHE did not say anything, busy collecting her money from the table. We were done. I left the woman who gave birth to me behind without saying another word.

Walking away from the house, I encountered a solitary smoking teenager and bought his lighter off him for twenty pounds. Then I took the Wheel of Fortune out of my pocket and set it alight.

* * * *

The day's memories have left me feeling tender, so before I can continue I need my physical self to feel the hurt that the rest of me is feeling. The time to think and reflect is over—now is the time for the action. I know just where to go to engage in physical pain, and it is not that far from here. I know you should never return to the scene of the crime, but I have never adhered to that saying. As long as you are smart about it you will be fine. Looking down on my naked skin I want to be covered in blood, I wonder what color it would look like under moonlight. Clothes do not make a man—it is the opposite—being in your natural state, naked, answering your true nature makes a man.

"But the hour cometh, and now is" runs through my mind as I get dressed and remove any signs that anybody disrupted the apartment since it last had anyone in it. Fully dressed, I might as well still be naked for what I am about to embark on. I do not have any weapons in my possession, not that I could not kill with my body, but now is the time to let fate decide. To take the physical pain, which I deserve, without any resistance and see what happens. If I am lucky, hopefully I will be killed and this will all end. SHE would be wrong and Alex and I will be happily reunited. Someone else can fulfill the role SHE has foreseen for me. It is time fate decides, but he is a cruel master and I do not really believe I will get the wish I desire.

Twenty minutes later I find myself in the housing estate next to the Drunk's, the one where he got mugged. This is not my intended destination, which is the Drunk's housing estate and a date with my Polish friends. I thought I would take the scenic route to get there; after all, I am in no rush. I would stand a better chance of encountering destiny if it was later at night. My casual stroll took me through the common where I was hoping to meet some homophobic bastards to start this journey earlier. Instead, I just came across, well, heard, my peers fornicating in the bushes. Then I realized I would not be a target even if there was a predator about because how would he or she know? To get that abuse I would have to get with a guy on the common, and mince around together until some drunk closeted guy on his way home from the pub decided to goad his mates into beating us to hide his own shame.

I think about Six and how he would have been the perfect partner in crime for this activity. He is so desperate for sex; he has suggested the common himself for want of a better place. Also, for his first time he would probably scream the place down to undeservedly get us the thrashing I am looking for. Six will have to wait on. If I survive the night I will take care of his urges. By the time I am finished with him, he will be praying to Lady Gaga herself to save him, and wish I had not survived the night.

My plans for Six are interrupted by the two figures that have emerged from the shadows. On closer inspection, I see they are walking over. I know them. They are not where I expected to find them and in the number I had hoped, but they will have to do.

"Guys, do you fancy a fuck?"

I motion first with my tongue to my cheek a blow job, then I jerk my waist to the motion so they are fully clear. This is greeted with a baffled look, so I blow the one with a goatee a kiss. Not because I fancy him but the uglier one would not have been as upset, as any compliment would do for him.

"Is that an erection in those tight jeans I see?" I taunt Ugly. "Do you want me to liberate it for you?"

He steps back as I step forward. *Fucking coward.*

"Don't you want to fuck me over, like how I fucked over your little dog? You know, he yelped like a little puppy bitch when I cut his head off."

They both look shocked now, searching my face for signs of recognition.

"Brutus, my ass. More like Bunny. Like a little floppy-eared bunny."

I hope they can understand my English.

"I'm the guy you threw a bottle at and wanted to mug in the shit-hole over there. You guys been demoted to this scum-hole now?"

I hold my palms out open towards them and then hold them up to say I have surrendered. *Do something, you cocks.*

"So are we fucking or not?"

Perhaps the cowards need their full force. Perhaps they are not used to dealing with anyone answering them back. Or maybe they are just so fucking stupid they cannot understand me. I do not want to fight, because once I start in that mode the years of training will automatically kick in and I will not be able stop myself. These Polacks will not stand a chance against me if I decide to engage them in that way.

"Come on then, you fucking Polacks, what you waiting for…? Me to fuck your mum? Attack me with everything you have!"

I step forward. The goatee one steps back while Ugly stands his ground. We are in striking distance of each other. He is sizing me up, or is it eyeing? Maybe he wants that fuck and if his mate was not around he would have been trying that. Normally a situation like this would call for a kick to his abdominal section, and as he doubles over

156

a knee to his face. However, I am not fighting today, I need to pay for my sins. So instead I slap Ugly hard. He was not expecting it. His hand moves to his hurt face. He looks at me insolently and smiles.

That is when I feel the sharp pain in my back. It is overwhelming, causing me to stagger forward. Ugly steps back and his friend joins him. The pain moves to the top of my back across my shoulder blades as something hits me. Both the Polish men in front of me come forward and start punching me. I drop to the ground face down. Punches and kicks are being rained down on me, the punches to my head and the kicks to my body. The noises they are making are animalistic, intertwined with shouting in Polish.

"We go to fuck you over so good, motherfucker. For Brutus."

I manage to roll over so that I can look at my attackers, and to let them have access to my more vulnerable face and the front of my body, which has not been hit yet. Above me are the four original members of the gang and a girl. Maybe the other two were shagging their little whore in the shadows and spunked just in time to join their friends.

"Make sure you finish me off and kill me. If you don't I promise I will hunt you down and bury you instead!" I let them know as I spit out some blood.

I am punched flush in the face by the fattest of the gang, the one who seemed the most upset about the dog's death. This causes the back of my head to violently connect with the concrete. My vision is blurred but I can make out a knife above me. I want to tell them to stick it to me good but I cannot speak, I cannot think anymore. I manage to make out some more Polish as everything is shutting down. My last thought is for them to just end this.

12

HE SEDUCES MEN WITH EASE

The time for debating and angst is done. These notions and secret desires to stop and live a regular life are over. The idea that not living would prove to be a happier state of existence is finished. No more shall I be weak and second-guess my destiny, something that SHE laid out to me as a child; a path that, even though I have questioned it at times, I have always known was mine to walk. I gave the world the opportunity to get rid of me, in essence to free me, if it wanted to. But like the cruel bitch who bore me, it refused. I am meant to be who I am for the purpose I do, and nothing will falter me anymore. The Polish gang should have killed me; I did not fight back. I was prepared to die and they wanted to kill me. But it was not meant to be. Even though both parties—myself and them—wanted it, it could not happen.

Instead I am a prisoner, drugged and barely able to move, somewhere I do not know, held by someone I do know. I feel certain levels of pain in my head and down my right midsection, and my left leg is aching like a bastard, so it could be broken. Pain is good, though. It reminds me I am alive and on a mission. Plus, as I did not die I deserve to feel some pain as retribution for my previous actions. That is the assessment I was able to give myself during one period of consciousness. How long I have been here I do not know. But it must be a new day from when the attack happened, so my day of self-sacrifice is over. I can now let my training and survival instinct kick in, if I could only stay awake long enough.

The next time I manage to wake up, I feel less groggy. Maybe past experiences of recreational use has given me a tolerance. My captor should have at least tried restraining me to some extent, instead of just relying on drugs. The hunter-being-hunted notion amuses me; the situation would be like that of man capturing a wounded tiger and caging him, but once the tiger is given the right chance he would rip the man's head off. I manage to get up off the bed, putting all my weight on my right leg, which is currently the stronger of the two but smarts as the weight is put on it. I do not have time to register the feeling, as I am distracted by two mumbled voices.

That changes the situation somewhat negatively for me. Given my current physical condition I would put myself at sixty percent, which would be enough to deal with a normal man, but not factoring in I could be dealing with a trained killer. But for two unknowns I would need to do a little reconnaissance first. I sit back on the bed and try to listen to the voices coming from the next room. If I can pick up the language I will know if it is my Polish friends. My hearing does not seem to be so good, as I am straining to hear beyond the voices that just seem like background noise. Instinctively I put my hand to my ear and feel something that should not be there.

I trace the foreign object on my ear. It goes the whole way around my head, and it feels soft. Maybe they have removed my skull and I am sitting here poking my exposed brain. I stop poking, just in case, and decide a mirror would be good. Remembering everything I have been taught to do when in danger—prioritizing knowing your environment, locating an exit strategy, determining what could be used as a weapon—I take my first real look around my cell.

It is not a cell but a bedroom, quite a clean and tidy bedroom. It is what I am guessing is a new build, with its low ceilings, spotlights and an en suite bathroom. I no longer think my captors are part of the Polish gang; this place is far too upmarket for them. Which raises the question, where the hell am I?

The mirror in the bathroom reveals some clues to my current predicament. I have never seen myself looking like this. Currently I am not smoking hot. My head is bandaged up, and that is what I was feeling earlier, as are my ribs and my left leg around the knee. In the bathroom there are bloodstained towels, the blood belonging either to me or a previous victim, for all I know. Besides the bandages I am naked, apart from some Emporio Armani boxers, which are not mine. I slide my hand inside the underwear and rub my finger along my Jap's eye; it is dry. I run my finger along the top of my leg, keeping it in the loose Italian underwear until I reach my crack. I gently slide the finger between my cheeks and into my hole; I do not feel sore or tender, so nothing untoward had happened in my unconscious state.

There does not seem to be an immediate threat, so I take a pee and go back to the bed. Walking around feels good in the sense that I could, and it allows me to fully gauge the extent of my injuries. Maybe one last little rest to get myself up to about seventy percent before the real challenge comes—opening the bedroom door. That is, if it is not locked.

Next to the bed I notice a glass of water and some medicines. I scan the labels and notice that they are aboveboard painkillers like tramadol and very low dose sedatives like diazepam, no flunitrazepam. A precautionary sip of water tells me that it does not seem to be laced with anything. It tastes mineral as opposed to tap (one can always tell the difference), so I guzzle it down and go back to sleep.

Four hours later I wake up. I know this because I checked the time on the clock in the room. I get up. My clothes do not seem to be around, but in the wardrobe in the room there are lots of clothes, presumably of the owner(s) of this place. Some are all right, and I would actually consider wearing them, but I decide against that. If a guy that I was looking after did that to me I would probably go over to him and just snap his neck. No, I will have to face this as he has prepared me, in his own boxer shorts. I walk over to the bedroom door, and before finding out the moment of truth I listen for any sounds from the other side. There are none. The door opens without any resistance.

As I move out of the bedroom into the rest of the flat, I drag my left leg along, exaggerating the extent of damage, so that I will be perceived weaker than I am. The flat is tidy and adequate for what I presume is an average degenerate. There is a folded duvet and a pillow on the corner brown leather sofa. No one seems to be in. I stop shuffling around the place and stand still and listen. I cannot hear a thing; I believe I am alone. Having investigated the kitchen, which besides revealing a clean-freak, there was nothing to report. I try one of the closed doors; it is the bathroom. This should reveal something—the state a bathroom is in is always a good tell. But again, nothing much is given away. The last door before I would have seen the whole place is now in front of me. All signs from the rest of the flat are pointing to my exploring being a fruitless endeavor. Maybe I've gotten the whole thing wrong and I was found by some good Samaritan, but there are still questions to be answered. Like why I am not in a hospital. This thought causes me to have a vague recollection about shouting at a guy "no hospital" and to just take me home. I open the door.

In my wildest dreams, which are generally horrific, I have never seen what is laid out before me. This is utter sick shit—even by my standards. The darkness draws me in to what was the second bedroom but is now a...the exact word of what it is does not come to me. I cannot actually tell if the room is painted or wallpapered due to the unique art adorning not just the walls, but the floors and the bed. Someone has been a very busy boy. Moving closer to some of the pictures I do what must be done and touch them, tracing the outlines where the details allow for that. There are just images, there are words, lots of them. So I start reading. "Crazy" no longer seems so crazy once the words are read. This scene is very precise, very organized.

The pages of words, reports, match the pictures they discuss. The more I read, the more apparent it becomes that each section is ordered in what must seem to the arranger as logic. The reading is fascinating; in some cases this unique point of view is even better than the graphic visuals, but do not get me wrong, the pictures tell a thousand words, each one stirring something in me. Some of the reports are just plain boring. These I gloss over. Some I read like my life depends on it; these I take such time over. The personal connection makes my heart beat fast—it is truly exhilarating. I must have been looking at the materials for over an hour, maybe two; it is so absorbing I have no concept of time. I finally get to what's on the bed. Was it worth the wait? Was the best saved until last?

Yes and yes. These are more shocking than everything else in the room, partly because they require me to turn them over to get to the source. Until that moment I had no idea what they would reveal. But mainly because they are the worst; even the host found them too devastating to leave them face up. I am no psychologist but I understand things at a deeper level than degenerates. After all, they are such emotional beings. I would have to say these bed items mean something to the guy. Which means I am in bigger trouble than when I first assessed this situation.

I totally get lost in the room, this hallowed place, and while away my time captivated in this man's seclusion. I am not sure how much more time has passed when I get interrupted. I have my back to the door and never see him approach. When he first speaks, breaking me out of a trance his goodies had left me in, I do not comprehend what is said. Maybe something like "what are you doing in here?" I close my eyes and truly listen as he continues to speak.

"You shouldn't be in here."

His accent is a very neutral London one; every word is enunciated in a way to get his point across without giving anything personal away. There was no panic in the "shouldn't" that would mean I had stumbled across his big, bad dark secret, just a calm statement that I should not be in this room. With my eyes still closed I sniff the air. He smells of Emporio Armani "He"—not the standard one but the white limited edition version that you can no longer buy. He must like that brand, or he has a thing for Italians.

"How are you feeling?"

Ah yes, he is still here. I open my eyes and turn around to look at him. He has jet-black hair and a natural tan. He could actually be Italian, apart from his perfect English accent. Half maybe, growing up here?

"I am Marco, you are in my flat."

I glance around the room and pictures I am holding while I sat on the bed, and then back at him.

"This must look fucked up. Come with me and I'll answer your questions." He is next to me now, taking the pictures out of my hands and placing them back on the bed face down. He grimaces while he does so. He takes my hand to help me up. "It's okay, you're safe. I'm not going to hurt you, I'm a policeman."

As I start to pretend-hobble out of the bedroom and have my back to him, I can tell he is scanning the room to make sure his catalogue is still there. Once in the living room he shuts that bedroom door, then gives me the once over, maybe to check I have not stolen anything or to appreciate me in his boxers. When I catch him staring at me.

"Do you want some more clothes to wear?"

"Yes please, that would be nice."

"Most of yours could not be salvaged, a doctor friend and I had cut your t-shirt and sweater off so as not to go over your head. Your jeans are in my dryer and should be dry by now, but I thought the denim might be a bit too tight to slip on over your bandaged leg. Your jacket looked like it needed specialized cleaning so is at the dry cleaners."

I nod. He helps me dress, as I was fumbling somewhat, in his Abercrombie sweats—not something I would personally wear but as the staple lounging around the house for any gay man they are comfortable. The zip on the hoodie is cold on my naked chest. This makes my nipples go hard, and I am sure this is obvious in the top.

"What do you remember from that attack?"

"Not a lot." He is going to get all policeman-like on my ass now. "How long ago was it?"

"Two nights ago. Was it homophobically motivated?"

"No, not really. I think they just wanted my phone and wallet." I cannot afford to be added to his little room of weird.

"Are you sure?"

"Sure of what?"

"Of what they wanted? It seemed more personal than a mugging."

"Well I guess the Polish, especially the gangs, aren't fans of us." He does not react to the label. "I think they were going to burn me, I remember that they stopped briefly when someone else ordered them to get the match."

"Zatrzymać?"

"Yes."

"That was me shouting at them to stop. They seemed surprised by my presence and ran off at that point."

"You speak Polish?"

"Yes."

He looks embarrassed; something is not quite right.

"But you are Italian?"

"Half-Italian, my mother was English."

Lucky bastard has a dead mother. "Well, thanks for rescuing me."

"You said you didn't want the police involved…you have nothing to be embarrassed about. It's not your fault; you can still make a statement."

"Can I think about it?" I decide to change the subject. "So you bandaged me up pretty well, I guess police first-aid?"

"No, I had a doctor friend examine you because you were adamant you did not want to go to a hospital. And if he had found anything suspicious, like it or not you would have been in a hospital."

"So I'm good?"

"Taylor said it was mainly bruising, there did not seem to be any internal bleeding or broken bones."

"I'm used to taking a beating. I used to be a cage-fighter." I get up and strike a stupid fake fighting pose.

He smiles. "You don't have any tattoos so I ruled out cage-fighter straight away."

"What did you come up with?"

"You're an enigma to me. Usually I would have just taken your identification from your wallet or a number from your phone and checked it out. But you don't have those items. I guess they were stolen. Which reminds me, do you need to call anyone?"

"My family is overseas and I wouldn't want to worry them, and I'm not seeing anyone special. Just need to call work and explain why I haven't been in." The thought of emailing them amuses me too much and I think of what I could say. *Dear Team, I got mugged and beaten up these past days. My head hurts! I am in pain and look like shit but as always I'm available on all channels—mobile, Blackberry, email, Morse-code and smoke signals. Yours forever contactable, Sebastian X.*

"You will have to cancel your credit cards, phone. It will be easier to report with a crime reference number."

Very sneaky, PC Plod, trying to make me capitulate to your way. "To be honest, I had a cheap pay-as-you-go phone on me which was nearly out of credit, and just a bit of cash." Actually they would have taken one of my phones but it would delete all information once the pin had been mis-entered twice, and they got no wallet as I do not carry stuff like that to be traced back to me when out at night. I must sound like a criminal to him now; I had better deflect this. "I only recently moved here from the States."

"Is that why you're staying at a hotel?"

"Yes." Crap, he knows a lot. "You could have just taken me there, I have really put you out."

"You kept insisting on that when I first found you, but in light of your no-hospital rule I thought it best you had someone to watch over you."

"You are too kind, seriously."

"It has been nice. Given me something else to think about."

We both glance towards the second bedroom.

"Is that why you really want me to report it? To add to your collection?"

"That must have totally freaked you out. Sorry."

"Not the nicest thing to find in the stranger's spare room after waking from a mugging." *Let me make this about you, so you do not look too much into me.*

"No one was ever meant to see that."

"Look, you seem like a nice genuine guy. I cannot presume to know you but from what you have done for me, I know you just want to help. Maybe too much, by bringing that stuff into your home."

He looks ashamed. "Someone has to."

"It looked highly confidential to me, and I'm no expert, but wouldn't all those different types of crimes fall under different categories? So unless you are a super-cop you can't be working all those cases."

"I need to find out the truth no matter what it costs."

"Your sanity?" Maybe too far. I could lose him. I move over to sit next to him. "I'm not judging you and I think it is awesome that the gay community has someone like you on our side, so thanks." I kiss him on the cheek.

He looks at me; behind his hazel eyes is a certain innocence. This time I kiss him on the lips. He responds with a hunger that says he really wants this. As I open my mouth his tongue enters, I start responding, and he pulls away.

"Sorry, I can't."

"Can't what? I was just thanking you for saving my life."

"I haven't been with anyone in a while…I promised

169

myself the next time I do anything like this, it has to mean something."

He is actually not joking, I should strip back into the boxers. "That's perfect. Given my current condition I probably shouldn't be doing anything too heavy. It's just I do not want to be alone tonight."

"I'm just outside on the sofa; you'll be safe here."

"Sure, but it's your bed, so I'll take the sofa. You've done enough for me already."

"Don't be silly."

"Okay, we share your bed—nothing untoward."

He is staring back at me, I can tell this is what he wants. His passion is saying yes, and his logical part that made whatever promise he made to himself is grappling with a way to justify the actions that will happen. He likes to be the hero, and in keeping with that role he cannot say no. I get up and stumble a little, causing him to get up and support me. Touch me. Usually I hate playing these types of games but more is happening underneath the surface of Marco than has been revealed. I am never one to shy away from a challenge, especially when it seems like I am already playing some role in his life, so a little gameplay seems sufficient.

Reaching the agreement to "just share a bed," we both know we are lying. Getting into the bed we both instantly take off all of our clothes, including underwear. The kissing starts up again. His body is nicely toned, not overly muscly but very athletic. As he gets on top he is taking care not to put any of his weight on me. We start humping each other, not in a penetrative way but laying on top of one another and grinding our cocks together. Conscious that I am still sore and that he wanted to take things slowly, we end up climaxing by jerking each other off. It was pretty intense as we remained locked, gazing into each other's eyes. After cumming, we continue to kiss each other and touch each other's bodies; he is being very careful around anywhere that is bandaged up. Presumably, aware that he might hurt me, he moves into the big spoon position and molds his body against mine. His arms wrap around me protectively and he starts talking. I listen and respond when it seems appropriate. I keep the details mainly to places I have been, the sights I have seen in those places and my job. I tell him about the locals; it is always good to put a human face on things. It turns out that he knows Nat too, small gay world and all. Eventually he falls asleep; either prowling the nights looking to stop gay crime has taken its toll, or the sofa is not comfortable to sleep on.

I cannot sleep even though I am tired. It is not because I am missing the pharmaceuticals which have had me pretty much out of it these past two days. But my mind is racing with the reports from the various crime scenes he has collected. The forensic detail, the investigator and technician perspective, the pictures in those documents are all fascinating, obviously some more than others. The gay guy having his stuff stolen from his gym locker—not that engaging. The gay guy on the common getting verbally abused—the fact that he reported it was more amusing than anything else. The gay couple beaten up for just being themselves—now we are starting to get to the intriguing stuff. My bedfellow seems to have taken every crime against gays over the past few years concentrated in the area and nearby, and is doing his own personal investigation into them. Even those that are solved have made it on to his walls. What his endgame is, I do not know. I know it is not a case of admiring his own handiwork, as I know he did not commit these crimes; it is obvious he wants to be able to help others, to atone for something. Also, the fact is that I know who committed some of the more recent ones. The fact is, it was me.

13

HE IS PROUD

The room of hidden delights has showed me something new: there is a picture of a penis stump from a guy who shoved his cock in a glory hole and had it cut off. I never imagined what the finished product would look like, all washed up and made as acceptable as surgically possible. Of course I was there when I cut the cock off, and saw the bloody stump pumping fluid out. The slice was so easy, so clean, I doubt it caused the man much pain. That was not in the report—only how he was traumatized by the incident. After the cut he fell backwards, maybe fainted, so I could see no more. An accompanying medical report would have been a nice supplement to this. Maybe I should wake the guy gently breathing asleep next to me and ask. The fact that Cockless was taken to what seemed like a very able hospital, with the ability to make the remainder not look like a fanny, shows me that I was right to grind the lifeless slug of cock that fell into my cubicle into the floor with the heel of my boot. The memory of how it was much more elastic than I thought it would be comes back. For the sake of completion the file should have probably included a picture of the guy's face. But it did not, maybe for some privacy reason. This is a good thing because I do not want to know who sucked me off that night, in case he is absolutely rough. But also a bad point, because a picture showing the face of a man knowing he would never have a working cock would have been priceless.

The good policeman (he must be more than that—Inspector?) reads too much into these cases. One case, clearly a crime of passion, does not seem to have him convinced. It is the incidence between My Tramp and the Drunk, which I left neatly tied up so as not to waste police time. My version of events, had I been writing this report, would have been: Drunk hates himself and his life and has very low self-esteem, then meets a nice guy who happens to be in his league albeit a tramp. The tramp moves in with him and they are living very happily together. Drunk sends relevant emails informing "friends" in his life who may or may not have bothered to read the actual emails once they saw who it was from, that he has met someone. He does not go into details, e.g. that the someone happens to be a tramp, as he wants to hang on to the minute bit of self-respect he has left. The tramp brings his dog to live with them. Drunk is jealous of the attention the dog gets so cuts its head off, never to be found again. I bite down on my lip to stop myself laughing and waking Marco once I hear the "where's its head?" in my own head. Tramp is upset about loss of dog's head so cuts out Drunk's tongue (possibility exists he gave such bad head the tongue had to come out) and eats it, proven by later autopsy. The two continue to indulge in kinky sex including bondage and emetophilia until they both manage to strangle each other.

Now, the actual report is not as clean-cut as my version of events, but due to no forced entry into the flat and no third party presence, they have to go with the occurrences as they could evidence them. They summarize that the Drunk felt sorry for My Tramp and gave him money. My Tramp's possessions included money, which could be traced back to being withdrawn by the Drunk. A weird sort of escort thing, or desperate loneliness, are mentioned as possible options. My Tramp followed him home where he was fed and watered. They had sex; it was thought that My Tramp raped the Drunk repeatedly, as there was evidence that the Drunk was restrained. Here they mention the mental capacity of both parties. My Tramp is thought to be mentally unstable and the Drunk has issues about being raped and attacked, documented through counseling. Claiming mental instability seems a bit of a cop out to me but seems to be the only way they can justify the tongue and head cutting, as it cannot rationally be explained. At this point the Drunk tried to escape, managing to free his hands, but was caught in the act and they strangled each other to death.

Tidy. Not really. No one cares, though according to the final report there are questions to be asked but no further investigation is warranted, that is apart from the guy in bed with me. Is he only concerned because of the personal interest he has in all these crimes? The case that was on the bed—it was very horrific, even by my standards, and even though that particular incident was also nicely wrapped up the perpetrator is still at large. In an earlier conversation with the deceased, he'd mentioned a guy named Marco, and seeing the file center stage on the bed could only lead to the conclusion that it was this Marco. Any further clarification is provided by the fact that Marco knows Nat, Nat was very close to the deceased, so Marco also knew the deceased. What was it he'd said? Before his Spanish lover there was one guy, Marco, whom he thought was his life.

The Italian suddenly disengages from holding me and turns to face the other way. I guess he is not used to sharing a bed with someone. He moves to lie on his back, and is tossing and turning. He starts mumbling, chucking the duvet off himself, all while asleep. The part of me that is still touching him skin-to-skin feels that he is hot and very sweaty. The mumbling starts to be more coherent, as does the shaking. He is apologizing for not being there, and then spasmodically he jerks awake, calling out a name.

"Joe!"

I pretend to still be asleep but stir a little for realism. I can sense him examine me with his eyes.

He gets up and goes into the en suite. I keep my eyes closed, but listen. Having removed the bandage from my ear earlier, I hear the tap is running. He is splashing water on his body, and when he turns it off I hear it clearly: "I am sorry, my dear sweet friend, that I was not there to protect you. But I will find your murderer and kill him."

A chill runs down my spine, not because I just did intimate things with this guy, nor I am scared, or think I am undeserving of death. But the conviction of his statement makes me believe him. I remain feigning sleep.

When he gets back into the bed, he lightly kisses my back and goes back to spooning me. I can tell he needs this intimacy; he needs to be able to hold someone to erase those images and stories of abuse, violence and hatred stored next-door but more so in his head. Deep down he could well be as tortured as I am—like me, he has seen the disturbed world. This is comforting. He wraps his arms tighter around me and sidles up as close as he can get behind me. I dare not open my eyes, because I am not sure what to do with the information I have just heard. I cannot risk giving away that I am the guy he is looking for, that he could accomplish his mission by moving his hands to around my throat and strangling the life out of me for his revenge.

I needed to kill him spectacularly, to put others off from buying the apartment next door. I never thought that the repercussions of my deed would be lying in bed next to me, sworn to hunt me down. There is a suitable scapegoat, who admittedly fled (according to the newspapers and the police report) and might be the object of Marco's bloodlust, so I just need to remain levelheaded about the situation. That night when I met the deceased I had drugged the wine and fully intended to make it seem like a drug binge gone wrong. However, meeting the little chap provided me with a golden opportunity. It was not like I was doing anything wrong; he fully satisfied my criteria for help.

From a young age I had realized that the good would always suffer, and I could help them by beating up the bullies at the zoo and on the bus. But what would happen next...? There was always more evil in the world than good. It would be impossible to wipe out everyone bad, no matter how hard I tried. Then I knew it was those already hurting who had to be terminated. Killing those in pain is the humane act, saving them from a world of misery. A bonus I had not really thought about until now is that it would bring about the Marcos of the world, justice givers eliminating vermin.

The deceased had hurt, his whole life—unloved by his family, selling himself to try and become important, shacking up with the first man who would have him. Yes, he needed help. After getting him to write down his history and current fears about the owner of the apartment, which would provide the perfect motive and where the police should look, he fell asleep drugged. This time the killing was tidy and everything pointed where it should have. The owner came around with drugged wine, gave the deceased some, then disappeared for it to take effect. The deceased—frightened—wrote his letter to his friend and hid it, then fell asleep because of the pharmaceuticals. The owner reappeared at this time using his keys (no forced entry), and proceeded to murder the victim.

What had happened was I had to make this good. A simple murder might not have had the desired effect, so I had to make it horrific. After he was knocked out I stripped him naked, turned him over and fucked him hard. I did not personally penetrate him, so I used the wine bottle. This caused him to stir. Once the neck of the bottle was inside him, I smashed it. Thick red blood started to pour out of him. It must have hurt, because even drugged on sedatives he screamed out. The little shards of glass cutting the inside of his anus, ripping the delicate tissue apart, would mean he would never be able to have sex again. With his most prized asset gone, he would surely want death more now.

The most dramatic pieces stir up emotions in as many people as possible. These emotions need to be controversial. Looking down at his pale white ass seeping blood I decided his death should be religious. I picked up the whimpering soul and laid him on a rug; he was still half out of it but not enough to be totally unaware. He curled up in the fetal position, eyes shut tightly, trying as he must have on many an occasion to block out the cruel world. I lifted the king-sized bed up by the head end, no easy feat for just one. When the bed was standing fully upright I pushed it against the wall to support it.

I removed the belt from his jeans and tied it around one of his wrists, then dragged him over to the bed. I shoved one of his socks in his mouth as a gag because the flight instinct was beginning to override the chemical effects. The apartment is soundproofed so his calling for help was not a situation that I was worried about, but more that, I wanted to give him some dignity by not allowing him to beg.

I picked him up again. His face was wet, as he had started crying. I tried to comfort him. In his current state he was weak, not quite sure what was happening, wondering if it was a dream, but the cold harsh reality of pain remained.

"Shhh, it will be over soon. Unfortunately it will hurt but you are serving your purpose."

As I tied the other end of the belt to the metal rungs of the headboard, he looked at me with his wet doe eyes asking why.

This is what I do; I cannot be ashamed of my nature.

Extracting a pillow from its case, I used the cloth to tie his other wrist to the headboard. Both arms were stretched out fully now, and his weak arms supporting his whole body. In this crucifixion position he looked at peace. He wanted this. His legs were not thrashing about trying to get free, probably because if he moved another piece of glass would tear at his insides. I did not hate him or hold any malice towards him but the supposed perpetrator did, so that left me with no choice but to beat this defenseless guy. Bruises would definitely tell the real horrors of this apartment. I started with a right hook across his face because the way he was strung up this was a good foot above me. I could not get enough power in the punch to knock him out again, so he had to endure. I moved to his soft, skinny midsection, which was at the ideal height to use as a punching bag, so I did. Every time I connected with his flesh his body shocked back to the red splotch that was growing larger on the mattress behind him. The only thing left was for me to grab his thighs, grip them vice-like and spread his legs open to leave behind the evidence that he had been forced to have sex against his will.

He was being crucified against a soft object, the mattress, which would allow the rhythm of breathing; he would not asphyxiate and die. In the kitchen I found a Lakeland filleter, which I took back to the bedroom to show him. His eyes were shut. As I approached him he tried to kick me. Judging by the grimace on his face this last act of defiance came at a great cost to himself, but I saw it coming and sidestepped it. He was staring at the knife and looking down at his naked vulnerable body. "Please don't," his eyes begged of me. I was standing right in front of him. Now would be the time to try to kick me again, to try and mount some kind of escape. But the instrument in my hand had pacified him. He tried to talk but the sock in his mouth prevented that. I did not want him to taint my earlier perception of him, so I decided not to remove the sock which was now red; I might have broken a couple of his teeth when I punched him in the face.

I placed my gloved hand on his chest and rubbed it until I found the bottom of his sternum. "This will set you free," I told him as I pulled my other arm back to get momentum before I stuck it to him. The knife was not driven deeply into him, but far enough. Once in, I pulled it down, cutting to his belly button and beyond, stopping only at his pubes. I was not sure which organs were cut. I just put my hand in the opening and grabbed whatever I could and yanked it out. The smell meant I did not want to hang around, so I left the crucified boy with his innards hanging out behind. I barely looked back. But I am getting a good look now, via the pictures in the report. It enables me to read that his death came hours afterwards; where he bled out and would have died in lots of pain.

* * * *

It was now two weeks since my chance encounter with Marco. Between first meeting him, finding out that he is secretly hunting down abusers of gays in his own time, and then being intimate with him, I met him again. Someone cannot "save" your life and you just blank them out; that would be suspicious, and I guess I live by the adage of keeping my enemies close. So we met up for dinner. He returned my jacket and I thanked him by treating him to the meal. I told him to pick anywhere he fancied: a Michelin-starred restaurant, the trendiest gay-friendly eatery currently on the scene or a new expensive place he wanted to try. He opted for a low-key place, which meant we had to talk to one another, something I felt was a novel concept for him as it was for me. That night we ended up back at his place; the date had gone well, and we ended up back in bed together. We did more of what we did the first time we were together, only this time we introduced oral sex into the mix. Maybe he thought I was still injured, as he wanted to take it slowly; he only liked doing this in sex, as he could not work out who is the lock or key, or he did not trust me. Who knows? But going the whole way with each another never came up.

Today we will meet for the third time, just for a coffee, after I finish some volunteer work I do. Even though it is a Saturday and the collective masses of gaydom will want to party all night, neither of us wants that. He said he had to work, and conforming to the norm is not my style. So it is just a lunchtime coffee. This is better for me, as there is something wrong between us (not the fact he wants to kill me), which I have not been able to identify yet.

The volunteer work I started since I arrived back in London and passed all the compulsory checks is something I enjoy doing. It puts me in touch with my humanity, and to be honest, in my life anything that does that can only be good. I am at the local cinema, Flicks, where some other volunteers and I are chaperoning children with special needs to give their parents and caregivers some respite. One of the other volunteers is a dyke who is the manager of the cinema and who has arranged this Saturday morning private screening of a new computer-generated animated film. I use the term "dyke" because she seems to overtly go out of her way to not be feminine—with her unflattering clothes, her personal appearance including a lack of make-up and a butch haircut, down to her vast size. Nevertheless, I think she has done a great job organizing this, even though it is the smallest screen and the cinema is not actually open to the public this early, because the children love it.

Being able to be themselves and not have to worry about some cock taking the piss out of them must be very liberating. Not that all of them would understand when they are being abused, but that is beside the point: everyone should be able to be themselves and be totally safe in their own skin without fear of any reprisal. We are paired with same-sex kids for when we have to escort them to the toilet. This works for me because I do not think I could handle being with girls. It should be one-on-one, but there are not enough volunteers for that. At the back of the screen I glance at the three boys I am watching over; they are totally engrossed in the film. If only they could live their whole lives this peacefully. But the world is too cruel for that.

Ben (point proved) the dyke is taking one of her girls to the toilets. If only we had had someone to watch over us when we were younger, I start to think, our lives could have turned out so differently. Then I banish the thought. Something exciting must have happened because the small group of children are suddenly cheering and clapping. It looks like the mythical animal hero of the story has gained the ability to do whatever he always had the potential to do—he only needed to believe in himself. I should really pay more attention to the film, because when we take the children back they will bombard me with what did I think of that bit when, who was the best character, did I like when etc., and I do not want to lie to them. Ben and the girl, Cathy, eventually return but Ben does not take her back to her seat; she is talking to her at the back by the door. I go over to make sure everything is cool. It turns out it is not.

After a bit of hugging, which is technically not allowed but was definitely needed, Ben, whom I have a new-found respect for, takes the girl back to her seat. She holds Cathy's hand as she settles back into watching the film. It turns out that in the cinema (now open to the public) toilets, Cathy literally bumped into a stranger. The woman in question overreacted like she had been slapped in the face or something, and shouted for Cathy to watch where she was going. Cathy apologized as she went on into the cubicle, after which the stranger muttered under her breath "stupid mong" which Ben heard, as the skank-bitch's mutterings were not quiet. Ben asked the woman what she said and was called a fat bitch—fair enough—for her troubles. So then Ben told her to leave the cinema, as she was the manager. This is when the woman got rowdier, telling Ben to keep out of her business. Cathy came out of the cubicle, heard the shouting and saw the altercation take place, and thought it was all her fault.

"She's better now. I explained it was nothing to do with her and we were playing."

"So what are you going to do now?"

"First, I'm going to get Cathy some popcorn, and then find that woman and kick her out of my cinema."

Feeding the kids popcorn is also not allowed, but I

know the girl deserves some comfort so I do not say anything. "Well, can you point the woman out to me?"

She eyes me suspiciously. "What are you going to do?"

"Show her the error of her ways."

"I'll just get security to kick her out."

"It will be better if I speak to her first. Where can we find her?"

"There is only one film scheduled to start soon and doors won't open for another fifteen minutes. That's in Screen One upstairs."

The queue did not have many in it, and without needing to have the slag pointed out to me I could tell which one she was: a skinny woman in a purple tracksuit. Her hair was scraped back so tightly that it gave her a facelift, and her giant hoop earrings jangled as she chewed on some gum. She was chatting to a muscular, tall, good-looking black man (clearly punching above her weight), who could pose a problem. Everyone else in the queue was standing away them.

"Purple tracksuit?" I ask Ben.

"Yes. Wait here while I go and get security." Ben must have sized up her companion.

She obviously does not know me if she thinks I would just wait around. So I approach the target.

"What?"

"I believe you have a problem with my daughter. What did you call her? A mong?"

She eyes me up and down. "Mate, did you stick it to that rough bird? She looked, well lez, a right dirty gay..."

"Do not pick on those less fortunate than yourself, especially children. And just so you know, I'm a dirty gay too, so don't be such a homophobic bitch." I interrupt so she cannot finish her sentence and simultaneously head-butt her flush on the face, leaving her sitting on the floor holding her face and nursing her potentially broken nose. The vileness coming from her gob meant I had to just teach her a lesson.

14

HE TIES UP LOOSE ENDS

This is ridiculously boring. It is at times like these I wonder why I actually bother. For the entire day I have been practically locked up in a room with a bunch of wankers; food is brought to us at designated times and toilet breaks are strictly scheduled. The other inmates are trying to be friendly but they all disgust me with their bravado about why they are here, the up-the-ass backslapping to say you did well so let's be friends, and the overall fakeness they are exhibiting. In this prison, the guy I know the most is the one who is annoying me greatest: he just does not know when to shut the fuck up and stop being such a cock. Maybe he thinks that to survive in this place he has to behave as he is. I am starting to feel sick, due to the combination of cheap clothes and unsuitable aftershave. Clothes from the likes of Next topped up with one standout piece like Prada glass frames, to try and falsely convince others that the whole ensemble costs more than it does. And over-cologned nasty odors, the cologne bought because that is new at the moment and is being over-advertised, not because it smells good on the wearer.

Why oh why? Actual incarceration would be preferably to my current situation. At least real criminals would have genuinely done something with their lives. Maybe even something commendable, something which would cause an uprising against the machine.

My confinement is being stuck in a room with a bunch of cocks, specifically managers, in the latest PR painfest called calibration. This involves all the line managers sitting together for a few days, with their human rights apparently stripped away, deciding the fate of all the employees. Instead of just being able to say this worker is doing a great job and deserves a promotion at any time in the year that is warranted, we have to hold it all in until one of these twice-yearly meetings where said employee is graded using feedback from co-workers. This is then compared to that received by everyone else in the company at the same level. Then everyone at that level is scored on a crude grid consisting of nine squares. Most employees are plonked in the middle square—performing to expectations—the weak (ones the company wants rid of) are shoved in the bottom lefthand corner so that they can be given a warning and designated on their way out. Then, to meet targets, those who have sucked enough cock are placed in the top right corner saying they are doing a bang-up job and should be considered for a promotion, and a junior account executive gets the not-so-massive jump to account executive with a couple of grand extra per annum.

Is this a just, honest and reliable way to treat the staff? No, it is anything but. Based on profits, a certain number of workers should be placed on warnings in case numbers have to be suddenly cut. In addition, even if everyone is performing way above and beyond there is only a certain percent that can actually be promoted. Promotion is then based on extra factors, the number one being how much you went down on senior management; then items like years of service and time since last promotion are factored in. The management would try and put those employees in their department in a favorable light, only highlighting the good aspects of their feedback, not because they care about said payroll number but because ultimately it will make them look good. So everything we are hearing in this room is bullshit. Why not call the employee in, let them represent themselves and give examples of where they have excelled? No, that would seem to be fair. Individuality is not allowed and the hierarchy must be respected at all times. They must instead be judged against one another so that we can all listen to ourselves talk more. I am sure this company is not unique, and every other major corporation across the country operates a similar corrupt system. The weak and poor will perish while the strong and rich will screw everyone else over until they achieve their small goals in life.

It would be better to just herd the masses like cattle going into a slaughterhouse, randomly pick those who look the weakest and stun them between the eyes, putting them out of their misery. The prize stock, usually the ones making the loudest noise and doing the showboating, would be able to lord it over the rest, demonstrating their superiority. They would then be taken somewhere else and be allowed to stud. The majority left behind would be in a state of limbo, slouching around and grazing at the grass until the next slaughter or breeding session when everything that has happened before will happen again. What makes this so disgusting is that the degenerates allow this to continue: they are happy to be treated like livestock, serving their masters however they can. There is no respect for themselves, no demonstration of self-worth, no taking up the opportunity to end this system.

Just now something was said and addressed to me, as they are all looking at me. I look at the image being projected on the screen, which is of Cindy. Obviously we are far too important to know everyone in the building by name, so in case said worker ever looked at a member of senior management in the wrong way their biography, meant to be used for new business pitches, is displayed in front of us. Of course this has the added benefit of providing us their full background, so we can factor where they went to university into our decision making process.

"She understands the company really well." She knows who to kiss up to, quite literally. "The clients she has been exposed to like her." The old men, coming from the old school PR ways of strip clubs and cocaine, who we parade her in front of, appreciate her inappropriate dress sense. "Her colleagues have an excellent rapport with her." As she spreads the "bitchy" gossip they hang on her every word. "There are certain areas where she can improve but those will come with time." Like time management, attention to detail, strategic awareness and business acumen.

They move on to Roderdick, who reads out the feedback he received about her, and I can return to sitting in contempt of the room and this joke of a process. I could have been more honest and told them that yesterday she spent the entire day talking to Jay about reality television shows. They both have a shared passion for these and I quote "explorations into real people's lives." When they first started talking with depth and intimacy about the "celebrities" I actually thought they were real mutual friends with them. Bunty had to inform me that these friends existed on the small screen. The level Jay and Cindy cared about what happened to the participants, if they would get together or cheat on their partners, bitch, bully etc., was beyond belief.

This reality television phenomenon must have passed me by. Why do degenerates care what other degenerates are up to? Is it to somehow validate their own lives by saying "look, that is normal behavior," or to say "I'm better than all that because I don't act in that way?" The untalented stars of these shows are the glory hunters wanting their fifteen minutes of fame, an escape from the mundane. So you cannot really blame them for participating. The creators know it is a cheap product to produce that can fill the ever-expanding multi-channel schedules. So the inherent problem lies with Jay and Cindy, in other words the masses, who watch the crap. I am sure the numerous different versions have a bit of eye candy or a unique selling point. But seriously, is there nothing better to do with your time?

If my two colleagues and everyone else woke up and really opened their eyes, they would know that the real life situations unfolding in front of them, the ones they can actually influence, are far more interesting and dynamic than the televised wank. This is where THEY have a made a mistake: allowing the growth of these voyeuristic shows just to save money could be THEIR undoing. Of course, I know it is not just a money-saving exercise and that by allowing their selected clones to rise up through the ranks of celebrity in order to eventually exert control on the masses is another way of THEM being THEM. However, these shows demonstrate the drama that can happen in real-life, and as more and more degenerates realize participating in the game of life will be better than watching it, we might all be saved.

The talk about these shows continued between the two of them all day, only briefly stopping for some self-esteem building. I will presume, as I stopped listening, that Cindy had said what a mega body one of the guys on one of the many shows had. This resulted in Jay re-telling the whole pod about this diet he is on, going over to Cindy, lifting his shirt up and asking her to check out how firm his abs were. In all my years working in companies, I thought I had seen it all: sex in the toilets, drug and alcohol abuse, homophobia, racism, bullying…this was a totally new one to me. But in PR the lengths that are taken seem to be pushed further and further all the time. After all, it was calibration the next day and Rod had just appeared. Cindy purred as she stroked away on his abs, and he looked constipated like he was straining to get his muscles to be harder. After she had finished, Jay moved on asking everyone else if they wanted a feel. Raj declined because he was now seeing someone, a relationship he has been keeping very quiet, and so did I. All the others went to have a stroke for some bizarre reason.

Bunty messaged me afterwards saying she had felt firmer. To which I replied "Auf wiedersehen." Since the reality show debate, I started watching clips on YouTube, as did she, so we could message each other lines from them in a piss-take of what was unraveling before us.

She'd responded, "You are the weakest manager,

goodbye."

"You've been evicted from the public relations house."

"Sashay away." She started laughing uncontrollably at that one and sent me the accompanying clip. It is a show about drag queens; I knew I must deliver an equally cutting one.

"You are no longer in the running to be America's, Britain's, any country's, next top model."

"Now fuck off with ya, yeah."

"You're fired!"

As Raj's face pops up on the screen I am interrupted from thinking about yesterday and the state where being talentless with nothing to say dominates the lives of the populace. Some of these shows are sugarcoated, where the participants are trying to learn or demonstrate a skill. But in essence they have the same goal as the others—cheap thrills for the masses. Who cares that some artist who had a number one hit ten years ago married a glamor model and are choosing to showcase their lives together for the betterment of mankind? Or that some corrupt politician is trying to show everyone that they are in fact decent, honest and just like Joe Public by joining a twenty-four-seven show where they get no privacy. It is all PR, spun so that the creators will have the winner they want; and yet it is watched in droves. The droves are those who care, but now there is the glimmer of hope, as they want in on the action.

The brown face currently being projected seems to be staring down on me, begging for forgiveness once again. The rest are discussing his future, and without me having to stick my oar in he is judged to be progressing as normal and will not receive a pay raise or promotion. Guess he should have whipped up his top and got everyone to stroke his abs. Or better still, not break the mold by trying to be different. Actually, I respected him for that, for not capitulating to his stereotype and becoming a doctor, dentist, accountant, lawyer etc. However, I am the only one in the room that might have stood up for him, before the betrayal. The others are all old school, and while they can tolerate the odd Indian spice they would not actively add it as an ingredient. PR is a predominantly white upper-class job; the more creative of the Oxbridge types end up in this world, and they are the ones who will survive.

Is this punishment enough for his act of betrayal? I would have to answer no. It is personal between us now, and while I should let it go, forgiving is not part of my nature. Fortunately for him, rationality is, and that is preventing me from planning his death.

"He is hard-working but needs to put himself forward to take on responsibility for running some of the various projects we have going on in the department," I add. That is the type of crap they like to hear. I get back to plotting vengeance.

* * * *

I decide it would be better not to go over to the source of the coldness that has sent a shiver down my back, no matter how tempting it is to see the sight of the dead body from this height. It carries the risk that I would be spotted, so it is best to be cautious. I will have to pacify the urge to see the glass-embedded splattered body from my first defenestration by looking at it at from ground level with the rest of the morbid spectators that will crowd around. I walk out of the dark room, stepping over the jerking body at my feet, thinking that how when I planned these activities earlier in my work prison-cell I could not have hoped it would have gone this well. The one doubt in my mind is that this will definitely be making it onto Marco's wall of gay, and there is the obvious link back to me.

Outside, even though I know the recently deceased well enough, he is unrecognizable. The fall and impact has truly fucked him up. I wonder how this would have played out on a reality show, because the reality is very different from what is seen on television. There is no pretty body with a few scratches from the broken window and a bit of blood, with one limb sticking out at an awkward angle. Instead there is a mush of where the bones have caved in; in other places the bones have torn through the skin. The head no longer exists after exploding on impact and creating a general mess all over the place and not all landing in a neat little pile all together. The reeking stench of the innards being splattered and leaking out their contents is another thing that would not come across on the screen. As I walk away from the scene and the increasing crowd, I replay the events that have just happened in my head to make sure I have not missed anything or left any clues to my involvement behind.

About three hours ago, I'd entered the high-rise. All the gays seemed to want to live locally to gay-town and if this means they have to sacrifice a nice place which they could not afford for a scum-ridden estate, so be it. This particular one in Battersea, a stone's throw away from Vauxhall, was not particularly hot on security: dummy cameras were in place to act as a deterrent but they did not film anything. (I got Matt to check this out when I first started coming here). Actually, the security measures are needed less than they are in the Clapham housing estates. The general community living here seems to be mid-twenties professionals trying to be accessible to the center. Most of the "unsavories" who would have been given the places for a very cheap rate by the council had sold out a long time ago when they had the chance to do so and make a massive profit. Knocking on the door to the flat I wanted to enter, I could tell the guy standing at the peephole was not expecting to see me and wondering what I was doing there. I had never been a threat to him and maybe he hoped I wanted sex, so it did not take long for him to allow me to enter.

"I got you a little something to show there are no hard feelings," I said as I handed him the bag.

He accepted the gift graciously and took it out of the bag; it was not wrapped or anything but was still in its box, a box I would later take and stuff in his wardrobe. "Thanks." He turned the box over in his hands. "Why don't you make yourself at home?" I guess he wanted me to take my jacket and gloves off. "Do you want a drink?"

"I always thought this area was a little rough and I worry about your safety, so I got you this when we were still going out. But never had the chance to give it to you then, I still want you to have it. After all, it is a dangerous world out there."

"About that..."

"Don't worry about it. I mean, we never said we were exclusive or anything and you and Raj seem like a much happier couple. Were we even actually a couple or just two guys who dated and fucked a few times?"

Haunted cracked a smile. "Thanks for being so understanding. It just seemed to happen." *Betraying me just seemed to happen…what the fuck, you cock?* "We sort of hit it off when we met at his charity party." *So you guys got drunk in the bar, went to a club and fucked.* "Then he went away and did his trek and it was so exciting."

"You don't have to explain anything."

"I thought I should, and after all you got me this gift." He held up the box. "And I missed his company, and you were absent."

"I was getting mugged, remember."

He looked closer at the gift like it made sense now. "Even before that, though, you were always distant. I just don't think we were compatible. And then he got back from holiday." *Yeah, you admit it was a stupid holiday and not some charity thing.* "We started hanging out and just seemed to click. One thing led to another, but before anything physical happened between us I had already ended it with you." He was trying far too hard to justify himself: he was guilty.

"So what was happening to that drink you were getting us?"

He got up to go to the kitchen to get us something. I swiped his phone, which was on the armrest of the chair he had sat on. I entered the pass-code, which I had seen him input a few times. It was a touch screen smartphone, usually the type that did not work if the user wore gloves, but these were special ones fit for this purpose. Like ninety percent of gay men with a phone like this, he had FAF on it. It said he had not used the fuck finder in weeks; I reactivated him and changed the information in his profile to say: "looking for NSA fun now." His picture was the same one from the dating website.

As he returned and passed me a glass of rosé wine, I hid the phone on myself. I toasted him and my colleague. "I am glad that the two of you are happy together." I did not drink the wine because I was sure it was cheap and nasty.

"You'll easily find someone else. I mean, look at you."

Who says I want anyone, dickwad? "I'm not really looking for anything at the moment."

"Why were you on that website then?"

"So do you like the color?"

Haunted looked puzzled, not sure if I was referring to his brown boyfriend or the yellow stun gun. "It looks really cool. I'm not sure about using it though."

"I hope you never have to but it's better to be safe than sorry. Get it out, and I'll show you how to use it." I left it as a sexual innuendo just to make him uncomfortable. While he was digging into the box, a box that had already been opened by me to fully charge the Taser X26 ahead of this moment, I excused myself to go to the bathroom.

In the bathroom I whipped out his phone, which had been vibrating away in my pocket, and responded to all the guys who had messaged him. Now was not a time to be choosy—there are so many time wasters on these sites. "I'm naked and alone, just need my hole filling. Come over—the door is open, the lights are off and I'm waiting." After sending that to the first guy I copied and pasted it and sent it on to everyone else. Waiting for the replies, I went online. The phone was already connected to his Wi-

Fi and was reacting quickly. I looked up some porn and screen-grabbed body, cock and ass pictures that could pass for belonging to Haunted. He did not have these pictures in his photo albums; I had checked, for authenticity. When I got back online to Find-A-Fuck, the few responders (I guess the directness put off the younger inexperienced guys) wanted to see pictures, know where he was, if he was into chems, if he was totally submissive. I responded to these next-stage candidates with the pictures I had just taken and sent his location map. Then I contemplated texting Raj and asking him to come over.

Haunted had the Taser out and was flipping it over, playing with it in his hands. He did not notice me re-enter the room. I stood right behind him when he noticed me, and that was only because I had my arms wrapped around his. From this position he stood up so I could show him how to hold the yellow plastic gun, to change and reload the cartridges. He was not paying much attention, probably enjoying the fact that I was behind him again, and wanting me to fuck him. He was pressing his ass hard against my cock, my embrace would have been better than anything he had with his boyfriend because I was taller and stronger. His lack of diligence in the task at hand did not matter—all I needed was his fingerprints all over the device.

I sensed that he wanted me to make the first move; he probably thought from when he spied me at his peephole that I had come over for a last bunk-up. While I might have been emotionally distant from him, the rare times we were physical had left him wanting more. Would it be enough to just start an affair with him and then let it slip to everyone at the office? No, I was cheated on, and such a betrayal from two guys I know cannot go unpunished. Plus, I had moved on and needed to erase him from my past. I kissed the back of his neck, which caused him to exhale in delight. He started to turn around. When he had nearly completed his turn and we were practically face-to-face, I punched him as hard as I could. I was aiming to knock him out, and I was successful.

15

HE CAN MANIPULATE ANYONE

He went down like the cheating cock he was, and did not move. I took out his phone to check the messages; there were a couple of responses. One guy wanted more pictures—he seemed like a total time waster, whereas the other guy—the perfect choice for this—had no pictures of himself up. He said he was married but wanted to try ass, wanted the lights to remain off, and he just wanted to fuck and go. I told him to hurry over and gave him the full address. He wanted my assurance that it would be totally discreet; I guaranteed on Haunted's behalf that after this night he would never be contacted again from this profile.

"Now that we have some time, let me go back to your earlier question," I told the body at my feet, not caring if he could hear me or not, as I started to undress him. After all, he did promise his guest that he would be ready and waiting. "I was on that website to meet guys like you, victims of life, to put you out of your misery so that the world could no longer abuse and hurt you. I misjudged you; you were not as pathetic as your picture made you out to be, so I was going to let you go. But then you stabbed me in the back by choosing to go out with a fucking work colleague of mine. How do you think that made me look?" He was now fully naked, so I neatly folded his clothes and put them on the chair.

"I could not let such a blatant disregard of respect for me go unpunished. Raj should be punished as well but he is too close to me, too many questions would be asked. Never shit on your own doorstep; even you being a sort of ex might lead back to me in a small way. But enough time has passed since we dated, plus the scapegoat will arrive soon. The second rule in this business is always have a sacrificial lamb at the ready."

His phone buzzed to say that the guy was on his way and would be here in about fifteen minutes. I replied by telling him to hurry as I was gagging for cock. I used this time to put the Taser box in Haunted's wardrobe and plug the charger in a socket in the bedroom. When I returned to the betrayer, I gently kicked his body to make sure he was still out of it, and then looked out of the window.

"Even though you live by yourself, you should pay more rent for a river view. Why live this high up and just have a view of the streets below? You should have asked your boyfriend to move in; he's desperate enough to do so. But judging by your earlier actions, I guess you weren't going to stay faithful to him." He started stirring, so I picked him up and propped him against the window so he could look at the view when he came to.

"What are you doing?" he slurred at me

"Weren't you listening to me before? Poetic justice."

The unlocked door opened and we saw a silhouette standing there. "Come in," I ordered him. The room was dark (not pitch black but dark enough that features could not be made out), as he wanted it. He must be really ugly—just wanting to shove his pathetic penis anywhere that would have it. Or did he hate being gay so much, going along with the lie that it could be a woman he was fucking was easier? He entered the room, shutting the door behind him. I told him I was by the window, so that he could use the light as a guide. Haunted was about to speak when I covered his mouth with my left hand. In my right I held the Taser.

"So is your cock hard?" I demanded of the stranger as he fumbled over. "I want it so badly, I hope you're taking your clothes off."

"Is your pussy wet? Is your..."

I shot him with the Taser the second he got close enough. He fell to the ground instantly, writhing in pain as his muscles locked in a spasm of hurt. I held on to the trigger to deliver the maximum shock. Haunted bit down on my middle finger that was loosely covering his mouth. This came as a surprise to me—they never fight back— well, hardly ever. I stepped away from him and shoved him as hard as I could, pushing him through the window. The room filled with a sudden burst of cold air, sending a shiver down my back. Part of me wanted to go over to the window and look down to see the masterpiece below, but this was too risky in case anyone looked up and saw me. The wind seemed to have roused the stranger on the floor, so I ejected the cartridge and shot him a second time.

At that point, I dropped the gun and walked out of the flat. I never planned to defenestrate Haunted but it happened, and would work as well as them killing each other. The stranger would take the blame: some sort of erotic game, a lover's tiff, a meeting that had gone wrong between two strangers disappointed when they eventually met up, or a sick murderer striking down an innocent. If no one found the stranger in the flat the phone, left conveniently on the sofa, would indicate who he was. They did not need his picture, just the data of who received the messages. If I was lucky, the stranger would be found in the flat and arrested for killing Haunted; he would deny it, but it would be a convenient open and shut case.

* * * *

This is the second funeral I have been to. Surprisingly, I had killed both of them. It was not my choice to come here but I need to keep up appearances. Usually you kill and move on, not go to the fucking funeral. Haunted has got a better turnout than I could have ever imagined; his family seems to be large, and I think since his kinky side was revealed everyone has come out of the woodwork to have a good gossip. The rumor mill is in overdrive because of the wisely chosen closed casket; as I'd walked away from the scene there had been bits of him splattered all around. I wonder how much of him actually made it into the coffin. Maybe about less than half, if that much, of him probably made it into the box.

He is being cremated, probably the only option available to his family. This is a good thing because if the dead were ever to rise, as so many current films and shows are telling us, you would not be able to be part of the walking dead as simply shattered bones with no skin or muscle holding you together. Raj, sitting next to me, starts blubbering, as it seems proceedings are about to get underway. Why he is so bothered is beyond me; as far as he is concerned his "boyfriend" was spectacularly cheating on him.

Haunted's family are making their way to the front

now, and we all automatically stand up to show our respect. Suddenly I am back at my only other funeral. I was sat in the front row next to the woman who had spread her legs to bear me and who was holding my hand as the sperm donor and some others carried the coffin down. I had wanted to help carry Alex but the whore had told me I was too young and vulnerable. SHE had held tightly onto me, not out of love or compassion, but to make sure I did not run over to the coffin or shout out the truth, but SHE did not have to worry, as that boy that was me was already dead.

Maybe the fact that I got away with it too easily had confirmed that it was the right thing to do. There was no bruising around her mouth or nose, her eyes were not bloodshot for the police to think that anything untoward happened. It was as if she wanted to go, or that she had protected me until the last by not showing any of these signs. Then of course SHE backed me, not that I was ever a suspect, but more likely covering her own back. SHE'd said that Alex always slept badly and would wake in the night gasping for air, which was true. Her breathing had always been a concern, evidenced by all her inhalers. So I, correction, we, got away with it.

When I had first put Alex to bed that night, I left her briefly to get a drink of water and saw SHE was in the kitchen. Our conversation is still vivid in my head.

"How was your sister's birthday?"

"Do you care?"

"Of course I do. Seb, look, I might seem distant but it is because I do not want to get too close to her or you. She is not long for this world, and then you and I must part ways. I have seen it all."

"You see nothing, stop pretending; it's all an act."

"She has the gift from me, you know."

"The only gift she wanted from you was for you to be there on her birthday. You could have made the effort."

"Because of her disability she will never be able to understand it; it will scare her for the rest of her life."

"It is just nightmares. She'll grow out of it."

"She will be locked up, you will not be able to protect her and she will be abused and scared all her life."

"I won't let that happen."

"How many of them insulted her today? Judging from your bruises, more than one. Who came to your rescue?"

"If you had been there, no one would have had to."

"We cannot always fight her battles. The only thing we can do is help her on her journey. The cards have shown me what we must do. Tonight we will help her peacefully move to the other side."

"You're joking, you're sick."

"How much more do you want her to suffer? The visions, her syndrome, the world out there will cause her to have a miserable life. Today she is happy, tomorrow she will not be. I will help her find the light. It is her destiny."

"You can't."

"I think she would prefer it if it was you, but you're too young and she is my daughter and I love her immensely. It will be painless, just as she sleeps."

"Stop talking like this! Look at the cards again. There must be another way."

"I have already told you what the alternative is for her."

"What if we…"

"Shh…"

We were interrupted by screams; Alex was waking up. "I'll go and calm her down," I said. "Then we can look at the cards again or call Dad."

"She will get worse as she gets older. Go now and comfort her, as it is you who she loves the most. It is you who should save her."

* * * *

My thoughts are interrupted as we all start signing a hymn at the present funeral; I stand up to mouth the words. At Alex's funeral, which was heavily musically based, I sung my heart out because she loved music so much. Out of respect to her I will not sing at this stranger's cremation. Thinking about it, I don't think I ever sung after that day. Raj, like I did when it was someone I cared for, is belting out the numbers, albeit out of tune. It seems common decency is to sing at the top of your lungs so that the one who has passed away can hear you in heaven, even if interspersed with the odd outburst of sadness and tears. All these mourners here to pay their respects seem like a bunch of hypocrites to me. If they really cared about Haunted so much, why did they not pay more attention to him in life? In our time together he never mentioned having so many close friends or a tight-knit family. Once again it is all lies. THEY have decreed that when one you knew has passed, to show you are a decent human being you shall go to their funeral and shed crocodile tears—in contrast to the reality of a guy you bullied at school and have not spoken to in over five years, a friend of a friend who you met once, a colleague at work whose job you coveted, an ex you cheated on and that you came here for the show, not because you actually care. Ironically, those who care and have the right to be present because they had true feelings, which they constantly showed to the deceased before death, are the ones that do not need to show up.

The wake is even faker than the actual funeral: Raj has attached himself to me, the only other individual he knows here. He does not seem to think it is inappropriate to hang out with the ex of the guy he coerced into bed and started dating, behind the back of said ex. I might as well have some fun with it.

"He was never that risqué with me, much more vanilla. Did you bring out this kinkier side? Was it something you encouraged?"

"What? No. It was a robbery he interrupted."

"Well, I say he was vanilla but he always talked about wanting to participate in an orgy, though I never thought he'd go down that road. He seemed satisfied with me and left it as just discussion. I thought with you, you might have encouraged it so that's why he had guys over."

"We never did anything like that."

"No one is blaming you for his death," I tease. "That would be the stranger he invited in to have sex with, but that side to him seemed new only after you two got together."

"Why did he Taser the guy? It was a break-in."

"I heard there was no sign of a break-in, that he invited lots of guys around regularly. But the others didn't lose it when play-fighting together. This time his luck ran out. I don't know…we were happy together. If only you had been there that night…"

Raj's face is blank. "We could've tackled the intruder together and he would have still been here."

"Or you could have been included in the role-play and found yourself dead too. Just imagine if your parents had to answer the door to the police who told them their son was found dead. Killed during a sex game with another man gone wrong." He looks like he is about to cry now. "As I said, no one blames you for your part."

"What part?"

"As you said, you guys weren't into role-play, which he obviously liked, so he must have felt the need to do it behind closed doors. It's not your fault."

I move off to get him some tea; no alcohol is being served, I do this to leave him alone to dwell on my words. Hopefully, it will put him off any relationship for a while and teach him not to betray me. I am not sure, though, that I said enough to properly traumatize him to the level I want. I spot Mommy Haunted and decide now would be the most appropriate time to pay my respects.

"I am so upset at what has happened, I can't believe it. I can't begin to imagine what you are feeling."

"Thank you, so how do…er, did you know my son?"

"We dated briefly. And I just want to say there was no weirdness that went on, like how the newspapers are talking about him. Part of me wishes we had stayed together so he would not have been led astray by other boyfriends."

I give her a hug and leave her to stew on what I said. After that I go find Raj. When I see him, I remind him that he should go and pay his respects to the parents. He seems reluctant at first until I reassure him that Haunted was out to everyone and his folks would have liked to have known he was dating a nice boy. I watch him walk off into the lioness's den.

* * * *

The day is done and it has taken its toll on me to some extent, mainly having to remember the other funeral; the only satisfaction was setting up Raj to get publicly shouted at by Haunted's mother and his father asking him to leave. If I had emotions, I guess I would be upset about having to attend a day such as this. I am not. But for appearance's sake I must pretend that I care, so I arranged to meet Marco, which is where I am heading now. I must come across to him as innocent. Though he is hunting down the wrongdoers of gay men and a lot of the recent incidences are a result of my actions, I do not think he suspects me in any way. He cannot even know I had any link to any of the cases—only that I dated Haunted a while ago and coincidently I had viewed the apartment next door to where his best friend was later killed. So it is better for me to play being normal, and this would mean I visit him after the emotionally draining day any normal guy would have had.

Deep down he knows I am not normal, just like I know he is not. I have seen in his eyes something dark. I think he is a killer like me—not quite like me, but he has killed before—maybe in the line of duty. But then what is his duty? He cannot be a run-of-the-mill policeman on the beat if he has killed and if he has access to all those files. When I have some time I must look up the various ranks of officers and see what he really is. Then there is his behavior towards guys. He told me he used to sleep around, lying about his name, never discussing anything personal (just like my attitude to men) and absolutely never having a sleepover at his place. He told me these things the last time we were together. He said he was being truthful with me because he wanted to change, and was fed up living the way he did in the past. I think it was because he saw in me what he could become and he liked it.

At the cinema he saw part of the real me. I had just head-butted the skank bitch and sent her to the ground cradling her bloody face. Her guy was sizing me, deciding if the shag with her was worth the hassle, when Ben reappeared, not with security but with Marco in tow. She had found him in the bar and thought a policeman was better for when she evicted them from the premises. She must have told him about what happened and the vileness that came from the ho's mouth because he was unfazed by the situation, unlike Ben, who looked worried about what had occurred and what would happen next. Marco positioned himself between me and the guy, and identified himself as a policeman. As I saw his face I could detect the faintest hint of a smile.

Ben ushered the mounting spectators into the screen and told us all to go to her office. Marco led the way. He knew the place well. The man held on to the woman and followed Marco. I brought up the rear as I did not want to give him my back. The woman was given a seat, which annoyed me. I would have preferred she remained broken on the floor where I left her. Ben came in soon afterwards with a makeshift ice pack. Marco asked what happened and she told him her version of events, how she was attacked unprovoked; the guy did not say anything. I let her speak. I just presumed she would not go legal in case it affected her benefits or whatever scams she had going. If she did I would just pay her off. When it came to my turn, I did not even bother going into all the details. I just said I head-butted her. Ben stepped in, saying that I only did so after being provoked by the homophobic woman insulting a little disabled girl. Marco said both sides had a legitimate case, and that if either of us wanted to take it further we should. But in terms of legality, it would be judged as two wrongs not making a right and we would both be punished, probably with community service and having to pay our own legal fees. She decided not to take the matter any further and left the cinema, after being told never to return.

I've never had anyone stick up for me or have my back like those two. I've never needed it, but to a certain extent it felt quite satisfying. Ben left us alone, and Marco moved next to me. He gently placed his hand on my forehead and asked if it hurt. When I said no, he gently kissed it.

"What is it with you, trouble and bloody broken bones," he asked me jokingly, and without waiting for a response continued, "I think I'm going to have to keep an eye on you."

We had skipped the coffee and went straight back to his, once all the children I had been watching over had been collected. At his place we ended up sleeping together again, continuing along the same lines we had started before. When I tried to take things further sexually he stopped me. He told me he used to be a player, having lots of endless sex, lying to the guys about himself, and that he promised himself he would not go the whole way until there were proper feelings between him and the guy.

* * * *

Now, at his place, he has made dinner in case I am hungry. I sit down at the dining table with a big plate of risotto in front of me and a large glass of red wine. I play with the food a little to make it look like I am contemplating the day's events, whereas the smell of it has made me realize I have not eaten much today and I am now really hungry. To appear human I decide to tell him about the funeral and how it made me feel—the version he needs to hear. I tell him how this funeral brought back the memories of my sister's, and I tell him all about her. Not our fucked-up family and upbringing or how I murdered her, but how close we were and how we felt about each other. I am always in control, but I tell him more than I have ever told anyone. As far the majority knows, I am an only child. I do not have to act much as what I am telling him is the truth. He listens patiently and seems genuinely interested. I think he felt the need to return the raw sorrow I was sharing, for when I was done he told me about the funeral of his close friend, the one who I killed at the Phoenix.

Neither of us has had this level of emotional intimacy before with a sexual partner, and it results in us ending up in bed together, skipping past what we have done together and taking it to the next level. I do not want to say we were fucking; rather, we were making love, because providing that level of support and closeness to another has to go beyond the regular fucking we have both done with other men. Afterwards we end up talking.

"I hope you don't feel bad breaking your rule about

having full-on sex with a guy."

"I haven't broken the rule. I said I would wait until there were feelings."

"Didn't you say those feelings had to be reciprocated?"

"Aren't they?" And he kissed me before getting up and going to the bathroom, not waiting for an answer. Maybe he knew already.

I just lay there, slightly paralyzed, thinking, *I am going to have to kill you.*

16

HE HAS NO BOUNDARIES

Seriously? Is this really happening?

I am on a plane that has just landed at its destination, and most of the cabin is clapping. This is definitely a cultural phenomenon, one that I have rarely experienced before and one which I find absurd. Who exactly are they clapping to? Themselves for just sitting there knocking back some drinks and arriving at their destination in one piece even though it had nothing to do with them? The airline for delivering them safely because flying is so dangerous, even though it is not, and because driving a car would probably end in a worse situation than catching a flight? God for watching over them (even though I doubt they regularly clap to their deity every night for allowing them to survive another day)? Or the pilot for just doing his well-paid job, even though he probably cannot hear them as he is locked away in his secure little cockpit?

As the stampede to grab their bags from the overhead lockers begins, I sit there wondering if it was for the pilot they were clapping. Do they go around and applaud other professionals for doing their jobs? Do they finish having their teeth cleaned by a hygienist and start clapping for a job well done? Okay, that is a bad example as I doubt they are the sort of ones to get that service done. A doctor informs them that the recurrent headache they suffer is not due to a brain tumor, which they had feared, but due to drinking excessively every night and being dehydrated—would they clap to that? Yes, I could actually see that happening.

Maybe I have been going about helping them in the wrong way. Picking weak degenerates and erasing them from their miserable lives does not achieve wide-scale changes. Perhaps it would have been more humane to have blown up this plane mid-flight and saved all these pathetic clappers in one go. I can see it now: an explosion in the baggage hold would be the easiest way of getting something on board given the heightened security now in place. Set off by remote detonation, the question is would I stand up and tell everyone what is going to happen, or just set it off? Which would be more satisfying? Watching the reaction as I explain to everyone that they are about to die and as they ultimately realize these are their last few moments left on earth, or just do it quietly and take in the fear and panic in the cabin as the unknown unfolds? In a state of emergency it would be every man for himself; the air stewards and stewardesses would be totally useless, as during a normal flight they can barely get the tea and coffee right, and would only try and save themselves anyway. I guess any explosion in the hold able to rip through to the outside and thus cause the plane to go down would have to be of such a high yield that it would impact the passengers, killing them before the crash. That would take away the fun element though, and there would be my own survival to think of.

Those actions would be seen as acts of terrorism, but you know what they say: one man's terrorist is another man's freedom fighter.

What did SHE say…? Somehow I am to be involved with thousands of departed… Maybe it is time to leave the old ways behind and move on to something new. A new order to facilitate many of those in need in one go; maybe this new order could mean that the scummiest degenerates out there would be the targets. I started on this path because it is more difficult to select evil than the targets of evil; under the new order I could blow up a prison, getting rid of many of the worse kind. But really, what good would that do for the masses? Those types are already off the streets and should not be hurting anyone anymore. If this new dawn is to come, some more thought is needed to find a way to select the actual hurters, criminals, intolerants, bullies, deplorable and wicked villainous types for expulsion from this world.

Six walks by, he winks at me and brings me back into the now, meaning those thoughts will have to wait a while as there is still an old-way task to take care of now. He tries to wait for me to get up and get my bag and join him in the aisle, but the rush of passengers carries him off, making waiting impossible. He looks back at me, unhappy; I remain seated. He should be satisfied that we have finally come away together. Admittedly it was not what we had previously discussed, but tough shit. Okay, it is quite a step down, but from the beginning he was, "I just want to spend time with you," so he needs to suck it up now.

When I was "mugged," that gave me a reason to put off our little trip away, as since that time I lost all interest in going to Amsterdam; it no longer had the same appeal for me. Then, I'd told him that if we were finally going to fuck he should be tested for all sexually transmitted diseases. He had sworn to me that he had not been with anyone, but got tested nevertheless, and was clean. So I had to man up and arrange our getaway. This is how I currently find myself sitting on the skankiest budget airline around, having just arrived in the former Eastern Bloc state of Lithuania.

Hardly the destination for a nice couple's retreat or the mecca of gay-friendly activity which Six had in mind but there must be lots to do here—otherwise why would the UK population of stag-doers descend here? Also, Six could learn to be more charitable and take some satisfaction in that we are helping the economy of a country less privileged than his own. Annoyingly, he is waiting for me outside the plane. Such desperation is making me regret not just killing him and being done with it. When we get to the passport control queue (I use the word control lightly: more like some makeshift booths that look mobile and are moved around the airport as needs must) I leave my passport in my pocket. I am not worried about him finding out my real name, as I am using one of my fake passports, but Six is the sort of guy who would snatch it out of my hand and want to see what my middle name is, laugh at the picture and other crap like that. In an instance like this I would have made sure we got into different queues, but here there is only one for all non-residents. I let him go ahead of me so that there would be no chance of him seeing my passport or hearing any conversation I might have. This is a trip I do not want traced back to me in any way.

It is more secure for me if he never knows my real

name or any of my aliases. This one is new, and I want to keep it totally untraceable to me just in case I need to leave, given my little Italian friend and his investigations. That said, it is always good to test a forgery in a safe manner: you do not want to be fleeing a country for countless homicides and get stopped at the airport because your passport is a blatant fake. It is best to check it at least once in a situation like this, where nothing is really at stake. The man scans it and barely looks up at me; he must hate this thankless job he has ended up in. I doubt he would get a little congratulatory clap for his efforts.

Six is waiting patiently as I clear immigration. I inform him that we have to go and collect my hold luggage. He looks worryingly at the tiny rucksack he crammed all his clothes and items for the weekend in. This is the type of flight that is cheap as chips, but they charge you for every element, for instance from if you want to take hold luggage, get a snack or glass of water, to practically having a dump on the plane. For me, used to business class travel for work-related trips and first class for personal journeys, this was at times shocking. Not one to squash all my belongings in something small to be shoved in the overhead lockers, I paid the extra ten pounds each way for the privilege of taking a suitcase with me.

"You should have told me you were going to bring proper luggage. I would have done the same."

"It was a last minute decision; your special surprise would not fit in my carry-on."

"Ohh really? What is it?"

"The clue was *surprise*."

"I'm really excited now."

"All good things."

"It was such a shame we couldn't get seats together on the flight, we could have planned our trip." He pulls out a library-borrowed traveler's guide to Lithuania. "I've selected some places that would be good to go and see. And there is even one gay club which is an apparent must-see."

"What's it called and where is it?"

He hands the book over to me. I look at the club which could be all right for me to go to, once I have some free time after getting rid of him. The baggage conveyor belt kicks into life and he starts to prattle on about how it would be great if my bag came out first (*it fucking does if you travel first class*, I think to myself) and what does it look like? This is the most time we've spent together since starting this trip, and it is now getting too much.

The idea of the trip had been totally different when I originally mentioned it to Six, and as my desires changed I was going to abort the whole thing. But then, having someone looking for certain patterns in my territory, I'd decided to revisit this. The premise was changed and the ultimate conclusion would be different from what I had planned, but it should be adequate. The cheaper destination and budget airline meant that Six could pay for his own ticket and book it himself, which he did once I told him where and when to book. This had the advantage of removing me totally from him. There was nothing linking us together in this trip. Budget airlines tend to fly from skankier airports on the outskirts; I had used this fact to make him travel there on his own, as I had to go straight from work and would be cutting it close. I told him to go through security and wait for me in a bar after he had done his duty free shopping. There was no point hanging around for me, and he should start his holiday as we meant to go on, with shopping, eating and drinking.

When I got to the airport, I had managed to check myself and my suitcase in without him knowing about it, and then went off to the private airport lounge. He kept texting, asking where I was as I sipped a Jamieson's and ginger ale away from the masses. The lounge had been nothing special as there was no spa or special treatments and just basic food and drink, but it did afford the privacy of not having to mingle with the majority of airport users, which included Six. After the last call for our flight I'd told him I had just arrived and that he should board without me. I then causally strolled to the flight and took my reserved seat by the emergency exit, which I paid extra for. So all in all, up until this moment, we had not spent any time together on this getaway. As I pick up my case, I think the taxi ride to our hotel is going to be a ridiculously long trip.

Now, the door is barely shut before he is all over me, trying to kiss my face with his arms draped around my neck. If I walk, I think he will swing like a pendulum hanging off me. I guess the moment when you first go through puberty and have sexual thoughts is nearly upon him. I give him a little peck on cheek, and say maybe we should have a shower. The words are barely out of my mouth before he starts to strip off. I should have clarified that I meant separately, but in his dash to undress I do not think he would have heard me. Why he hurried is a complete shock to me as his body is nothing special—

skinny and hairless, with no redeeming features. Looking at him, he must have taken the hint and felt a little self-conscious, as he moves one hand to cover his obvious excitement and the other across his chest.

"So once you are ready you should probably have a bath to get you nice and clean and relaxed for our session."

"Shouldn't we have one together?" He is trying to sound sexy.

"No. I'll run the bath for you. And when you are in there, you might want to knock one out. Just so you don't ruin the moment by cumming on my hand or something."

"Don't you want to do that for me?" He attempts to be alluring.

I stand behind him, grab his dick roughly and start jerking it like it is an inanimate object with no sensation. I whisper in his ear, "If you really want our first time to be like this." Then I stop and leave him there to go run his bath for him.

When the water is running at a nice warm temperature I go back into the main room, get my wash bag and go back into the bathroom. He was sitting on the bed looking like he had a bit of a bad mood. I finish getting the room ready, and once the bath is suitably filled I go and get him. He is being a bit resistant, so I kiss him and tell him that I want everything to be special for his first time. I cover his eyes and lead him into the bathroom, and when I remove my hands he gasps.

"Oh my god!" he shrieks. "It's, it's so nice." He turns around and starts kissing me. I delicately escort him over to the bubble bath. "It smells so good too."

"I wanted to get candles and put them all over the

room but I thought it might set off the fire alarm, so you'll just have to settle for this."

"There are pink and red rose petals, so many bubbles you can't see the water. And such delicious smells. I love it and I love you."

"Well, get in." I go over to help him in. He rests a hand on my shoulder for support as he dips a foot in. I watch him carefully.

"Ohh."

"Is it too hot?"

"A little, I'll get used to it."

"Get in and appreciate the whole bath."

As he slips in, he tells me that it feels like there is something in the bath with him.

"That must be the bath bomb dissolving. Do you want me to rub your back?"

"Yes please."

I start rubbing his shoulders. "That's just for starters. Now relax, take your time, we have all night." I reach down into the water and feel around for his cock; he is hard, so I start wanking him, much more gently than before. "Remember what I said about taking care of yourself so our first time won't be over too quickly." I leave him to it. As he is having his bath and wank, I unpack the special item from my bag and wrap it in my towel. I then repack my case, ready to leave at a moment's notice, and include his passport and wallet in it.

Twenty minutes later he emerges from the bathroom. He sees me fully naked and stares. I grab my stuff and head for a shower. Six tries to grope me as I go past him. "Get comfortable," I tell him, nodding in the direction of the bed, "and I'll be with you really soon."

Alone in the bathroom I lock the door, step under the shower and rinse myself off, washing away the grime of the budget flight and any of the other passengers that I might have come in contact with. Once I am done with a shorter-than-usual wash, I get out of the shower stall but leave the water still running. I quickly dry myself off, take some talcum powder from my wash bag and pat it all over, and when this is done I get out the surprise for Six that I snuck in here under my towel and start getting ready.

Six is lying on the bed under the sheets watching television. At first he does not notice I have emerged from the bathroom and am standing in the doorway waiting for him. I do not say anything; we are now done with words. Eventually he looks up and sees me standing there. He shrinks away from me and pulls the sheets tighter around himself. His face looks scared; the television is sporadically flicking beams of light on his visage and must also be lighting me up a treat.

"What's this?" he asks in a trembling voice.

I respond by placing a finger over where my mouth would be if it were visible, a way to tell him silence. I move slowly to him, not taking the direct route but walking around the whole bed to get to where he is. I time this movement to coincide with the illuminations from the television so that he can carefully take all of me in, in all my glory or horror depending on your outlook in life. He was disturbed at first—that much was written all over his face—but now his adrenaline has kicked in and the exhilaration of what is to happen next is coming around. This is of course helped by the fact that my beautiful body is being displayed in all its glory, with every muscle exaggerated to perfection via the black shiny rubber.

"I never knew you were so kinky." There is still some nervousness in him.

My next step moves me next to the bed and in touching distance of Six. He kneels up in the bed and kisses the rubber above my right nipple.

"Could we do it without the mask though?"

I shake my head to say no. *If you want me, want this; you will have to have me clad from head to toe in this suit.* The thought of what is to happen amuses me more than any fetish or kinkiness of the total rubber gimp suit persuasion. He'd thought he would be romantically made love to, with lots of kissing, blowjobs, and his anal-cherry being taken ever so delicately. That the feelings he has for me would be reciprocated, and I would caress his body and make sure his first time was a magical experience and that the memories would be something he could cherish forever. Instead, I am standing here without an inch of flesh on display, access to my mouth is closed, and I am ready to show him how brutal the world is.

He is taking what enjoyment he can from the situation by continuing to suck on the rubber where my nipple is. His hands are running over the skin-tight cat suit exploring my great body, or he is looking for the zipper. His attempts to romanticize the situation are ended as I shove two rubber fingers in his mouth for him to suck on. He does so obediently. I turn him around so he is no longer facing me. As he is now lying face down, I straddle his naked body and continue shoving the fingers in his mouth to suck on. My other hand is running through his hair, grabbing it and pulling his head backwards to control his mouth. Taking the now wet fingers out of his mouth I shove them both up his hole. If he was not an anal virgin I would not have bothered doing this, but trying to get a cock up there without it being broken in first would be trying. He is grunting along, enjoying what he has been begging for since we met.

I continue with the fingering until he is juiced up and I am hard. I spread his legs with my knee, liberate only my cock from the suit and shove the head in him. His hands clench around the pillow; he is gripping so tightly his knuckles go white. I shove myself further in him until he screams out to stop, which I do. I do not withdraw, just hold still for him to get used to the size. If I was doing this with compassion it would involve lots of lubricant, foreplay, words of encouragement and reassurance, taking my time, allowing him to control how much and when, and general intimacy. Unfortunately for him, he was stupid enough to pick someone with no compassion to be his first.

I lean down to lie on top of him so he can feel my entire rubber-encased body against his naked flesh. A few minutes later he is trying to move his ass up and down my shaft; he is ready to continue. I start fucking him, not slowly, but hard and fast. He cries out, first in pain then in groans of sexual ecstasy until he cums. I remain inside him while I maneuver myself on to my knees, carrying him with me, then I lie down and he is sitting on top of me facing away from my hidden face. He uses this opportunity to swivel himself around so he can face me, well, the rubber-suited man who has fucked him. I wonder if he got off on this after all, or if he had imagined it was me or anyone of his fantasies all along. This new position is unbecoming of him so I sit up and wrap my black shiny arms around his sweaty body. I push him down and start fucking him in the missionary position so he can stare at the black mask and the memories of this moment can forever haunt him.

After I have finished with him, a couple of hours later, I put myself away so that none of my skin is exposed. At that moment he tries to speak but I put a single finger to the mask again, to indicate this is a time for silence. Then I get up and collect my stuff from the bathroom and chuck them back into my suitcase. I grab the case and leave the room. The door to the room next to ours is unlocked, so I go in as planned.

"Hello, James," the guy dressed like me but without a mask on greets me.

"Hello, Adolf," I respond. We both know neither of us are using our real names but it does not matter. "He is all yours."

"Did you break him in?"

"There is still work to be done."

"Good. I like to sample the goods before selling them."

"Have you already got interest?"

"Yes, you know how to pick good ones. He will make a good sex-slave for an aging Russian or a fat Arab."

"Perfect. And remember our deal that once his masters no longer want him, you will dispose of him appropriately."

"Once the masters are done they usually prefer to get rid of slaves themselves. But if for some reason he lives, he won't for long afterwards."

"I know. Then I bid you farewell until next time."

"Bye."

I watch as Adolf puts on the headgear that fully covers his face and hair. I wonder if Six will realize the next installment is not me. I mean, the guy is shorter than I am and nowhere near as well built, but Six could be fooled. Where I showed a level of restraint, this trafficker will not. He will do as he pleases with Six, and when he is done he will sell him to some weirdo who will do whatever he desires with this young, innocent English rose before taking his life. In some ways I should have killed him myself but I think this education will better suit what remains of his miserable life.

17

HE ENJOYS HIMSELF

Moving day was scheduled for just over a week ago; that was the day we completed the sale and the Phoenix apartment became mine. Since that time I have stayed in the hotel while my bespoke modifications have been made to the place, but not repainting the color of the walls or anything I could have done myself. These customizations are more of the technological and structural types which I could not do myself, so I had to pay for them to be very discreetly done. When the completion date was a month away I had purchased the furniture for the place. This was done working with an interior designer, not because I trusted the queen's taste or opinion—I'd picked everything myself—but I had wanted someone to organize the delivery and assembly of everything, as I do not want to deal with manual worker-type degenerates. Ten days later, all the remodeling I wanted done and furniture I picked were fully operational in my apartment. Once the workers had finished, I moved in with all my clothes and whatever else I was keeping with me at the hotel. Then my specialty items that were in storage I had delivered, mainly so I could supervise their arrival and make sure no one else opened them.

I presume this is the stage where a degenerate would have a house party so that they could lord it over the other degenerates they know. "Look, I am better than you because I have purchased my own place and you have not, the pad I have moved into is better than the shithole you call a home, my things are newer than the crap that you have in yours, I am more popular than you because more guests turned up to my party than ever turned up to one of yours." It might be better if you just invited a guest around, both took out your cocks and compared the size; then each show their bank balances just for good measure.

Obviously I am not doing any such thing, nor do I have any inclination to mark the occasion in that sort of way. However, Fatty is coming over. She seemed to invite herself once she heard I had finally moved in. I could not be bothered to put her off, so I thought what the hell. Bunty also wanted to come around but I thought it best not to mix acquaintances from different aspects of my life. Plus, because Bunty is a work colleague it might be better that she does not see where I live and report it back to others, who I would not want to know what the color my bed sheets are. Maybe the only work associate I will let know about my sheets is Nat, and that would only be from first-hand experience just to fuck off Roderdick. That cock has it coming.

Due to the nature of my guest, I decide to order food in. I have a local caterer make and deliver a few canapé selection trays. "Nice pad, mate," the delivery lad lets me know as he places the trays down in the kitchen and removes the packaging. "So are you having a party?"

No, just one guest, but she is large. "Something like that."

"Cool. If you need a server I could provide that service."

"We should be okay."

"Well, happy to help in any other way you might need." The way he says it is very suggestive. He leaves a card behind, a personal one and not one from the company.

"If I need your services I will let you know." He was attractive enough and it is always nice being hit upon, so I give him a large tip. He eventually leaves, after loitering far longer than he has to.

Moving into my own place should involve a celebration to provide some enjoyment befitting me—maybe going to a sauna and having lots of meaningless sex, walking around and being blown in the numerous locations in the sauna, through the glory holes, in the hot tub and swimming pool. Then going into the little rooms with the plastic mattresses and seeing if an attractive guy or guys are in them waiting for someone to join them. That would seem like a fitting way to celebrate the purchase of my first home, since when I was homeless and did not have much money many a night was spent in a sauna, admittedly a lot lower-brow type than the one I would visit now. This was much cheaper than a hotel; once the ten-pound entrance fee was satisfied it meant you could shower there and bed down, find an empty room and try and sleep. In the beginning the trick was lying down in front of the door so when someone pushed it, it would not open and they would not try to join you. Then I taught myself to pick the locks so I could just lock the door once I was in, and not have to worry about being bothered.

* * * *

"It's lovely," Fatty reiterates as we settle down on the sofas, a thought she'd gushed since we started the tour, which began in the private swimming pool downstairs.

I pour two glasses of the poor man's champagne she brought around with her, Veuve Clicquot. In between gulps of bubbly she is picking at the canapés. "I could order some proper food in, if you are hungry." Joy, as she faces this dilemma. "You're my guest, I should at least properly feed you."

"I'm okay for now."

Yeah, right. "So last time we met up you were about to go on an Internet date. What happened?"

"The guy turned up and he was ginger. Not a mild strawberry blond, but fierce red."

"Did he not have pictures of himself up?"

"Yes, but they were all in black and white. Now I know why."

"So you don't like ginger men?"

"Well, if I wanted that I might as well shove a carrot up there. That way I can at least pick a decent size." She laughs.

There is hope for her yet. Here I was thinking she would be grateful for whatever came her way, but instead she is being fussy and making quips worthy of me. "Carrot, good one." Have we been spending too much time together?

"Just imagine if the bloke and I got together: the fat red-headed kids we would inflict on the world would be too great a burden. I just couldn't do it."

"True. Though you could have just slept with him, protected of course, and see if the freckles are all over his body and on his genitals."

She winks. "Who says I didn't?"

"Did you?"

"A girl has needs."

Geez, even she is taking advantage of all the opportunities around her. Unlike me. What is wrong with me? "Was the carrot adequate?"

"I'm seeing him again next week."

We both burst out laughing. The fat minx has somehow lured the poor unsuspecting bloke in. And over time, me too. She is still a degenerate, but seems to know about the game and plays the hand she has been dealt well, making her above the others. Perhaps here I have met a degenerate who can be elevated above that status. Actually, she would be the second currently in my life out of the new ones I have met since I returned to the UK that deserves to be above that level, the first being Marco.

The Veuve was finished ages ago along with the canapés. After a bottle of Krug is nearly polished off, the conversation, which was largely based on sex and sexual conquests, has moved to our first times.

"I lost mine late."

"Last week with the carrot."

"That would have been more memorable. It was the skinniest, spottiest boy in the sixth form. It was the end of year party celebrating that we had finished our exams and would be moving on to the university. We were at this party together: no one would do him, no one would do me. So we did each other. He barely got in me before he came. It was all over so fast I am not sure it counts. Yours?"

"To a stranger on Clapham Common." This was actually the truth. The build-up to the occasion I omitted.

I had gone to some dingy club, the Common, and was moving between the popular dance room and the techno music room, neither of which was more than a third full. This was post-Alex and I just wanted some company, so I continued walking around the club when I happened to glance up and see an older guy looking at me. Before I had a chance to decide what I wanted to do, the guy had come up to me and offered to buy me a drink. I accepted, and watched as the man went to the bar. I told myself that the older gentleman was attractive and that he looked like Indiana Jones, albeit from the Last Crusade. I placed him in his mid- to late forties.

As Indiana sidled up next to me with the drink and started making small talk with chat aimed at someone around my age, I found the whole situation to be a bit desperate. Desperate on the man's part for trying so hard with someone so much younger, but also desperate on my own part for going along with it just to have a companion briefly. Next thing I knew, Indiana had placed his hand on my leg and was gently rubbing it. I was not sure how it happened, but we started kissing. The man, obviously experienced, knew exactly what he was doing and was a really good kisser. I was really enjoying the act so I went along with it. Indiana started to get more physical with me and was groping me and moved himself so that we could rub against each other. Then the man whispered in my ear that he wanted me to come back to his place.

I felt my hand being held and I looked at Indiana. He told me we only had to do what I felt comfortable doing if I went back to his place. My cock wanted to be relieved, but I would only be going with the man out of desperation so I said no. He tried to convince me, but when he saw I was determined not to be swayed he stopped and offered to make sure I got home safely. I politely declined and made my way to the cloakroom to get my jacket. Standing outside the club, my minimal alcohol jacket had not been strong enough to protect me from the cold wind so I zipped up my actual jacket, shoved my hands in its pockets and started the journey home.

Suddenly a vehicle appeared. "Sorry for startling you," the driver said. I looked up and saw Indiana. "I wanted to make sure you got home all right."

I thanked him for the kind offer but said I wanted to walk home and it was not far, just across the Common—a lie. The older gentleman drove slowly around the corner, parked his car and jumped out, saying that he would at least walk me the rest of the way because the Common was no place for an attractive young man to walk alone at night. Before I could say I was all right and did not need a bodyguard, Indiana matched my pace and started talking and walking with me. I found out that the guy was called Alfred but preferred Alfie, probably because it made him appear younger, and he worked as a banker. Back in the bar I had determined Alfie had a good body for his age. But was I really attracted to him or just desperate to get physical with anyone? As we were now walking through the Common I heard the hushed tones and sounds of men I could not see, and noticed individual men just standing around and waiting. I was about to assess if any of these cruisers were fit when Alfie put his arm around my shoulder and said how much he had enjoyed kissing me. I enjoyed the kissing too—this experienced partner knew what he was doing.

I let myself be led into some bushes where Alfie started to kiss me. Soon I was on my back and Alfie was trying to undo my belt and jean buttons. I closed my eyes so I could imagine it was someone I fancied about to go down on me. Alfie had finally undone my belt, and as I lay there I heard the noises from the other couples dotted around the Common. I touched the man's face, felt the wrinkled features and knew I could not go through with it. "Stop. I can't," I said. I pushed Alfie off me and started to button my jeans.

"What's wrong?"

"It's just this place; it feels seedy, I can't," I replied not willing to say the whole truth.

"Let us go back to my place. We can take things slowly, just kiss and cuddle."

After I declined again, Alfie turned nasty, called me a childish cock-tease and would not let go of me. In the end, to get away I had to loudly declare that I was going home and could I just be left alone? He left and I got up. That's when I noticed another guy had been watching us all the time. He was younger, from what I could see. I lay back down on the grass, and he came over and finished what Alfie had started. I never knew his name, his age or what he looked like in daylight. We did not even get fully naked and there was no intimacy. It was just sex to take care of the physical urge.

"But now it's all different. Now that you are loved up with your Italian."

"I am not *loved up*." I do not have the ability to feel that emotion. But since Marco and I slept together and went all the way, we do seem to be meeting up with regularity and repeating the experience. I am doing this not because I love him but I like to have good sex, and it is mainly to check up on him and make sure he does not get close to finding his Jean Valjean. By spending more time together, the unexpected effect that he seems no longer as committed to his quest has occurred. Now that his guard is dropping, maybe I can find out all his secrets.

"Since you met him, you've been different. I think you're falling for him."

"Really? Different how?"

"You seem more settled. More calm."

"I think he likes me more than I him. He asked me if I wanted to be exclusive with him."

"You gays have all the fun. That conversation would never happen in a straight relationship, it would be a given."

"I think it's because he has never been in a proper relationship. Neither have I."

"Wow, you have to be with him then. It would be perfect, Romeo and Romeo."

"I like him, but there are other factors."

"Like what?"

I murdered his best friend and go around killing others to save them from their miserable lives. And he is hunting me down, so every part of me is telling me to kill him soon. "He's a few years younger than I am."

"That doesn't matter. You don't look like you're in your mid-thirties."

"Early thirties, dear. He acts a lot more mature than I do."

"And?"

"Shouldn't I be the one asking about exclusivity and being the mature one?"

"You're just uncomfortable because you aren't in control."

"Do you think that's it?"

"Yes."

"So if I took control, then I would be more contented?"

"I guess so. Why are you putting all these obstacles in the way? Do you like him?"

"Yes." *He is the closest man I have ever met to being my equal.*

"Is he good in bed?"

"Very." *He makes me cum and I do not feel sorry for him.*

"Is he attractive?"

"You would." *I really fancy him.*

"Could you take him home to meet your mother?"

"I wouldn't inflict that on him, which I guess means that I do care for him more than any others."

"Sure you don't love him?"

I chuck a cushion at her. "Shall I open another bottle of champagne?" *Could I love someone?*

"No. I had better get going, I feel tipsy already."

"I can order us a pizza?"

"No. Work tomorrow. Let's do this again on a weekend. Bring the Italian Stallion and get him to bring a brother."

She gets up and kisses my forehead bye. I get up and give her a hug. I am also feeling quite tipsy. I did not eat anything. But most of all I am feeling horny. I want to celebrate all my accomplishments. Once I am alone in the apartment, I pick up my business mobile and call the guy I think would be there for me now.

* * * *

Outside the club Delivery Lad (DL) had told me to meet him, I scan the queue to see if he is there. I cannot see him, so I head to the front of the line and say I'm on the guest list. This not being the hours when a guest list would be operational, the bouncer just looks at me and smiles. His grin gets wider as I slip him twenty pounds, an hour's pay for letting some arrogant jerk in ahead of the rest of the losers, and he steps aside. Inside the club, I want more to drink because now that I have already started it seems fitting to continue.

I am at the bar ordering when I vaguely hear, "I hope that you are going to work those calories off."

I turn around and see my personal trainer (PT). I haven't really bothered using his services, as I have been too busy. "Let me get you a drink so you can't guilt trip me."

"Okay," the inebriated guy tells me. "Now we both have to work it off."

"So, a session tomorrow after work."

"You mean today?"

It is after midnight, he is correct. He does not bother waiting for my response.

"We could work it off in other ways." He looks me up and down as he says so.

Our drinks arrive. He grabs both of them and heads over to the dance floor. I follow him, as he has my drink.

"Is dancing the way you had in mind?" I whisper in his ear.

He looks down at my crotch, which I think he would have groped had he not been holding two drinks. "No. You and me. A bed," he informs me. "You can fuck me however you want."

There is the lack of confidence in the bloke that I saw when we first met. Sure, he is being very forthcoming at the moment, but I believe that is the alcohol talking. Seeing himself as a piece of meat just for my pleasure is the real him.

Suddenly I am being kissed, full on. My eyes are closed and I go with it. When the kiss ends and I open them and I see DL is the co-kisser.

"There you are," he says, beaming. Somehow he managed to block out PT, positioned himself in front of me and decided to go for what he wanted.

PT pushes himself back into my field of view and hands over my drink. "Sorry we don't have one for you," he hisses at DL.

"That's all right I'll just share." DL takes my drink out of my hand and has a sip before glancing back at PT.

"I'll go get another," I tell them both. At the bar, I look at them both standing there, not dancing but talking to each other. I am no lip reader but judging by their body language, including poking one another on the chest, I would say they are arguing about yours truly. This is amusing. Watching them, I start thinking which guy would be better, even though a little voice in my head is telling me not to bother with either. Then a louder voice shouts what the old me would have done, and I realize this is the correct course of action. If a new dawn is approaching the old ways should be given an appropriate send-off.

"Gentlemen. Is everything fine?" I ask them on my return.

"I was just giving him some tips on how to bulk up his skinny frame," PT remarks quite snidely.

"Yeah, and I was just asking his opinion of the political situation in the Middle-East," DL quickly comes back. "I think he was about to tell us."

We both look at PT for his response. He has a gulp of his drink. "I love this song, let's dance."

At that, the three of us start dancing away. Perhaps to give himself an advantage over the competition, PT peels off the T-shirt that might as well not have been worn as it was so tight.

DL starts dancing closer to me so that we can touch, which he starts doing, draping his arms around my neck so he can stare into my eyes. Not one to be outdone, PT moves behind me and holds me too; he is grinding away. He kisses my neck and turns me around to face him where he joins his mouth to mine.

After the long warm kisses from PT, DL comes in for his turn. I take DL's hand and place it on PT's chest. I think DL must have pinched PT's nipple hard because I hear PT mutter, "Ouch." But they realize if they want to play with me, they are going to have to get along. So, once I have finished with DL, he takes the initiative and starts to kiss PT. PT responds with kisses and groping, I presume the latter is to grab him hard as payback for nipplegate. I rejoin the guys and we start alternating our affections between each other, interspersed with more drinks. None of them go to the toilet; I guess they do not want to leave the other alone with me. It is flattering, but pathetic.

We are now in a cab heading back to my place. At first PT was reluctant when he heard the location, but seemed to offer no resistance once DL was so happy to oblige. PT says he has already done the whole threesome thing before. DL says that he has too, and added that everyone has, as another put down to PT. DL suggests he could film the event on his phone: he could put it somewhere to cover the whole bed. That new dimension would make it more fun. The narcissist PT, who probably only loves his body and nothing else about himself, jumps at this idea. They are currently kissing each other while I am wondering what I am actually doing. Is this really what I want? Do I really have something to prove?

Screw it, I finally think as we approach the Phoenix. I might as well enjoy myself now because tonight I could very well be dead. I made a vow and now that I have my sanctuary I intend to keep it. Blood will be shed and death will arrive; I just need to make sure I am not on the receiving end of the horrors to come.

18

HE DESTROYS THE EVIDENCE

It is over twenty-four hours since the threesome. In the shower, Alex is washed dry. I watch as the blood washes off him, dilutes with the water and swirls down the plughole forever to hide the events of the night. When the water off the sword is running clear I carefully carry him out of the shower stall and place him on a towel on the bathroom floor. I leave him to drip dry for a while, then I will dry him off properly and apply the various oils and treatment to him. As he lies there in all his glory, I step into the shower stall for a shower myself. Fully clothed under the hot water, I start to rub my face clean. The outer layer of clothes I am wearing are waterproof to a certain extent, but everything feels heavy. My body ends up sliding down against the wall until without really knowing it, I am sitting on the shower floor. I cross my legs, shut my eyes and remain there as the water rains down on me.

I must have been sitting like that for a couple of hours when I finally have the desire to open my eyes. I strip off all my clothes in the shower and leave them there. I get up and clean myself; the hot water on my skin feels comforting. Somehow liberating. When I have finally fully washed, dried myself, and changed into some something more comfortable, I take care of the sword. He has done his job to perfection but now he must rest. I carry him, fully sheathed, over to the mantelpiece where I kneel down on the floor. As proud of him as I am and of my own skills and how they held up, I cannot display him for anyone entering the apartment to see. I reach up into the non-working fireplace where the special "decorators" custom-made a home for Alex, digging out a cavity to fit his dimensions. They did not know what would be going behind the keypad-locking panel, hidden away. Using my fingers to trace the outlines of the numbers on the hidden keypad, I enter the code. I hear a dull swoosh noise as the panel opens. I take the sword and carefully feed him up the fireplace, and when he is at the correct level I bring him towards me and into his own alcove where I delicately place him. After entering the code again I stand up, stare at Bloody Adonis that was left behind by the incompetent estate agent.

In the next few hours I will have to wake up and go to work, but I cannot be bothered with that. In bed, I compose the relevant emails, one privately to Roderdick saying that I am still not feeling very well, and as there is nothing pressing if it is okay with him I will work from home. The next email is to the group telling them I will not be in later, but to please feel free to disturb me on all contactable channels if they need to. Hopefully they will be good little cocks and manage to get through a whole day using their own initiative. Then it will be Mulberry bags all around—on me. As my computer is out and I have time to kill I start to watch the threesome that DL filmed. I had let them film it because I knew it would never see the light of day, as after the event I stole the phone, downloaded the relevant part to my computer and then destroyed it. The idiot had the bloody nerve to call and ask if he had left his phone behind. I told him no, and not to bother me again. Maybe I am getting too old for this shit. While I look good and hold my own, the video shows the younger guys to be much more into it and taking far more pleasure in the activity than I. When it is "waking-up" time I send the work emails and then proceed to go to sleep.

I am awoken on the following day, Saturday, by someone at my door. The CCTV I had installed has pinged up the image on my computer. I recognize the guy carrying a large flat object, and as I have slept for over twenty-four hours I decide I might as well go see what he wants.

"Hello, I'm Ricky," he says, extending his hand to greet me. "Welcome to the Phoenix."

I prefer not to have my picture out there and I always intended to find Nat's photographer friend and pay him off for my photos he took on that charity night, especially any of me with Haunted. And here he is with the decency to pay me a visit. "Come in."

"Sorry to bother you, when you have only just moved in but I need a bit of a favor." He holds up the object, which is an identical copy of the "art" above my mantelpiece. He goes on about how that was the first print of his best piece of work, and his ex-girlfriend would never return it, and he wanted to swap it for sentimental reasons. I stop listening.

I agree to the swap on the condition that I get to see more of his work, as it is so impressive, and he might sell me another piece discounted. He informs me that he is staying in the building with a guy and that I'm welcome to view his work anytime.

"No time like the present," I tell him, and go to the bedroom to get something that I keep hidden from him before I accompany him down to his apartment.

The apartment he takes me to is so familiar, yet different. It appears I have come full circle now. I made the right decision moving here.

His computer is on; I guess he was working. He starts showing me some of his other pictures. They are all crap; well, if I had the right camera, I would be able to recreate them. As he moves between folders I can see one named after the charity night.

"Could I bother you for some water? My throat is dry after one too many last night."

"Sorry, I should have offered."

Once he has moved away I plug the special USB device into the nearest available socket. I watch as the bar on it lights up indicating it is at work. Once the single row of lights have all turned red the complete set goes green, telling me I am good to go. I pull out the stick and wait patiently for him to return. I guess I will sit here and drink my water and preview his plop little pictures so as not to rouse any suspicion. Basically, in twenty-four hours the virus I just uploaded will activate itself and completely destroy the hard-drive. Nothing will be recoverable. As this is his livelihood, I guess he would have backed-up his main works, but I doubt he would have bothered about some event he did for a mate. If not, tough. The beauty of this not-cheap technological wonder is not the time delay, but the fact that the computer does not even have to be turned on for it to work, and if it is connected to a network it will bring them all down.

＊＊＊＊

Later that day I go to Marco's place because I have unfinished business with him that needs to be completed. In my possession I have another of those technological wonders on me. The only issue is I have seen he has two laptops, one for work and another personal one, I presume. He has never used either in front of me, so before I can let the device work its magic I need to find out which computer is his work one.

"How would you feel about us taking a trip away together?"

He starts getting affectionate towards me. "Like a dirty weekend away?"

"Yes. We both work such long hours, and having this alone time will help us unwind and decide where we want to take this."

"Sure. But not Italy."

"You don't want to introduce me to your papa? Or is your family like some sort of mafia clan?"

"Don't worry, you won't wake up to find a horse's head next to you, just this other horse meat." He points to his groin.

I smile. "Barcelona or Lisbon?"

"Either is fine with me."

I get out my phone and start playing around on the Internet. "Barcelona has a better scene. You know, this would go quicker on a laptop."

"We can't book anything now, I'll have to get time off work. We don't all work in public relations, darling, and can jet off whenever."

"Grrr, don't mock my very important job. If I weren't

around, who would be able to tell the clients they are fabulous? But we could look up hotels and pick where we definitely want to go."

He picks up one computer and switches it on. During its booting up cycle I ask for a drink. When he disappears to comply I shove the stick into the other computer. This process will take longer to work as that computer is switched off, so I need to distract him and make sure he does not notice the device sticking out of his work laptop. When he gets back he passes me a glass of wine and settles with one for himself, he logs onto his computer. The password was random letters and numbers, which I could not make it out.

The obvious distraction would have been to initiate sex, but I need to stay near the stick. I decide to bring up the subject of the elephant in the room between us. "Will you never come and stay at my place?"

The pain registers on his face. "That place just has too many bad memories for me. I think it is cursed."

"Do you believe in that sort of thing?"

He looks at me. "No. I was joking. Do you?"

"I knew someone who was into all that." I must have sounded too serious when I asked him if he had faith. But now is not the time to go into that. "I don't want to make you uncomfortable."

"I just need some time."

"It's okay. I'll wait for you. If I have to spend our time together here I had better Sebastianize this place." I wrap my arms around him, because I feel that is what he would have done next and I need to start taking more control.

"So what does Sebastianizing involve?"

"I am a simple man, so nothing. You get off lightly."

"Speaking of getting off, shall we go to the bedroom so I can show you how grateful I am for your understanding nature?"

I glance at the USB; the green lights show it has completed. "You're just making up for all your lost time after your self-imposed ban."

"Are you complaining?" he asks as he heads off in the direction of the bedroom.

"No," I tell him as I swipe the stick out of the machine and follow.

A couple of hours later, after the sex and a post-coital nap, we are back in front of his computer because he wants to pick a destination. I guess he thinks I really did want to go away together. His computer must be in idle mode, as pictures appear and disappear. Some I presume are of his family with their typical Italian looks; others presumably are of his friends. Then one image comes up that catches my interest: it is a group shot, a group I seem to have been all too familiar with. I did not realize he was paying any attention to me, but my interest in this one cozy friend shot has not gone unnoticed. Somehow he tends to notice most things about me which others would not even register. That is why I have to remain so guarded and think it is best to sever all ties.

"I seem to recognize mostly everyone in that picture." The computer has moved along to the next one.

Marco taps the keyboard and opens up the picture folder, scans through file names and opens the album from which the visual representation of my judges awaits me. It is now displayed on the screen, static, not about to go anywhere and move to some other less uncomfortable (for me) scene. All those happy smiling faces seem to be mocking me, looking at me in their pixelated form saying "we knew him first. We are going to tell him. You had better run or kill him. But do it quickly because he is on to you. Save yourself, bury us all. What you fear the most is coming."

The last comment from them snaps me awake. "Yeah, so there's Nat. He looks really happy compared to now, where he always seems lost." I add, to explain my apparent shock at seeing them. I need to act my ass off as my adjudicators continue staring me down.

"Those were happier times."

"Oh."

He smiles. "Don't get me wrong, I am happy now, with you. But when that picture was taken life seemed so much simpler."

I need information; I am bursting to know now but I will play the slow game because that is what you do. "So is that guy his boyfriend, I mean the one before Rod, the one that overdosed?" I point at the mixed-race guy standing next to Nat.

"That's Jason. They weren't going out when the picture was taken but they went on to, and were really happy. I didn't think Nat talked about him anymore."

I try to look sheepish. "He didn't. Others at work gossiped about it." And the fact that one of my main critics blabbed all, before I crucified and gutted him. "So how's he doing?"

"There's been no change. Still in a coma."

"Will he ever recover?"

"They don't know. Sometimes because of his state of limbo I think it might have been better if he had just died. I visit him and tell him everything that is going on, but I could do that at his tombstone."

"Do you visit your friend who was murdered?"

"Ah, Joe." Hearing his name feels like I have been cut somehow, while Marco touches the screen where his friend's face is. "I can't. I should have been there for him and I wasn't. He died believing I was angry and upset at him, and I have to live with that."

"Is this why you feel you must find his killer and avenge his death? To be honest with you, I'm sure your friend would not want you to live your life like this. Maybe you need to just let it go. Go to his grave and make your peace and move on with your life, with our relationship."

"I don't want to lose you over it, but I can't let this go yet."

"So how did Ben make her way into this picture? She doesn't seem the type to want to hang around with a bunch of queens like you guys."

"She definitely brought a new different dimension to the group. She worked at the cinema with Joe; they were like two peas in a pod."

"That's Richard, whose apartment I bought," and whose career I have probably fucked up. "Is that his ex next to him?"

"Yeah, that's Carmen. I guess he never came out in the right way. But he had to follow his heart."

"The guy next to them, I don't know."

"Actually you met him, but I guess you were really out of it. His name is Taylor and he's the doctor who saw to

251

you after your mugging."

"He's not what I expected. I guess when I heard "'doctor'" I presumed some old grey-haired man. Maybe we should take him out for dinner, my treat, to thank him properly. And I guess it would be good for me to get to know your friends."

"Yeah, I'll arrange it. I've been a bit disconnected from everyone."

"I know Tim, he's my personal trainer."

"Ha-ha, small world."

"So who is this guy next to Tim?" This is what I have wanted to know since I first saw the picture; I must find out about the only one that got away. Having to go about it in such a roundabout way is harrowing. The moment I saw the guy I wanted to shout out, "Who the fuck is *that* guy?!" Because when I knew him, he was younger and innocent.

"Bobs. His real name is Robert but I never used that. He was my best friend, who I knew from school."

No one at my school was openly out. There were a few classmates who were quite camp and were relentlessly picked on for being so, even though they denied it, but there was no way anyone would openly invite that level of abuse on themselves. So I never had the opportunity to have gay friends. When I was at school there was a guy in the upper sixth who came out, well, was outed when he got drunk at a party and tried to kiss another guy. Whenever he walked by, the rest of his class and the one below it would make the exaggerated gesture of covering their asses and quickly move to stand against the wall. Prior to his outing the guy had been popular, but this did nothing to help him. The anti-gay behavior around the school escalated and was concentrated on this guy. When his name was called out in assembly to receive an award, someone shouted "gay" and the whole school started sniggering while the lad had to walk up to collect his now tainted award.

I hadn't laughed; instead, I went bright red on hearing the word and hoped that no one sat next to me noticed.

Because we were in different classes and I was not allowed in the sixth form center, I just heard the rumors that went around the school about the guy. I knew the injustice had intensified to a physical level when the beatings began. I'd witnessed it once, when the guy was walking to his next class by himself and I was looking at him thinking that he was fit, and desperately wanted to speak to him. Suddenly someone threw a coat over his head. All the lads nearby rushed him and started throwing punches and kicks once he went down. When the coat was removed and I saw his ruffled hair and messed-up uniform I wanted to run over and help him, but I felt paralyzed—I just looked on. The guy got up from the floor, obviously trying hard not to cry, and happened to make eye contact with me. I was frozen to the spot and could not move to help him, even though I desperately wanted to. Instead, I had to watch as he picked himself up with no one coming to his aid, and hobbled off.

I heard someone laughing behind me saying that this was a common occurrence. I wanted to turn around and punch the speaker but I was rooted to the spot. After that incident, I only saw the guy one more time before he moved schools. But I was left wondering if the guy told his parents the truth, and if he did, how great it would have been to have parents like that, ones that wanted to help.

"So you were out at school?" I asked.

"No. But he was the first person I came out to. It happened at the end of the summer holiday just before we entered the last year of school. We came out to each other simultaneously, and being horny teenagers just wanting to lose our virginity, we did. It was more of a spur-of-the-moment decision, not one based on a deep sexual attraction."

That sounded a lot better than my first time. "So what happened? How come you aren't friends anymore? Did sleeping together ruin your friendship?"

"No, the deed cemented our friendship, actually. It was the perfect first experience for both of us, and neither of us regretted a thing. But it was not something we planned to repeat with each other."

"That sounds nice. Maybe I should have picked someone to come out to at school. It must have been nice to have that trust with someone."

"We both seemed to know the other was gay but we were both so paranoid. Doing what we had done ran the risk of coming out to someone who might not have been gay. Then that person would surely blab the fact that the other was, to the whole school. Once the majority of our peers knew, it would get back to the teachers and then ultimately our parents. Bobs was worried because his father, Mister Ashton, paid handsomely on top of his school fees to make sure he was kept well abreast of anything to do with his son. If I had come out, the stuff at school would have been harsh and my dad would have flipped—but that would be nothing compared to what would have been waiting for Bobs if his father, a strict homophobic disciplinarian, had found out he was a dirty ass bandit. He would have probably received a beating, followed by disinheritance, then been kicked out of the family home, and as he was tossed out on his ear another beating thrown in for good measure."

"That sounds cruel."

"Bobs's father was a cold, heartless bastard who was always disappointed in Bobs. Bobs said at times he wished he was not an only child, just to deflect some of the attention from himself. His sadistic pig of a father was a closet case, using rent boys and abusing whomever he could. He was the one who killed Joe."

"But I thought you didn't believe it was him, and thought something else had happened."

"After his father disappeared straight after the murder, Bobs contacted me and said his dad spoke to him, said he was innocent and that it was a setup. We've been friends for so long I believed him, and also because something about the whole situation did not quite feel right."

"Don't hate me for saying this, but are you looking for more because you feel guilty?"

"It's so fucking shit. Everywhere is misery."

"So where is Bobs now? And why are you no longer friends?"

"He's in Australia. He said it hurts too much to be back here. But I think he owes it to Joe and me to help find his father and the truth, unless he used our friendship to manipulate me to see more than there is to the murder. Maybe it was his dad all along, and he filled my head with all of this bullshit; he could even know where his dad is. Now, after the events at the Phoenix, two of my friends are dead to me."

"You've been through a lot, so much pain. But none of it is your fault. You should just let it go."

"I want to. But it still feels raw."

"There is something I need to tell you, well, confess to you." As I say these words to him, I can feel his body go rigid next to me. "I just want you to hear me out before you say or do anything."

19

HE LIKES TAKING RISKS

"I don't actually know how to say this so I am just going to say it. You see this guy here…?" I touch the computer screen. "Something bad happened. I did something that was not out of character but represented the old me."

"Go on." He is very calm.

"It represented how I used to be. I want to change, hopefully with you, but if we are going to make a go of it I guess you have to know the truth. Because I have wronged you. I know the timing of this is really shit too, after everything you have said and what you must be feeling. But the guilt is too much."

"Just tell me." He sounds hostile.

"I slept with him. It just happened and I was very drunk. That is not an excuse, but I want you to know because I don't want to hurt you."

"When?"

"I had just moved into my apartment, I wanted to celebrate. You refused to come over. So I had a few friends around. Then we went to a club and I bumped into my personal trainer. He was all over me. I was very drunk and one thing led to another. At the club, some other guy started to join in and it just sort of happened."

"I trusted you."

"I know. It was wrong. I don't know why I did it.

Maybe I did it because I was feeling low, as you would not visit me, and it happened because at times you are so distant with your extra-circular investigations."

"So it's my fault."

"No. I was scared about our exclusivity talk. Part of me wanted to say yes to you. But you have to understand I have never done the relationship thing, and it scared me. Being with those guys meant nothing to me, just drunken sex, which I was not even involved in much. It cemented the fact that I do want to give us a try. I would like to go out with you, exclusively."

"It took a threesome to show you that." He states it as a fact, without emotion.

I am not intimidated although I feel I may be about to lose him. "Yes. I guess part of me wanted to prove that I could still pull and was desirable. I had to say goodbye to my old ways. But now I promise you I want to give this relationship a try. I will never cheat on you again."

"Just leave."

"I don't want this to be the end of us…I understand if you can't forgive me...but can't we just try?"

The expression on his face seems like a mask. I back out of the door, he just stands there watching me go.

Outside of his flat I jump into the nearest taxi and head to the computer geek. I text Marco and tell him to call me if he can find it in his heart to forgive me, because I want to make it work with him.

In truth, I needed to get out of there sharp. I need to find Robert Ashton and kill him—properly this time. It was very clever of him not to use his real name when we chatted online. Just like I used the alias of the man I was staying with, he had also used deception. But seeing him, the only one that can link me back to Martin Fealy, the Nightingale Hall fire and all that business, really spooked me. Marco, who is used to watching my reactions and expressions, would have known something was up once I saw that picture. Rather than saying "I kidnapped your best friend, tortured him and was about to kill him ten years ago but he escaped," I thought it better to reveal my little indiscretion with PT. Anyway, if they know each other it would come out eventually. That little sacrifice is for the greater good.

My mind flies back to that time in the Year of Wealth where this rich older man, Martin, liked to use me. Little did he know he was being played. Yes, I'd put up with his sexual advances, even pretended I liked them and him. He liked having a young, good-looking, college-educated man in tow. When I first met him, even though I had just finished my degree, I was still uneducated in the world. Do not get me wrong; I was not a naive innocent. I had killed, slept rough, done sexual acts with others I was ashamed of in order to survive, and I knew we were all pawns THEY play with. But I did not know what to do about it then. Then Martin came along with his bags of money and nice little home in Nightingale Hall. With Matt, I hatched a plan to steal all his money. This involved sleeping with him, making him fall in love me, and experimenting with various drugs until I could get him in a state he would be compliant. We tricked the Old Bastard into opening a company, which basically entailed getting him to sign papers when he was off his face. The company did not exist physically, no premises or staff, but on paper (actually online) it did. Using our fake identification, Matt and I became board members. Paper trails, fake identification, offshore accounts—they were not my thing, but that of my little associate.

The hardest part was having to stay with the Old Bastard and keep him sweet, which I only managed to do by amusing myself, cheating on him with guys from Internet forums. I fooled around with many guys, mainly out of boredom. I did not use my real name or face pictures in case any of his old pervy friends were online. My body got me all the attention I needed. Then I met the one that got away…he called himself Logan and would not reveal his real name, which I only just found out was Robert Ashton. He was different, shy in a way, weird in others, but mostly he was just pathetic. Rich daddy might cut his allowance if his wrist went too limp; he was the epitome of a wasted life. He disappeared for a while. I had assumed he was getting some in real life and had grown up, but he came back more desperate than ever. That is when I decided to kill him, to erase such a miserable weakling from existence because life is tough and he had no chance of survival.

The added effect was that all of Old Bastard's money was now in my possession, and then it was time to cover all traces with him. Of course I realized a scapegoat would be needed—Little Logan seemed like the perfect choice—two gays, one stone. He practically begged to meet up, he was so willing. I could probably have had him axe Old Bastard for me just by asking. Logan and I were together in the normal sense first, then things moved to the perverse. I guess I had wanted to teach him a lesson, what it truly meant to be a victim of life. My lesson worked because somehow he managed to escape his bonds, incapacitate me and liberate himself, not just from my clutches but from his weak, pathetic life. The way Marco told it, Bobs had become a strong individual, the alpha male of his group of friends, no longer a bottom-of-the-barrel degenerate. I had helped him, I made him. At the same time I was made. And it seems another was also made.

After Logan had hit me and I came to, I heard him talking to another, a voice I am surprised I did not place straightaway. Maybe part of me thought it was impossible, maybe the hunter aspect blanked all associations about the one that got away. But our dear Marco was there too, helping him. Back then I was not as trained and practiced as I am now. I did not know how next to proceed. I tentatively opened the door to see if they would jump me, but they had started a fire and fled. I could tell by the smells and the color that this was no ordinary blaze, but involved the chemicals I had obtained to pour over the body of Old Bastard who was incapacitated in the second bedroom. The plan was for Old Bastard to pick up Logan online, do all manner of abusive things to him. Then, as he is about to kill him by dissolving him in acid the young lad would fight back, killing his abuser. But not before the Old Bastard lands a fatal blow. Tidy.

I leapt over the flames, which had not yet engulfed the entrance to the room, and knew I had to get out. I did not have time to finish making sure no trace of me remained, so I splashed the remaining acid around the apartment in those places I thought I had been the most. The initial fire spread, feeding on the chemicals I had dashed around, eventually finding its way to the gas from the stove I had switched on before running out of there as quickly as I could. Retrospectively, I did not have to run because the explosion did not happen immediately. I was able to clear the building easily before that happened, before the glass from the flat shattered across the ground below. That is when the adjacent flat took the brunt of the damage, itself being totally destroyed along with the residence of Old Bastard. The owners of that flat, who happened to be in, had also died. Collateral damage.

It was surprising more hadn't died. A few were treated for bad smoke inhalation but they lived. I guess lots of the residents were out because it was a Saturday afternoon, and the fire brigade would have been on the scene sharpish; it was not like Nightingale Hall was full of local authority types. But I did not know any of this at the time, because I'd fled. I had the money and there was no way I was going to get caught. I left the country that night. At that time I did not know how easily I got away with it; everything was blamed on Martin Fealy. In the papers they did not disclose much about him like pictures or personal information because of the investigation, and we did not leave anything behind. Matt informed me that the investigation found traces of chemicals in Martin's place, which was the source of the fire; he had been conducting suspicious fraudulent and criminal activities and transferring his vast wealth into a company which was then moved into other ones, becoming untraceable. It was presumed he owed illegal company money through some sort of dodgy activity, and he either moved it to hide it from them or paid them off. But either way, they had terminated him.

I now had my money and never had to work, even though I eventually decided to do so to blend in more easily. So I needed something to occupy my time: molding and bending the wills of degenerates who had the misfortune to encounter me. Those events had made me who I am.

The unexpected dimension to the events that started on Fire Day was the making of the honorable cop. Thinking he was partly responsible for killing three, burning down a building, not being there to stop his friend getting tormented, and having to keep all of this secret over the years made Marco pursue a life of wanting to serve, help and protect others.

* * * *

"Find out everything you can about Robert Ashton."

"Who is that?"

"He's the guy who escaped when we robbed Old Bastard."

"Is that what has you on tenterhooks? That's old news."

"Just check if he has made any accusations to anyone."

"Stop stressing. We got away with fleecing all of Old Bastard's money."

"Just check, yes?"

"There's no evidence."

"Check."

"I tapped into your hotel security because you wanted to check up on the staff, and issued an emergency repair warrant for all CCTV in the Clapham area last week, causing them to be out of commission. There is nothing we can't do or get away with. Calm down."

"It's just so weird how everything is tying back to the Phoenix event."

"And…?"

"There is no 'and'. It was a surprise, is all."

To stop myself from becoming overly frustrated while Matt conducts his search, I switch on the television in the background to provide some noise and entertainment. The aptly named idiot box calms me, and I watch some advertisements. Public relations gets its fair share of being a useless service to the masses, but in my opinion advertising is worse. The workers that create this shit I am currently watching are much worse than the PR lot. Part of me thinks THEY control all the ads in another attempt to influence and order the masses and their purchasing powers.

One ad is trying to place its product over that of a competitor and ends with the line "Nothing works better than…" Well, if nothing actually works better than, use nothing. What a terrible line, horrible language that seems to have infiltrated numerous ads. Are all advertisers truly that dumb, or is more at work here than is openly evident? The next one has a mother of three aesthetically pleasing young children feeding them healthy food; fair enough, but the actress looks to be in her twenties. To produce all those sprogs she would have had to start when she was about twelve. And they wonder why there is a problem with teenagers getting knocked up. Next is for a sofa, a nice gigantic leather piece that could actually fit well and look good in my apartment, if only I bought mass-produced items. The issue is that the set is obviously a television studio; the majority would not have a living room the size of the one portrayed in the advertisement. So yes, the sofa, or bed (they also seem to do this in their ads) looks great in the spacious studio being shown to us but in reality, in the homes of the degenerates, it would be a tight fit getting that in their three-by-two yard living rooms or bedrooms with all the other accompanying crap that is already in there.

"Nothing is coming up about him making any police reports, no incidences. It's all about his father fleeing after murdering some rent boy. You know your other handy work?" Matt grins.

I feel better. I am safe for now, as Marco had said Bobs is in Australia and is not looking like returning anytime soon. Plus they are not speaking, so even if they somehow kissed and made up and my name came up as a fling Marco had, it would mean nothing to precious little Robbie as he never knew my real name. "Fuck off."

"I see you're calm again."

"I have a present for you. That USB device from the policeman's computer."

"Gimme."

The news is about to start, and something about a Blue Shadow scrolls along the bottom of the page. I switch the television off, lob him the device. "Let me know what you find. And start thinking about a trip to Australia," I add before I leave.

* * * *

Back at my place I decide to go straight to the downstairs pool changing room and my private locker. I realize that I have not even bothered to shower since having sex with Marco, as I rushed out of there and then had my mini-mission to look into. I do not bother getting under the shower here. I do not want to wash him from my life; I just change into my trunks and dive into the pool. Fifty laps later, balance has been restored. I feel fine and calm. I do shower now to get all the chemicals off my skin, before changing and heading back upstairs. Outside my door Marco is sitting on the floor.

"Hello."

"Hello."

"I need to speak to you."

"Come in." I open the door.

He sits down on the sofa next to me. "I'm not sure how to say this, but those guys who beat you up..." He pauses and is staring in my eyes. Instead of speaking he motions, maybe to lighten the mood or maybe he realizes in our relationship we need to move past darker tidings. "I thought you had a right to know."

"What...? Wow...I'm not sure how I feel about that. Christ...er, do you want a drink or anything?" I say, getting up to remove myself from the situation and break eye contact.

He takes my hand, not allowing me to walk away. "Hearing about them reminded me of when I first met you, all bloody and beaten, and how I fell for you straightaway and have now fallen in love with you. I know, I know it's only been months...but I do love you."

"I love you too." I think I do. "What I did, I did out of fear; I have never fallen for anyone."

"Me neither. I never thought I deserved happiness."

"Are we too alike for this to work?"

"I think that's why it *will* work because we are the same and complete each other."

"What about my little indiscretion?"

"You said we weren't exclusive at the time, and we weren't. And if you promise nothing like that will ever happen again then I can forgive you."

"Seriously? Just like that…?"

"Yes. I have to compartmentalize lots of aspects of my life with my work being what it is. I can do it this once, for your mistake."

"Your work, your hatred of this place. How come you're here?"

"When I heard about those guys that attacked you I was scared for you. I had to make sure you were okay. I guess in my mind I associate them and you together."

"What happened to them?"

"They were always destined to get into trouble."

"True. Gangs are always bad news."

"There were some eyewitness reports of just one person being involved, dressed in blue, who just disappeared into the shadows. The newspapers are calling him or her the Blue Shadow."

"That's the media for you; they prefer to exaggerate to sell stories. 'Group of men fought with another group of men' won't sell as many papers as the spin they put on it. What is the official line?"

"That's the thing. When I heard about it I called around, no CCTV was working in the area that night due to a scheduled maintenance. So it has to be all the words of eyewitnesses. The police are still scouring, looking for anyone who might have seen something."

He does not mention the motorbike. So, the old bags were not the informants. At least they respect what I did for them. "I guess I had better ask, was it you?"

Marco raises his eyebrows at me and smiles. "No."

"It's just with you and your crusades…you know, it could have been. You've already said you will kill Mister Ashton for murdering your friend next door."

"I'm going to let it go. Joe would not have wanted me to waste my life chasing down his killer. That's the job of the police." He is lying, telling me what he thinks I want to hear based on our earlier conversation.

"But you *are* the police."

"Not my area."

"So what is?"

"I just analyze and input data, really boring stuff." He is lying again, he knows way too much about everything going on. Never mind, soon his secrets will be mine.

I give him a kiss, which he responds to. We end up going to bed; we do not have sex. I guess we are both satisfied enough from earlier, or now we have admitted we love each other the sex dwindles.

He is spooning me while nuzzling at my neck. I am trying to figure why I said what I did. Am I capable of love? I play others. I am just playing him, right? This is all a game—my part is to string him along using whatever it takes to make sure he does not find out about the real me, but also because he has the potential to be the SOURCE.

Marco gets up and heads to bathroom. Not having his body pressed against mine makes me feel a bit empty. I am different now. I killed to help those in need to stop suffering, but that was my old way of thinking; now I will kill to help those in need by eliminating their sufferers. My ethos has changed and I, this Blue Shadow, plan to rid the world of the actual scum to inspire others to stand up against their oppressors. As this thinking has changed, maybe other aspects of me are to change. Maybe I can love.

Fuck! My clothes from that night are still on the shower floor. He will see them and work it all out; or maybe he will be too tired to pay any attention. No, who am I trying to kid? RoboCop will not miss a trick. He has probably suspected me all along and snuck his way into my apartment to snoop around.

I jump out of bed and rush into the living room. I go over to the fireplace and shove my arm up behind the facade. With my fingers searching for the keypad, I tap in the code. The panel opens and I grab Alex. Now I just have to wait for him to come out here and end this once and for all.

My instincts are right. He enters the room carrying the wet clothes. It looks like he has thoroughly examined them. The throwing knives were still in the jacket pockets. He might have taken them out. Will I be quick enough to deflect them if he hurls them at me? He looks up at me standing there in my underwear, holding the sheathed sword.

"It was you." He does not ask the question but says it as a statement.

"Yes. I hurt them. They fucked me over so I fucked them right back. I did it with this." I draw the blade.

"And what are you going to do with that now?" He

must be scared. Or trying to buy time. He has probably already informed on me.

Kill you. But first I need to know if you told anyone. "I don't want to go to prison." Shit, is that what I fear the most? Incarceration? The inability to be free, to be me?

He slowly puts the clothes down and holds up his hands. He is not holding the knives, that much I can see. "I haven't called anyone. Let's talk about this. They hurt you badly so you wanted to hurt them back." He takes a baby step closer.

"Why didn't you call your police friends?"

"I love you." He takes another step forward.

"But you can't condone what I did."

"Actually I can. I have done some pretty fucked up things in my past."

That is right, you murdering Nightingale Hall arsonist. "So you are going to let me get away with it."

"Did they not have it coming?"

"They most certainly did. But you are on the side of the law. I have broken the law."

"I know why you did what you did. Remember, I found you. You could have gone to the police and reported the incident, but you didn't want to; I guess you wanted your own revenge. But I also did not report the incident, because you asked me not to. So I'm as much to blame as you are." Another step closer.

"If I ask you not to report this incidence?"

"I won't."

"Really...?"

"Yes. I know the system doesn't always work. Look at Joe, you've read some of those other reports about all those other criminals who got away with hatred and abuse. In some ways you did the right thing."

"I know." This time I take the step forward, bringing my right hand forward and then raising it above my head. I swing Alex around in the air above us before shoving the steel into its target.

20

HE SEIZES THE MOMENT

How did I get to this moment?

What made him come to my apartment and catch me out?

What made me do what I just did?

It was just after the average threesome. I'd had better and I'd had worse. Once everyone had cum I had kicked the guys out under the guise that I had to go to work in a bit. When it was time to get ready and go to work, I decided I could not be bothered; plus, I needed some rest. So I emailed my delightful employers to tell them that I was not feeling well. Then I went back to sleep. A boy needs his rest when he plans to kill later in the day.

When I finally awoke after a good eight hours sleep, I felt alive and refreshed, that feeling when you have been waiting for something and it is about to happen. I felt extremely awake. If the place was not soundproofed I am sure I would have been able to hear the birds outside. That is, if birds make noise at four post meridiem. In this state all my senses were heightened. I could smell the other two guys still in the room. I called down to the in-house cleaner and asked for someone to come up to just change my sheets.

I used this time to go for a run, really a light jog because I did not want to overexert myself, to loosen up my body and clear my mind. I thought back to my time spent in Japan. After I had acquired my wealth, my first destination had been Tokyo. I decided I wanted to learn to fight, so I spent a day in a commercial dojo there, learning the basics of sword fighting.

Actually it was even more basic than that—a program designed for westerners. We were given bokkens and were shown the moves required to satisfy the ritual and etiquette. They'd told us it was to cultivate the right mind-set, and that every movement no matter how obscure was done for a reason. I guess they did it to wheedle out any wannabe samurai with a serious blood lust. We did a few katas and finished with getting to hold a real sword. Job done, the tourists could tick that off their list of things to do and move on to their next mundane task. I stayed behind and asked if they knew of anyone who would be willing to teach me the way of the warrior.

"It is a lifelong journey, not something that could be taught on a vacation," the guy who had held our class and who spoke the best English told me.

"I have a year. I want someone to teach me whatever they can in a year. And I am talking about twenty-four hours for each of the three hundred and sixty five days. I will be the servant and am willing to do whatever my teacher says. As a thank-you, I am willing to pay for the building of another dojo, if that will please my master."

The next day I started my journey to Sado, as I was instructed to do by another of our trainers. He hadn't spoken during the class so I presumed he did not speak English, nor did he speak up when I made my request. It was only after I left the dojo, empty-handed as it were, did he approach me and tell me where to find the one I sought. He told me to go to the island and get someone to take me to the northern mountain range.

"Once you are in the region, start asking around for the pottery maker."

"Can't I just go directly to him?"

"You will never find him; he lives up in the mountains. You will live up in the mountains too if he decides to help you in your quest."

"If he's in the mountains, how will he know I am there?"

"They will whisper to him."

"The locals?"

"No, the mountains."

Oh fucking great.

Three weeks later I was with my Kensei who had agreed to teach me. I never knew his name nor did he know mine. He did not want me to pay, which worried me at the time, as a bought man is a dishonest one, a man I could control. When we first met, he'd knocked me to the floor, grabbed my face and stared into my eyes. He told me I was tortured, and for that reason he would teach me. But I think he took me on because he was lonely, and for pride, to show off his abilities to another. I learnt this from reading his eyes. That was one of our many lessons, the ability to see what another is thinking without them opening their mouth, and to anticipate their next move.

Before the actual swordplay began, I must have spent a month running up and down the mountain and doing other physical labors to get my body in shape. It had hurt but felt good at the same time. I guess I learned to endure emotional pain from a young age, so feeling physical pain was nothing. Another advantage of his having me around was that I could go into the town and sell his creations and purchase the supplies we needed. Most of the locals would just do business with me quickly so that I would be on my way. On one occasion an elderly woman told me I was evil, and spat at the ground; now, if this was an insight into my soul or because of who I kept company with, I do know. My only other "significant" interaction with the islanders was when a young woman, who I had noticed always watching me when I came into the town, obviously wanting me, spoke.

"What are you doing with the exile?"

"I'll tell you, but first tell me, why do you call him an exile?"

"Thousands of years ago they used to exile prisoners here. Then decades ago he was sent here. The whispers say he was a murderous warrior who killed so many, who was too dangerous to lock up with any others and too deadly to be killed himself, so that he was sent here in exile to live out his life in solitude."

"Do you fear him?"

"No. I don't tend to believe what the elders say."

"I am his apprentice."

"Pot maker?"

"No. Killer." I smiled and walked off.

She giggled and called after me, "I don't fear you, either."

When I got back to my Kensei I did not ask him about the story; we did not sit around gossiping about out pasts. We both obviously had done unimaginable acts that were not for the ears of others.

Once my training with the sword began, there was little time for talking and thinking, just practicing. I was trying to learn a lot in a short space of time, so I had to be constantly at it. I did not mind, it was preparing me for my life to come. Besides teaching me how to use a sword, he taught me how to handle a range of knives, basic martial arts, some Japanese, and reading a soul through the eyes. In many ways he was like the father I never had.

When my year was up he'd asked me to stay on, saying that I was a good student but had lots more to learn, and I had only started this journey and should not leave it incomplete. I stayed on. When I eventually left there was no way I would be able to take on and win a battle against someone more practiced in the art than myself, but I did not intend to. He had given me enough to survive, to have a competitive edge against those I would face, and to be able to do everything I planned to. With him, he never said anything twice, so when I said again that I had to go, that was it. Maybe one day I would return. I meant it, because it was a peaceful place where I would never be found, if the need occurred. There was no emotional send-off. We bowed goodbye and I headed off. Before I did, though, he gifted me a sword. Not his most prized one—a Kensei would have to be buried with that—but a great one nonetheless. He told me to name it and let it become one with me. That was the rebirth of Alex.

* * * *

It was nighttime, and time to get ready. I had another shower, mainly so that as I cleaned myself I could massage all the muscles I could reach. Under the hot water I had also prepared my mind. Both the body and mind have to be prepared and act as one when vanquishing an enemy. After the longer than usual shower, I dried myself off, then I put on the top and bottom I had decided to wear. It was basically a special sports outfit, and was very tight. I looked myself up and down in the mirror, dressed neck to ankle in this second blue skin. I went for the blue one because white would stick out too much, the black one did not have the long bottoms in stock, and only shorts and grey is, well, just too dull. It is from Nike: I wanted something mass-produced in case I was spotted. The material is known as Pro Compression with Dri-Fit, meant to allow an athlete's skin to breathe when training while supporting major muscle groups, PR bullshit to sell to the masses. But it allowed for full flexibility. I'd picked it because being so tight, there was less chance that any of my hair or skin will be left at the scene to be traced back to me. Not that any forensic details about me are on file anywhere that I know about.

My body looked good, like it had been painted. I started getting a semi, which was obvious in what I was wearing. Now I knew why superheroes decide to wear their underpants on the outside—to hide the bulge, which probably grows a lot once they do their thing. I did not do that, as there was more to come over the base layer. I got some gel, not a product I like using, and slicked my hair back. Soon it went solid. I yanked a little bit of hair, and it seemed like it was joined to every other one on my head. Again, this was done so that I would not leave any hairs behind, plus it had the added advantage of not having hair covering my ears, my hearing which like all the other senses was vital on that night.

When engaging the enemy that night it would have been nice to have had music playing, like in a film when there is a fight sequence and the director chooses a piece to make up for a lack of dialogue, a song that completes the choreography as the blows coincide with the beats. I would have had "How You Like Me Now" by The Heavy as I kicked the shit out of those who had been warned that I will be back for them and had taken such pleasure when they had their turn on me. But needing my hearing, I opted for real music as I got ready. I had "Running Up That Hill" by Kate Bush playing in the apartment, because I'd made a deal with God so it seemed a fitting choice. I got out the face-paint I purchased, a red, white and blue set so you could paint the Union Flag, but I just went with the blue. Sticking to the theme now. I painted a horizontal blue stripe across my face where my eyes are as a kind of mask. But up close and personal, someone would have known it was me.

Once the blue line had dried I finish dressing: a pair of black leather trousers and a leather sleeveless hoodie, both with blue trim. I finished the outfit with a pair of metallic silver Alexander McQueen Puma Joust ankle-length boots; they have a contrasting ivory panel throughout and a rubber sole. I finish the ensemble entirely by getting the weapons I was going to take ready, and putting them in their allocated slots.

My preferred mode of transport is anything that gives me freedom, not restricting me to a little cabin or small space and trying to adhere to a timetable, which is so dependent on others that it might as well be redundant.

That night I decided it was time for my latest purchase to make an appearance. I realized it is better not to walk the streets dressed how I was, carrying what I had. A car would offer a lot more discretion, but if you are caught you are fucked, and you would never get away without getting stuck in traffic in London. The best way to travel in this instance was definitely by motorbike. In the Phoenix underground car park I took the sheet off the little run-around I had bought myself. It was not the fastest, most advanced bike on the market, as I am trying to be subtle. The Italian hunk between my legs was the MV Agusta Brutale 1090R. Based on the F4 Superbikes model, its powerful, high-performance serves my needs. It allows me to duck through the traffic, not that there was much at the time of night. But if I were to be chased, the 164.5 miles per hour maximum speed would let me get away. I have not even had to make any modifications to the bike; the only thing I had bespoke was the helmet, a little extra something to help me enter stealth mode. I got on the machine, started it and headed out to fulfill the promise.

The lights on the bike were now switched off as I approached the estate. I was using the night vision aspect built into the helmet to navigate. It was not like I was going really fast anyway, plus in these built-up areas there is ample street lightning. There is also lots of recording equipment but I was not worried about those, as they were taken care of. From a distant I spotted my targets. They appeared to be harassing an elderly couple. Why the oldsters were out this late at night was a mystery to me. To a certain extent they were inviting trouble on themselves. Of course, in a perfect world anyone should be able to come and go as they wish without having to worry about their safety, but this is not a perfect world, THEY make sure of that.

My intentions had been never to do it in public—too many witnesses—but it looked like things were about to get nasty. I switched the bike lights on, revved the engine and headed towards the gang. The light beaming straight onto them caught their attention immediately. They looked up at the bike heading towards them. I stopped a couple of yards in front of them. The idiots were trying to stare me down, but because it was me this would never work; I cannot be stared down. And given the current situation of them staring at a biker with a helmet whose eyes they could not see, it was a pointless action on their part.

The old bags were also looking. I kicked the bike back into action, headed towards them and drove directly between the gang (who seemed to have regrouped back together) and the couple. With the visual link severed the couple walked quickly off, as quickly as their arthritis or whatever afflictions they had allowed for. The woman turned around and shouted a thank you in my direction. The man ushered her on. As I drove circles around them the gang was herded together, not bothered about letting their geriatric prize escape; they had me to deal with.

One of them had found his balls from somewhere and lobbed something at me. On impact, I presumed it was a can of beer. This must have provided the inspiration for the rest of them to act, because another one, the really ugly one, had broken from the pack and tried to kick the bike on my next pass around. Seeing him head out of the group, I made a wider loop so he missed me.

I glanced back over to where the pensioners had wandered off. They were out of sight, hopefully safely back in their little flat with the lights off, twitching at the curtains to see what happened next. There had been the risk they would have called the police if anything kicked off just then. Or would they use their opportunity to get rid of the Polish infestation on their housing estate any way they could? This was the sort of place where the residents, once safely behind closed doors, do not give a damn about what happens on the grounds. Maybe in the beginning when they first moved there they tried to make a difference, but they learnt not to welcome any trouble onto themselves. Ultimately it is that apathy that needs to be addressed in the world.

But this was not the way I had wanted to end my former attackers. I'd made them a promise which I was about to fulfill, so I owed it to us all for them to see my face.

On my next circuit I drove right through them a lot faster than I had previously been going, but not quick enough so they could not see it coming. They parted desperately. I flew through them and zoomed off. Something hit my back; maybe I was going to have to take up some high-impact sport in the future to explain away all my bruises. I will do it with a nice gay group, the perfect alibi, as everyone would assume I am doing it to cruise for guys. I stopped the bike perpendicular to them, so they could see me in the distance. I turned my face to the side to look at them so they could see this helmeted guy in all his glory and hopefully understand what was to come. I decided not to linger further as we (the bike and I) were both side-facing them and presenting the largest target if they should try anything. I took off.

I parked the bike at the other side of the housing estate, near the road but hidden away, disembarked and removed the headgear, leaving it with the machine. I checked that the strip across my eyes was still in place, put my hood up and grabbed my sword, then headed back to where the gang had been. Breaking from tradition, I did not keep the sword at my side. As the weapon was attached to my back and sheathed, it would not be obvious what it was if someone quickly glanced my way. I stuck to the shadows and tried to remain inconspicuous, even though at that time of night hardly anyone was around.

Two feline green eyes appeared ahead of me. A cat came out of the darkness. It was jet black, and just stared at me. It pointed its head in the direction I was about to go, and meowed. It then darted off in the other direction. I hung back where I was, and listened. A couple were slurring at each other, I guessed coming home after a drunken night out. They were being annoyingly slow. Perhaps I should step out and just decapitate them both. I moved behind one of the bin sheds until they passed. I thought. I waited.

Finally, I was nearly at my destination, just a corner to go. The Poles were there; I could hear them. I walked around the corner and looked in their direction. None of them were looking my way. The four I'd originally met with Brutus were present, the same four that had beaten me. With the pale, tight jeans they all were wearing and beer cans littered around, I doubted I had to worry about any runners. I was almost upon them when the fittest one of the group spotted me.

"Hello," I greeted them.

They recognized me as the biker.

"I doubt you remember me."

"The fuck from the motorbike. You dead."

"That's me." I pulled down the hood so they could see my face. "I am also the guy who killed your dog, the man that you beat. Remember I told you to make sure you kill me, otherwise I would be back? Guess what? Your time has come."

One of them had strategically moved behind me. I pulled the hood back up and raised both hands in the air as if to say "I give up," but instead I asked, "Who wants to die first?"

My right hand griped the handle of Alex, my left the bottom of the sheath. I drew the blade out and swung it above my head. Combining an overhead with a side cut, I aimed for the neck of the Fat Pole directly in front of me. My plan was to decapitate him with the strike, so his head would fly into the air and blood would spurt up from the hole, spraying us, before his body fell over. But I hit the bottom of his chin before finding his neck, and the sword did not go all the way through. I was not sure if hitting the bone first had weakened the cut or if his neck was just too fat, but his head was still attached to his body, lolling backwards, hanging by strips of skin and muscle.

You are not meant to use force, merely guide the blade, which will do the rest. The sword was firmly lodged in his neck. I attempted to pull it out the way it went in, but it did not move. I dropped the sheath and let my left hand join the right one; together they managed to pull the sword out. I changed my right grip and using both hands, swung it into the air and then let it drive by my side behind me. It hit the Fit Pole who had positioned himself behind me. It entered his midsection, slicing through numerous organs.

The sword came easily out of him. Out of the corner of my eye I saw the gutted man crumpled on the floor in a pool of blood. I did not need to look to know that he was dead. I thought back to my training, these movements are embedded deep in my muscle memory—I must have been distracted somehow, by using them for the first time on actual human flesh. So I repeated the cut I made on Fat Pole a second time, letting instinct guide both my hands. I did not let power overtake the action, I let the weapon force its own way. I took his head cleanly off this time.

Goatee Pole, who had pissed himself, barely managed to stand; he was shaking so badly. He had his hands together as if to beg me or to pray. I slew him with a Kesa Giri, using my forward momentum to strike upwards at an acute angle. My right fist was slightly above my right shoulder and I made sure not to lean forward. Without pausing, using one continuous movement, I executed a return diagonal downstroke. It was textbook, it was perfect. He was dead. I had slain those three in under a minute.

Ugly Pole had started to run off. I unzipped my hoodie, grabbed the first throwing knife my fingers found, and hurled it in his direction. I did not bother to see if it hit him; I knew it would have. Because at that moment the adrenaline had taken over and I was in pure killer mode.

I grabbed another knife and sent it along the same trajectory as the first. Ugly Pole went down and was crawling on the ground. The third knife I had to throw differently to hit my moving target. I wiped the majority of blood off Alex using the jacket of Goatee Pole, before re-sheathing him. I calmly walked over to Ugly Pole. He had pulled out one of my knives, but instead of having the good sense to keep it as a weapon he had thrown it away. I stood over him now, peering down into his face.

"Do you have anything to say?"

"Please."

I did not respect the cock for trying to beg. Another knife from my jacket soared precisely into his open mouth. Four knife wounds from throws were not enough to finish him off. I liberated Alex again and drove the point down into Ugly Pole's heart, sending him to hell. As I withdrew the sword I placed a foot on his chest for leverage. His heart pumped its last contraction; the blood shoot out of the foreign opening made in that muscle and saturated his chest, and my shoe, in blood. I felt an overwhelming sensation of satisfaction that I had never felt before. I realized the new path I would walk, the new course destiny had laid for me.

EPILOGUE

"Hurry up."

"I'm finished, I'm coming."

"Sorry to rush you out of here, it's just that I have a dear old friend coming around soon."

"And you don't want him to see you sleep with prostitutes."

"You know I don't think of you like that."

"You love me, love all women. Wish we could be married."

"Here's something extra for you."

"You've already paid up."

"I know. I want you to treat yourself."

"Thank you, sweetie." She collected the money and thought to herself that she did deserve extra. Having the midget fuck her was bad enough. If only he had given her the bonus before starting the deed she could have been imagining all the stuff she would buy with the money, taking her mind off the revolting little man on top of her. Groping her breast with his small hands, darting his little tongue into her mouth. Yes, he'd paid the extra to be able to kiss. It is always the hideous ones that do, she thought. Her only consolation came from the fact he liked to do her from behind and take her up the ass, so she did not have to look at his face. Normally it did not hurt her as he was too small to get really far in or stretch her much. But today he took ages to finish, and she felt she might be sore after his few inches constantly prodded away at the same spot inside her.

After the door closed behind her, the midget ran over to his stool, jumped up on it and then onto the bench. He switched on all five monitors and watched the one showing the CCTV of the outer corridors to his loft apartment, so he could watch her leave. Not that he liked to watch her move; he merely wanted to make sure she buggered off. He saw that once she was away from his front door she practically ran out of there. *Am I that really that repulsive?* Even though she behaved like that, he did not regret giving her the extra money, because his mind was not entirely on the matter at hand. He was both scared and excited about something he had been recently tasked to work on. That task had consumed his thoughts, and he was not able to fully let himself enjoy his weekly indulgence. Now that she had left the building, he jumped down to shower and change so he could talk about the work when his guest arrived. In the shower he had a wank, because he'd never finished off earlier. Usually he could cum if it was up the ass as that was tighter than fucking in the front, which he always slipped out of, but this morning he'd had to fake it to get the session to end.

Once he had washed and put some clean clothes on he went back to his work station and waited for the only person who was allowed to come into his home besides the select prostitutes, and his cleaner who could not speak or read English. His friend was uncharacteristically late. A slight panic started to grip him. Not that he thought Sebastian would sell him out if he was ever caught, but because he genuinely cared for him. His agitation worsened when his thoughts reflected on the information he had found on the device.

What has Seb gotten us into? Matt thought, sitting at his desk working when he heard a sound.

"Boo."

He clutched his heart, turned around quickly to see the source of the sound. "You fucking scared me!"

"You need a better security system," Seb told Matt. He walked over to him and planted a kiss on his forehead.

"How did you get in? I have cameras everywhere."

"When are you going to realize how truly talented I am?"

I hope you are because you are going to need…

"I climbed up the drainpipe outside your bedroom window, which was not locked."

"So, your policeman friend. This is big. Sit."

"It can wait," Seb said very nonchalantly, kicking back and lying down on Matt's sofa.

"Wait for what? I have to tell you all about his secrets. Now."

"We hardly ever spend time together; it's always work. We could talk for a bit first."

"Seriously, what has gotten into you?"

"Remember at school, do you think I should have come out then?"

"What?"

"I was just thinking what it would have been like to have had a friend that I could have come out to."

"You could have told me. It is not like you didn't know my little secret."

"You never told me you suffered from achondroplasia, I had to guess." Seb smiled at Matt who rolled his eyes at the dry-wit. "Do you think things would have been different?"

"What if I had come up to you and told you I got bullied constantly so I spent all my time inside hiding from the world? I took apart computers just to destroy something, so I could vent my anger. But then out of boredom I put them back together, and learnt everything about them. They were kind to me, they were my friends. On the Internet people did not judge me for my small size, and it became my way of life."

"See, wouldn't it have felt better if this fucked-up world had let you feel comfortable enough to say those words to me all those years ago? So I could have understood you better and been there for you. I could have felt safe to come out, and you would have supported me."

"Not wanting to sound like your mum, but we *did* find each other. Destiny threw us together and we were able to help one another."

"Argh…enough. What did you find?"

"Are you sure you used it properly?"

"Shove it in the hole, it's not rocket science."

"I know the infallible Sebastian Bowman would not make a mistake. But I wouldn't make anything damaged."

"Did you not get anything? Was the computer too advanced for you?"

The dwarf grinned. "Even though the computer was not here my device still managed to pick some stuff up."

"Oh yeah?"

"The fact that the computer is not a police one, it's military intelligence. Your friend is a spy."

Seb sat bolt upright. "Really?"

"Please tell me you haven't killed him, because if you have you had better flee the country."

"What else did you find on the computer?" he ignored the killing part.

"Low-level files, the ones not worth encrypting, like the background check on you."

"Which I presume would be flawless since you constantly make sure my references, background information and personal details say what I want them to."

"I presume so. I could only get the file name, not the whole content."

"It's fine, he trusts me," Seb said, so his accomplice would not become ultra-paranoid.

"Well now, on to the good stuff."

"I wasn't the good part?"

"No, definitely not. There was an unencrypted language program on the computer. Looks like your lover is learning Persian."

"He's a very cultural guy."

"The only other file name I could retrieve was one named, 'The Invasion of Iran.'"

"What?"

"I'm not kidding. Looks like this government is planning to attack Iran. That's why he has to learn the language. Other military personnel are doing likewise. There are no more lessons in the Army for Afghanistan languages. It is all about Iran. I checked."

"Are you sure you're not in conspiracy theory overdrive? Why would they do that?"

"The oil. To stop them from launching weapons of mass destruction. To decimate the entire region so it will not pose a threat. To control the Middle East."

"Okay, okay."

"Either way, the sand niggers are going to get it."

"Who?"

"S-a-n-d nig-gers. You haven't heard that phrase before?"

Thousands of departed in a desert, SHE had seen it all. He pretended to be disturbed at Matt's vulgar language, rather than reveal the real truth of what had spooked him. "What next?"

"This is the moment I tell you a storm is coming."

"And I heed your advice and run."

"I can't tell you that. I need access to that laptop, I need to know everything on it."

"Somehow I will find a way to get you the laptop."

"Thank you."

"Do you think we are meant to intervene somehow?" he always liked to get philosophical.

"This government is fucked up, always controlling people. This will tell us what they are up to and how to defend ourselves against them. The least we could do is sell the information."

"THEY could be brought down if the information is true."

"There is one more thing."

"There always is."

"Because of how sophisticated the machine is, there is a chance the computer could detect the hack and notify the user."

"Oh."

"You will have to kill your playmate. We need to hatch

a clever plan to do it, as he is a spy and all."

"About that…"

"I knew it. You had a funny look about you when I joked about it before."

"No. I didn't. And no, I haven't killed him."

"What then?"

"He knows I killed that gang, and is completely fine with it. Maybe we can turn him." Seb had failed to tell Matt about the whole incident. That he was going to kill Marco but at the last moment, the last swing of the blade, the target was to re-sheath the sword. That for some reason he could not kill him. He could try and rationalize it, that Marco had the potential to be the SOURCE. That he is a policeman and that would make the repercussions too great. That he shouldn't kill in his own apartment. That he believed Marco would not turn him in to the authorities. But he could not kill him because he was in love with him. Unknown to himself, he had become one of those, someone in love. His greatest fear has been realized: he is now a degenerate.

ABOUT THE AUTHOR

Mark was born and bred in London and considers this intoxicating city his home. That is why his debut novel is set in the city. With a scientific background he then moved in to communications. He wants to write books that breaks the norm while exploring some of the darker elements of humanity, which he feels his debut novel 'The Degenerate Opportunity' does. To write this book he had to go to a dark place – a place that calls to him, one he will have to return to. Which means his stories are only just beginning…

Learn more at www.marklakeram.com

Printed in Great Britain
by Amazon